The Brothers Barnhart

The Brothers Barthau

The Brothers Barnhart

E.N. Klinginsmith

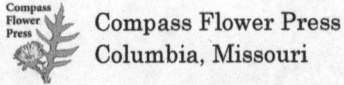
Compass Flower Press
Columbia, Missouri

Cover art by Yolanda Ciolli

Published by

Compass Flower Press
Columbia, Missouri

Library of Congress Control Number: 2021918807

ISBN: 978-1-951960-28-5 Trade Paperback

ISBN: 978-1-951960-30-8 Ebook

Dedication

To my wife, Barb; our sons, Mike, Jon, and Doug; and to their other halves, Erica, Megan, and Kerri; and to our granddaughters Kate, Claire, and Lorelai.

Prologue

SNOWING! Of course, it's snowing! It's the first Monday in February. It's Missouri. It's the first commute to my new job. What did I expect?

Before I left this morning, I checked the weather in Philly out of habit, I guess. The forecast called for 45°F and dreary. Okay, it didn't say dreary, but I am sure it is.

Two and half years ago, I went there to attend grad school. I chose Philly, because an acceptance letter from one of the Big Five schools was the first I received. Moving to a new part of the country was a priority at the time, so three months after I graduated from Mizzou, I headed to the City of Brotherly Love. I lasted a semester in grad school, not because I didn't do well—I did, but because college wasn't what I wanted to do anymore. I'd been in school for seventeen years, and it was time to grow up and get a job. I took a position at a bank, and it went well, until one day it didn't.

And so here I am on westbound I-64, making my way through the snow and traffic, ready to continue down a new path; one that began on a flight home last fall. The woman in the seat next to me struck up a conversation and we talked the entire time. I learned her husband was looking to hire some people at his business. She felt I would be just what he was looking for. A few weeks later, I was home for Thanksgiving, and he set up a time for us to meet on Black Friday. I drove to his office to have an interview. It had started snowing heavily that morning and the roads were getting treacherous, so we kept it short. Somehow, I did well enough that he made a job offer. Two weeks later, I accepted.

I left Philly last week, and now I'm back home in Missouri. Back home after things went south at the bank where I worked. Back home after the girl I had grown fond of chose nursing school over me. Back home and ready to see where this new road leads.

The snow starts hitting my windshield harder now, making visibility poor. There's always a challenge, it seems. Today, it's snow.

1

Monday, February 4

I'M GOING IN TODAY, a week earlier than planned. Larry Morgan, my new boss, called me on Saturday and told me he had some exciting news he couldn't wait to share and asked me to move my start date. How could I refuse him?

I make it to my exit in the Chesterfield valley and turn on a side street where I see a large Morgan*Plus*: Mortgages & More sign. I find the entrance to the lot, pull in, and park in front of the building. With all the snow, I'm not sure that I'm parked between the lines, but I make my best guess. I put the car in park and look at my new place of employment. It's a two-story brick building with Morgan*Plus* housed in the western two-thirds and an insurance company in the eastern third. Larry started his business five years ago and moved it to this large brick building as his business has grown. Eventually, he wants to grow it to the point that it will occupy the whole place.

There are only a couple of other cars in the lot today, one of which I know to be Larry's; having seen it when I came back at Christmastime. I'm ten minutes early, even with the snowy commute, but I see Larry, already at the door waiting for me. I get out of the car and trudge through the snow toward the door. He opens it and I step in, letting some snow blow in as I do. He greets me with a big smile and an extended hand. I shake hands while stomping snow off my shoes.

"Sorry," Larry says, "the guys who plow the lot haven't done it yet, obviously."

"The way it's coming down, they'd have to plow it again if they had."

"Glad you made it safe this morning. There's some crazy drivers around here."

"The drivers here aren't even close to the ones out east; trust me."

"Well, that's good then."

I nod as I dust the snow off my coat.

"So, Dale, are you ready to do this?"

"I am."

"Great." Larry gestures farther inside. "Come on in. There's breakfast in my office."

"With lots of coffee, I hope."

"Oh yes. Plenty of that, and eggs, bacon, hash browns; everything a guy could want."

If he's working on a coronary, it is, I think.

We walk through the lobby, take the elevator to the second floor, then walk down the hall to Larry's office. It's on the southwest corner of the building and has large windows which provide a panoramic view of the on-going snowstorm.

4

There's a conference table by the windows and food, catered by a local grocery, ready and waiting for us.

"Coffee to start?" Larry asks.

"Please."

"Cream or sugar?"

"Straight."

"I knew I liked you. Straight's the only way a cup of coffee should be," he stops for a second, "drank or drunk. Hell, I can never remember which way to say it."

I laugh and tell him that the word is probably drunk, He says that makes him picture some guy lying in an alley with a brown bag. We laugh. It's a good start.

He hands me a mug emblazoned with the Morgan*Plus* logo. It's filled with hot coffee, and it smells especially good on this wintry day.

"Dig in. Cooper will be joining us soon."

"Cooper?"

"My son. I don't know if you've met him."

"No, I've not. Forgive me, but I didn't think he worked here."

"He didn't, but I'm happy to inform you that he started last week."

"Oh, that's good."

Is it?

I continue, "I'm sure you're excited to have him on board. Is that what you wanted to tell me?"

"Yes and no. It's just a part of it. But let's enjoy our breakfast first, and then I'll explain."

My brain is trying to sort out what all this might mean, while at the same time trying to focus on the conversation.

After I had that interview in November, Larry called me in Philly and offered me an interesting proposition. He said he wanted to train someone to take over for him eventually. He would start by having me observe several people in the company and then, after a few months, take on ever-increasing responsibilities, until sometime, maybe three but no more than five years down the road, I'd be running Morgan*Plus*.

To be honest, I was a little surprised and flattered that he would see me, a twenty-five-year-old guy, as his heir apparent. My résumé to that point consisted of a couple of years handling loans at one of the larger banks in Philly. I was also surprised that there was no one at Morgan*Plus* who was a candidate to take over, but Larry assured me that none of his employees had an interest in doing so. When I asked about his own children, he said that neither his son nor daughter worked for him, so he needed to look elsewhere.

We fill our plates and sit down to eat and, needing something to discuss while waiting for Cooper, we launch into a conversation about sports. That's usually a safe place for guys. We start with the Cardinals (Larry shares four season passes with a friend), then Mizzou (he's not an alum but he's a fan), next, the Blues (he's a major fan and hopes this is their year), and finally, some talk about local politics and the weather (both are a mess, he thinks).

As we finish eating, he asks me if I want another cup of coffee and I decline. I'm thinking caffeine may not be my friend today. He gets up to pour himself another cup, and as he does so, there's a knock on his door.

"Come on in, Son." He assumes it's Cooper, and he's right.

Cooper is taller than his father, nearly my height, and maybe fifty pounds heavier than I am. He has on a very nice-looking suit, which probably cost him as much as my entire wardrobe, and his hair has been styled, not cut.

6

"Cooper, I want you to meet Dale Barnhart. Dale this is my son, Cooper."

We shake hands, and he has the exuberant handshake of a used car salesman, which, as I think about it, he was.

Larry says, "Sit down and let me catch you up some things. Coop, you know most of this, but there's some of it that will be new for you as well."

We take our seats.

"Before we start, Coop, would you like some coffee? It's not bad."

"Yes, Pop, with a little cream, please."

"Dale, you sure you couldn't use another cup?"

"You know I think I will have one after all."

"Straight, right?"

"Yessir, Mr. Morgan."

"It's Larry, remember."

"Then yes, please, Larry."

"Coop, why don't you do us the honors? You're younger than I am."

Larry waits as Cooper gets coffee for the three of us and takes a seat. Then he begins.

"My wife and I ran into an old friend, Cam Walker, at a New Year's Eve Party. While we were catching up on things, Cam told me that he still owns his family farm out by Wright City, but he may want to sell it. The guy who's been living there working it for him has done a great job, but he has his eye on his buying his own property. If he is successful, Cam would have trouble finding someone as good. So, like I said, it might be time to sell the place."

He takes a sip of his coffee before continuing.

"I told him we'd be happy to help in any way we could, and he told me I should make him an offer for the farm. I was interested, so I asked him what it would take, and he named a dollar amount that we could probably fundraise with a little help from some of our investors."

He puts down his mug and says, "But here's where it gets interesting. Cam is selective regarding what happens to the farm. His father inherited the place from his dad, so it's been in the family three generations, and there's a lot of sentiment attached to it. Well, the gist of it is that we *can* make an offer on the place, but before we do, we need to have a plan as to what we would do with it should we get it."

"Has he clarified what he might be looking for in such a plan?" I ask.

"No. He hasn't exactly said what he wants it to be, but he's been pretty clear about some things he *doesn't* want it to be. He told me that people have approached him in the past with an eye to developing it with homes or some type of commercial development. He also knows that a big commercial outfit, a corporate farm if you will, would love to buy it. For right now, all of those are no-goes for Cam. It's his family's farm, and he wants to do something better. He says he doesn't want to see a bunch of look-alike houses or giant hog barns or rows of Butler Buildings on the old home place."

I sip my coffee while I consider what I've heard.

"So, let me see if I got all that. You have a friend who thinks it might be time to sell his place, but he won't sell it unless the buyer assures him he's going to do something acceptable with the place. And, while we know what's not acceptable, we don't know what is acceptable. Am I on the right track here?"

"You are. And as he and I talked that night of the party, I thought of you. I could tell during our interview and in talking with the HR person at your old bank that you're a bright guy, and I believe you are the person to help put together a proposal that will convince him to sell and give us something new and exciting to work on."

"That's a big compliment—and a bigger challenge, I think."

"I think you can do it, and"—nodding at his son—"Coop here is going to work with you on it. After that night at the party, I was telling him about what was going on, and he indicated that he would like to come on board to work with you. Of course, I was thrilled to have him join the company, and I am excited to see what you two can do."

"Could I ask you what kind of time frame we would be dealing with?"

"I will be meeting with Cam Walker on March 1 to make our pitch," Larry says.

"March 1? That means we have just one month."

"Right."

"Mind if I warm up my coffee, Mr. Morgan?" I stand, looking to him for permission.

"It's Larry, okay? And sure."

It's not so much that I want more coffee right now, but topping off my coffee buys me a little time to process what I've heard and think of what I want to say next. I return to my seat with my refill and a plan.

"I think it would help me if I saw the place. Right now, I have a general idea of a farm in my head. I think I need to see the place to generate some thoughts for you to consider. Is there a time this week Cooper and I could go look at the property?"

"I'm sure you could do that," he assures. "Sounds like you are on board?"

"You're the boss, Larry, and if this is what you want me to do, then this is what I'll do."

"Great, I know you boys will be a great team. I'll have Cooper set up a farm tour. In the meantime, I want to share this with you."

He hands each of us a folder.

"I've had the staff prepare a folder for each of you. They've got photos and aerial shots, maps of the farm and surrounding properties, and some information on what governmental jurisdictions would be involved in permitting and the like, if we were to ask to change the zoning to something other than agricultural. Also, you'll find an appraisal of the property that my team worked up."

We open our folders, and there are pictures of the place in summer. These views leave little doubt that this is a great piece of property. Some of it appears to be hilly and covered with woods, but there is a considerable acreage that lies in the creek bottoms which is covered with crops and pasture. There is a house on one of the hillsides; the caretaker's house I would assume. In addition to the house, there is a large metal building and a barn. Up the hill from the house is a small lake. The farm appears to be surrounded by other farms, but there also appears to be a mix of uses farther away, with some commercial property and smaller acreages with homes. As I give the contents of the folder a cursory glance, I decide that it will be interesting to work on this. Partnering with Cooper should also prove to be interesting, but maybe "interesting" is not exactly the right word for it.

"Your staff did a nice job on these folders."

"They did, and I'd like you two to look through them

together later today. First, though, we need to do your orientation. You haven't met the team yet, as I recall."

"No, I haven't. I've been going through the materials you sent me, and I know most of their names and job descriptions, but it'll be nice to put faces with the names and roles."

"Great. The rest of the crew should be in by now. Let's go meet them."

I set my coffee cup down, grab my folder, and look at the view outside as I stand. The snow, which had let up while we ate and talked, appears to have intensified again.

Larry leads us on a tour of the second floor. We come first to the office of John McCauley, who is engaged in what seems to be an important phone conversation. Larry decides we will come back to him later.

I'd read some about John in the information that was sent to me prior to coming here, and I ask Larry to tell me a little more about him.

"Well, John McCauley, and Paula Smith, who you will meet in a moment, work with me to recruit investors. We sell more than half of our mortgage loans to them and get the rest of our money from banks. John and Paula are both good at what they do, and we've built some good relationships. They are big reasons we're doing all right."

When we reach her office, our luck improves; Paula is not on the phone.

"Paula, this is Dale Barnhart; the new guy I told you about."

"Hi, Dale. So, you're the Philly guy?"

"Not exactly, I'm from Spring Mill, a town an hour north of here originally. I worked in Philadelphia for a while after college, though."

She says, "So, what brings you here to Morgan*Plus*?"

11

"I was beginning to get the urge to look around a little, and fortunately I learned about this place, got an interview with Mr. Morgan and I'm happy to say that he was willing to take a chance on me."

"I see."

The way she said, "I see," was interesting to say the least. *There's something to watch for*, I think.

"So, Paula, tell me about you."

"I grew up in Overland Park, Kansas, and graduated from KU. I moved to St. Louis with my husband fifteen years ago. He's an executive with Ralston Purina or I guess I should say Nestlé Purina now. I worked at various jobs around the city, some in corporate and one as an executive director for a not-for-profit. Three years ago, I too had the urge to look around, and then I saw an on-line posting of this job. I felt that my background would be a good fit, so I applied, and Larry hired me."

She didn't mention children and I see no pictures, so I don't ask about that.

"Is your husband also a Jayhawk?"

"Yessir."

"Well, I'm a Mizzou grad, so I guess we'll have to work around that won't we?"

She grins and says, "We've gotten pretty good at that."

"Oh, I'm sure."

"We have converted to being Cardinals and Blues fans, so that's helped."

"Good. That'll give us a place to start. Larry was telling me you and John do a great job."

She looks at Larry with an odd expression and says, "It's always good to hear that you're appreciated. Thanks, Larry."

Larry, looking a little uncomfortable, says, "Well, you are, and I don't tell you that enough. Believe me, I never take your good work, or John's, for granted."

"I'll remind you of that when I ask for a raise!"

Larry fakes a look at his watch and says, "Oh, boy. We'd better get a move on guys!"

I don't know if I'd call it tension exactly, but there was something there. We say our 'nice-to-meet-you's and head next door. As we head down the hall, most of the people are working the phones. We get some nods, and one person mouths, "Welcome aboard." It's a little amusing that my tour has been more miss than hit today. I think if it had been up to me, I would have arranged a meet-and-greet instead.

Larry's cell rings and he checks to see who it is.

"Guys, I need to take this call."

He answers it and asks the person on the other end to hold for a second.

"Cooper, take Dale to your office and show him around until I get back, okay?"

"Okay, Dad. Will do."

Larry heads back to his office while we proceed to the other end of the hall. Cooper takes me to what must have been a large conference room that has recently been divided into three parts with a space for Cooper, one for me, and the remaining half of the office still set up as the conference room. The east wall of the area separates Larry's business from the insurance firm.

"I took the liberty of taking this space and you can have that one," says Cooper pointing me towards the middle of the three spaces. As I look at my new space, I'd estimate it to be smaller than the one Cooper has chosen, and unlike his there is no window. There was some advantage to being the first new guy on board it appears. We walk into the place, and I start to check it out. I take the opportunity to learn more about Cooper as I do.

"So, Cooper, you're here now. And if I remember you were selling cars before?"

"I was, and I was doing pretty well. It's slowed down a little though and I was starting to get bored with it frankly, so when Dad . . . I guess I need to call him Mr. Morgan, anyway when my dad and I were talking during a couple of weeks ago, he told me he had hired you and that he had a project he wanted you to work on. He told me a little bit about it, and that he was still looking to add one more employee. I asked him if he'd consider me, and he said he'd be happy to have me come on board. And here I am."

It's a slightly different version of the story than Larry's. I say nothing for a second, and Cooper, reading me and seeing that I'm not sure about all this, says, "I know this has caught you off guard. Dad told me the plan he has for you about you taking over for him some day. I'm sure you're thinking that if the boss's son comes on board that changes things. Nothing has changed there."

"Well, that's good to know, but for now it seems we have work to do, right?

"Right."

"I would like to see that farm, though."

"I have Jim's number, let me call and see if we can go out there tomorrow."

"Jim's the caretaker, I assume?"

"Yes. Good guy. You'll like him."

"Let's call then."

Cooper gets out his cell, pulls Jim's number up and hits the call icon. There's no answer, so he leaves a message.

After he ends his message, I say, "So, you've seen this place then?"

"Yes. Dad and I drove out there the day after he hired me. There was no snow, so we got a good look at the place. It was a typical cold winter day, and of course nothing was green like it will be soon, but even on that day I could tell the place had a ton of potential. I think after you see it, we will have some fun thinking about how we can make some money there."

"I'm sure we will."

His phone rings. He checks it and says, "It's Jim," then answers.

"Hey, Jim. Thanks for calling back. You get much snow out your way?"

Jim answers him.

"Wow! Sounds like even more than we're getting. Hey, Jim, another new guy at our firm and I are going to work on our offer to Cam and we were thinking about coming out tomorrow to check the place out. Is there too much snow to do that?"

Jim says something.

"I know, but we are looking at a deadline to put a proposal together, and it would help us to look at it, and I've got four-wheel drive on my Jeep."

Again, I hear Jim's voice, but I still can't make out what he's saying.

Cooper says, "That's okay, I'm pretty confident we can handle it even if the road isn't cleared by then. I'll check back with you in the morning, but plan on us getting there around ten or so."

Jim again.

"Great. Talk tomorrow."

Cooper hangs up, looks at me and says, "We're set. Hope you have some snow gear to wear. We might get stuck, and we'll definitely want to get out and do some walking around."

"I'll dress accordingly."

"Okay, then. It's time to get you set up here in your new office. Let's see if your computer is up and running and get you going on that."

"Okay."

We get my computer set up, and I set up my passwords where they're needed. I check my email and see that there are a couple of things that I still need to complete for Patterson Personnel Services, the firm who handles personnel and payroll for Larry.

"Let me finish this stuff, Cooper, and then maybe your dad will be ready to continue the tour."

"I just got a text. He says he'll take us downstairs after lunch."

"Sounds good."

He turns around to leave my area, stops, then turns back around.

"Did you bring lunch, Dale?'

"I brought some stuff from home, I'm good."

"I guess I'll have to order in if anyone is doing delivery. Well, I'll leave you alone. I'm thinking I might give the folder another going over."

"I'll do that too, when I finish this HR stuff."

"See you in bit. Oh, and Dale—"

"Yes?"

"I just want to say once again that I look forward to working with you."

"Same here, Cooper."

2

"YOU CAN'T DO THAT!"

I set my salad on the counter, move my tablet so that I get a better view of my parents, and say, "I can't do what, Mom?"

"You know what I mean. A person can't hire a relative. It's nepotism and it's not right!"

"Well, Mom. You worked at a public elementary school, so that would probably be the case there."

"I know it's the case. We had a principal who married a teacher."

"I remember that. It was all we kids talked about at the time."

"And do you remember what happened?"

"Well, I know the teacher wasn't there the next year."

"No, she wasn't. The School Board told the principal that either she went, or he went—that he couldn't supervise his

18

own wife. It's the same thing. Your new boss hired his son, and it isn't right."

My mom is obviously not happy with what she's hearing, and when Pat Barnhart gets righteously indignant, it takes a while to get her settled down.

"Help me out here, Dad. You run a business. What do you think?"

"I think I'd be happy to hire my son to take over *The Gazette*."

"I guess I walked into that one, didn't I?"

My Dad's paper, like so many, is going through tough times. Somehow, he thinks I have the business instincts to save it. It's a frequent topic of conversation between us.

"You did, but that doesn't make the sentiment any less true, and to your point I think the private sector is a different animal than the public sector with regard to hiring relatives."

Mom says, "That doesn't change things for me. You accepted the job there with an understanding about what would happen down the road, and on your first day, your very first day, your boss gives you a completely different kind of task to do and tells you his son will be working with you on it."

"I get your point, Mom, but here's what I think. First of all, I'm glad to have a specific project to work on rather than just job-shadowing people. And second, all I can do is take hold of this farm project and knock it out of the park."

"And if you do, who's to say you'll get the credit?"

"I have to agree with your mom there, Son. While I think Larry Morgan has every right to hire his son, I also know that it could change everything for you. Just keep your eyes and ears open and be vigilant. You have a little bit of a tendency to trust other people and to think they're like you. Sadly, they aren't always."

"So, you think I should have stayed in Philly, then?"

Mom says, "No we're thrilled you're back home. You know that."

"Okay. Let's just see how it goes tomorrow when Cooper and I go to the farm. Maybe everything will fall in place."

"Will you call us and tell us about it?"

"I can do that."

"Great. It's so nice to web chat with you."

"Mom, we could do that when I was in Philadelphia!"

"I know, but it's better when you're closer."

Dad and I laugh at that.

"You know what I mean!"

"Where's Dave—I thought he and DJ would join us?"

"Your brother's upstairs giving DJ a bath and trying to get him to settle down for the night."

"I'm ready to see that little guy. Oh, and DJ, too."

It's a classic Barnhart Brothers statement and gets the usual eye roll from Mom.

"You're coming up this weekend, right?" she asks.

"Sure I am. I'll be up Friday night or Saturday morning at the latest."

"And you'll stay for our Super Bowl party?"

"Yeah, sure. For most of it at least. The game goes on forever, and I'll probably leave early to get back here, but I'll be there."

"Great."

"Goodnight, Mom and Dad. I love you."

"You too, Dale, and we're so glad you're back home."

"You've said that about fifty times already."

"I know, but we are.

3

Tuesday, February 5

COOPER'S GPS TELLS US that we are nearing our exit. We're on I-70 headed west, and about thirty minutes into our trip.

"So, tell me about Jim Lynch, Cooper."

"Like I told you, he's a good dude. You'll like him."

"And he's going to be buying his own farm."

"Yes. Dad said he found himself a smaller place up near Hannibal. It's a place he can afford and closer to where he grew up."

"Do you know how long he's been taking care of the Walker place?"

"At least five years, maybe ten."

"Well, he must be doing a good job of it."

"Yeah, the best. The farm and house look great. As Dad says, guys like Jim are hard to find."

We take the exit and turn south crossing over Interstate 70. It's a couple of miles to the farm road now. The snow is piled high along the county road, and it's obvious they've had more here. The skies have cleared today, and the sun is up and starting to melt any snow that remains on the roadbed.

"You're quiet, Dale. What are you thinking about?"

"Just going back over all of this before we get there."

"What specifically?"

"Well, for one thing, remind me how your dad got first shot at this deal?"

"Dad and Cam used to work together before Dad bought the Mortgage Company. My parents have remained good friends with Cam and his wife and still see them from time to time. I guess they were all at the same Christmas party."

"It seems odd that Cam would pick us to do this. We're a mortgage firm. We don't do things like this ordinarily."

"No, we haven't before, but Dad wants to diversify, which I believe is another reason he hired you, and this is our first chance to help him do that."

"So why doesn't Walker just sell it to us, or sell it to someone else and let us handle it? Why are we doing this little dance?"

"I think he's had some offers on the place. Well, I know he's had one from a neighbor, Rusty Brotherton, and he doesn't want to sell it to that guy. They have never gotten along. As for considering other offers, Cam's afraid he'll sell it, and then the buyer will turn around and do something to ruin the place."

"It's not easy to control what happens after you sell a place."

"I know, but that's our challenge."

"I see."

We drive a little farther and the GPS tells us to turn right on Rolling Hills Road in a quarter mile. Cooper makes the turn onto the snow-covered road, and as we make our way down Rolling Hills, there are fences on either side with slight depressions between them and our narrow road. I assume the depressions are drainage ditches, and I'm hoping we don't meet another car. With all this snow, Cooper's four-wheel drive is going to be put to the test as it is. We don't need to see how it handles in a ditch.

Cooper takes it slow, but we still slide from time to time. He looks over at me and says, "Hey, what's the worst that could happen?"

"My dad used to say that to me."

"Yeah? Well, I guess today the worst thing would be we'd end up stuck in a ditch."

"I guess so," I agree.

"We would most likely survive that, don't you think?"

"I'm thinking we would."

"Then just sit back and relax and enjoy the scenery, and I'll do my best to keep us on the road."

I decide to follow his suggestion and check out the view.

We keep driving through an open area of snow-covered fields. In the distance, the fields are bordered by small hills covered with greenish-brown cedar trees growing where the old-growth hardwoods once stood. Their branches droop with the weight of the heavy snow. Intermingled with the cedars are a few surviving hardwoods whose dark branches are outlined by the layer of snow on them. It's a Christmas Card picture.

About a half-mile in, our route begins to curve south. There's a break in the fence-line and a road leads off to our right that I know from looking at my folder leads to the Roberts' farm.

We reach a steep downhill and Cooper shifts to a lower gear to maintain control as we go. When we reach the bottom, the road forks. The left road has a marker that says Brotherton Farm Road. Cooper takes the smaller road to our right.

"So, we've finally made it to the Walker farm, I take it?"

"Almost," Cooper says. "We need to cross that old bridge first."

"So, it's Roberts on the right, Brotherton on the left, and the Walker farm up ahead."

"Yes."

"And the road we just took runs between the Roberts and Brotherton farms?"

"Yes, I guess it does."

"I'm wondering whose job it is to take care of the road. I'm assuming the county maintenance stops on the black top road."

"I don't know for sure," he says, "but I would think Jim has to take care of the road from where the roads split, and maybe the other guys take turns on Rolling Hills—just a guess, though."

We approach the bridge, which like the road, has yet to be plowed. It's a one-lane structure made of heavy horizontal planks held in place by larger planks that run the length of it. I'm hoping those two bigger planks will keep us on the bridge. Cooper, still being cautious, crosses the bridge, and as he does, we can hear each board rattle under our tires even though the snow muffles the sound.

"I'm taking it slow, so you can enjoy the view as we cross the creek."

The view I'm eyeing is a stream that runs between snow-covered rocks, and if a guy doesn't mind the prospect of sliding off the bridge and ending up in it, the stream's remarkably pretty.

We make it across, and Cooper says, "Okay, now look ahead."

As I do, I see a sign over the road that says, "Welcome to Walker Farm." The sign is suspended from a cable that runs between two cut-off telephone poles.

"I like the sign."

"And the view?" He asks.

"Definitely."

As we enter the property, the stream we crossed veers west and hugs the hills, leaving a broad expanse of bottomland ahead of us. I can see the stubble of last summer's crop under the snow cover. About a quarter mile ahead of us there's a large barn with several head of cattle, some red and white, some black. A few of them have their heads poking through a metal fence and are working on a large bale of hay. Others are standing nearby at a water tank, watching and waiting for a drink while a man works to break the ice.

As we get closer, I can see he has on a bright orange stocking cap and Carhartt overalls over a sweatshirt. He's dressed for outdoor work, for sure. Covered up as he is, he could be forty—or seventy—and weigh between 140 and 250 pounds. His movements suggest that he's fit and closer to forty. His well-used farm truck sits just behind him. The guy, who I guess to be Jim Lynch, is either so engrossed in his work that he seems not to notice our approach or just chooses not to. It could be he's not all that excited about our visit today.

4

WHEN WE GET NEARER, he looks up and waves at us, then points in the direction of the machine shed on the other side of the road. We make the turn into its parking lot and stay in the jeep for a couple more minutes until Jim pulls beside us in his old truck. He gets out and comes to Cooper's side of the car, reaching through the now-opened window to shake hands.

"Good to see you, Jim. Thanks for making some time for us today."

"Good to see you again, Cooper." He reaches past Cooper to shake my hand. His hand, while not a lot larger than mine, is calloused and tough from hard work, and makes me self-conscious of my office hands and determined to get outside and do something—anything, to rectify the situation when spring comes.

"Nice to meet you."

"And you too, Jim. I'm Dale Barnhart."

"That almost sounds like—"

"I know, I know, and to make matters worse, I'm Dale Barnhart, Jr."

"Oh, man." Jim grimaces. "That had to be some fun when you were a kid."

"Not as much as you'd think."

"Well guys, get out and come in the shed. I've got the wood stove going and the coffee pot on."

We both think hot coffee sounds good and we follow him inside. Jim closes the door behind us, and we soon start to warm up.

The shed is approximately 30 feet by 40 feet, and we have entered it through a door in the middle. I look around and see that it is simple, neat, and efficient. It's divided into three unequal sections, the largest being on the left where there is room to park a tractor and pick-up. In the middle is a well-equipped work section. To the right is the smallest area; the living quarters of the shed with a small fridge, microwave, wood-burning stove, a table and some chairs, and a counter with our coffee pot.

Jim goes to the counter, finds three well-used and mostly clean mugs, and pours us our coffee.

"I don't have any sugar or cream, boys."

We say we don't need it, although the coffee, having been on awhile, could use a little something. I take a sip and decide that in this setting and on this day, it's perfect.

Jim takes off his hat. His face is old and young at the same time; skin taut and weathered like that of a cowboy or a ski-bum, and his hair a mix of brown and blonde and a little too long. His smile is the young part of it; bright and open, and it makes him look more like the forty-year-old I now think he is. People spend a lot of money to have a smile like his, but I think nature has spared Jim the expense.

I ask, "So how long have you been working this place?"

"I've been here seven years—ever since old man Walker passed." He pauses for a moment, then says, "It's hard to believe it's been that long."

"It's a nice place, Jim."

"Do you have a buyer for it yet?"

Cooper says, "It might be our company if we put together the right offer. Cam Walker wants us to have a proposal in front of him by March 1. If he likes it, then he'll allow us to proceed."

"You guys are a mortgage company. I bet there'll be a bunch of houses out here someday."

I say, "Not for a while I don't think. You're still far enough out of the city that people can find better options closer in." And for that, I get a look from Cooper that tells me where his head might be and a smile from Jim.

"Well, that's good."

I add, "Plus Walker doesn't want this to be turned into a subdivision or a corporate hog operation. So, there's that, too."

"Great," says Jim.

"Yeah," says Cooper, "but that just compounds our challenge. We've got to figure out what we *can* do that would meet his approval."

Jim sips his coffee and stares at us for a moment. "A farm is what this place needs to be."

Cooper looks at Jim and says, "Walker's afraid he'll sell it to someone who will *say* they intend to farm it but will turn it over in five years."

"Well how can he control that?"

"I guess it's our job to come up with a long-term plan that makes sure," Cooper responds.

"You boys may have yourselves a challenge."

I say, "I hear you might be buying some land of your own up north."

"I was, but I just learned that the deal fell through. Some people from Indiana outbid me. I thought about countering their offer, but it would have meant taking on too much debt. I couldn't see a way to ever make any money on that place if I did that."

"So, what are you going to do?"

"Well, I'm not sure. I guess I'll figure that out while you figure out what you guys are going to do."

None of us speak after that. Instead, there are a few minutes of coffee and thought.

Jim sets down his mug and says, "You came out here to look at the place. Are you ready?"

We both say, "Sure."

"It's not the best day to show it to you, but it should be fun."

"We're ready."

"Then let's go. I'll drive Shania and show you around."

Cooper and I finish our coffee and head outside to his truck, which is apparently named Shania. Jim gets in on the driver's side and Cooper offers me the middle seat, then slides in after me. Although Jim is slim, like me, there are three of us in the seat and we're wearing multiple layers, so the fit is tight.

Jim says, "Here we go," and turns the key. Shania starts with a little encouragement, and our adventure begins.

5

As we pull back out onto the road, a couple of cows with calves stand near the barn.

I feel the need to make some small talk. "I see you've got a couple of new ones there."

"Yessir; just a week old, and more on the way soon. Luckily these two came easy. That doesn't always happen."

Cooper asks, "So, do you call a vet when the cows are having trouble? How does that work?"

"Not usually. I can handle most of the births, but occasionally there's a problem. I've had a lot of experience with calving. When I was a teenager, my first real job was helping our local vet. I learned to do just about everything a guy needs to know on a farm. I can give all the shots, turn the young bulls into steers, and help pull calves if needed."

"You are one handy guy."

Cooper says, "That's just the half of it. You should see what he's done to the house."

"I'll want to do that."

I look across the road at the barn and it looks to be in remarkably good shape—freshly painted and with a good roof on it. Pop Barnhart thinks a barn is a proxy for the health of its farm. My granddad would love this barn; he would love the farm it is a part of; and he would understand why Cam Walker would want the right thing done by it.

We drive past the barn and take a road that splits off from the main one and climbs the hill to our east. As we do, we pass the farmhouse, which located as it is on the hillside enjoys a great view of the valley. To the north of the farmhouse there is a level area, which I guess to be a garden plot, although I can't be sure with all the snow.

"You two want to look inside the house first?"

Cooper says, "I don't need to. I've already seen it. Dale, you want to go inside?"

"No, that's okay. Let's keep rolling."

"As I said, Jim's done some nice things to the house. It's in great shape. You need to see it sometime."

"My girlfriend helps me out when she comes down."

I ask, "Does she live nearby?"

Jim says, "Oh no, she lives north of Hannibal, but she gets down here to spend weekends with me quite a bit. She loves this farm almost as much as I do."

"What does she do?"

"Her parents own a farm implement business, and she helps them out with that. She finished her degree in business a couple of years ago, so she takes care of their books and advertising and the like."

I look at him for a second, wanting to follow up on the "finishing-her-degree a couple of years ago" part. That raises some questions about her age. But I can't decide how to ask politely, so I don't.

Jim saves me the trouble. "Yes, she's younger than I am. My older brother is friends with her parents, and he introduced us. I took it from there." He looks at us and gives us a half smile.

I say, "So would you move back to that part of the state if this place sold?"

"Guess so. I was so set on buying that farm that I really didn't have a backup plan. I've done enough things over the past few years that I should be able to find work. I mean I could probably find a vet that needs a good assistant or go to work for someone in construction, if nothing else. Hell, I could even work on farm equipment if I need to, although it would be my last resort."

"What about finding another farm near the one you tried to buy?"

"I don't know if I will find anything as good as that one. The house and buildings were in good shape, there was the right amount of acreage I could afford, and they were going to include some of their equipment. I'll keep looking though. Maybe one just as good will turn up."

He looks as if he doesn't think it will. We continue up the ridge and pass a dam and, behind it, a small lake that was created by widening the crease between this hill and its neighbor to the south. We continue to circle to the eastern end towards a snow-covered cabin. It has a deck with what might be a grill on it, and near that, a canoe leaning up against the side of the cabin. We follow the road which runs between the cabin and a fence, that I would guess separates the Walker place from the Brotherton farm. Looking back across the lake, I see a dock with a diving board that's been pulled out of the lake for winter. They are snow-covered and out of place on this wintry day. It's hard to imagine there being a day warm enough for the dock to be in the water and kids diving off it. I make a mental note to come out this summer just to see that.

"It looks like the lake has all you need for some summer fun."

"You could say that. The fishing's good, and you can't see it under the snow, but there's a nice little sand beach right there near the cabin. Cam set it up for his kids and grandkids to use when they came out here on weekends. I've worked on it to keep it up, but it doesn't get used much now. I think they all have pools at their houses and the kids are all involved in activities. About the only people who enjoy it now are me and Ginny. We sometimes bring our sleeping bags up here and camp out. Her chocolate lab, Jake, loves this lake, too. We can't keep him out of it."

"And fall? Is it as pretty then?"

"It is. There's a little color in these hills. And when it gets chilly at night you can build a campfire and actually see some stars."

I can sense that Jim has a genuine fondness for this place.

"It will be hard to leave here, Jim."

"It will be. I won't find a place I love any more than this farm; that's for sure. My only hope is I'll find one that's close."

He circles along the ridge, and we have a great view of the farm below us. There's a curl of smoke coming out of the machine shed and it smells great. Cooper thinks it would make a good cologne, and I agree.

"Maybe that could be our new project—*Smoke Cologne for Men.*"

"I have a feeling if we pitched that to Dad, you'd be looking for a new job and I'd be selling cars again."

"Yeah, most likely."

Jim had stopped the truck to let us look at the place. He leans forward a little so he can see us both and says, "We've got two choices here, fellas. We can turn around and go back the way we came, or we can keep going. If we keep going this road will take us down the hill to where you can see the other valley, and from there we can catch the main road back to the shed. It'll be a bit of rough ride. Which way do you want to go?"

Cooper asks, "Do you think Shania can handle the hill? What with the snow and all?"

"Oh sure. I mean, we'll be going downhill. There's just that little jog around that mound on the way down."

I look at the road, check out the mound, and say, "Let's do it. I'd like to see the whole place."

Jim shifts to a low gear, and off we go.

The road winds down along the hillside towards the mound which sits to the left and is covered with trees and large rocks. Snow covers the whole scene making it another Christmas Card moment.

"What is that mound, Jim?"

"The story is, Dale, that it's a sacred Indian site, like a burial mound. Anyhow for whatever reason, it has not been touched by anyone who's ever owned the land."

We ease toward the mound, and the road veers to the right to go around it. To the right of our road, the hill slopes away from us. Jim taps lightly on the brakes, and we slide a little to the right. For a second, I think we might start sliding down that slope, and then, suddenly, the front right wheel drops off the road and we come to an abrupt stop.

Jim says, "Well, that's not good! Let me get out and see.

34

We might be stuck."

I'm thinking that we most likely are stuck, and stuck pretty good. Jim exits and I see him walking around the truck, and occasionally squatting to survey the situation. Within a couple of minutes, he gets back in.

"Yep, we're stuck."

He's so dry and matter of fact about it, we can't help but laugh. It appears that getting stuck today *was* the worst thing that could happen, and it's not that bad.

Cooper says, "I was going to guess that we might be stuck, what with the sliding off the road and not moving any more. You got a plan, there, Jimbo?"

"I'm working on it. I can tell you why we got stuck if you are interested."

I say, "Sure. I mean it seems like we have some time."

"Last fall we moved some dirt from the left side to the right and moved the road over a little to help a drainage problem. We just hit that soft dirt on the right side, and it sucked us in to where we're high-centered."

"And now we know."

"And now you know."

"Can Dale and I push while you drive Shania out?"

"We can try. But if you try to push me going downhill, there's a chance I might not be able to get back on the road and Shania would turn into a giant sled. You're going to have to push me *up* hill, I'm afraid."

"Okay then, Dale are you ready?"

"I guess I'm ready."

We walk to the front of the truck. I take the side that is still on the road and Cooper takes the side that's stuck in the soft ground. Jim puts the truck in gear and, as we push, he gives it some gas. Both tires kick up a combination of snow and dirt and rock, and the truck doesn't move. We continue this for a couple of minutes until it is obvious to all that this plan is not working.

Jim hops out. "Well guys, we need a new plan."

Cooper asks, "What do you propose, Jim?"

"We need to get just a little more horsepower involved. If you two want to, we could walk down the hill and get you back to your jeep so you can head back to town. I can get the truck out later."

I say, "No, we don't want to leave you like this. You're in this predicament because I wanted to see the rest of the farm. We aren't leaving until we get Shania back on the road."

"Well then, I'll go get the tractor out of the shed and we'll pull her out. It'll be twenty minutes or so before I'm back. Is that okay?"

We both say it is.

———————————

Jim takes off down the hill, then falls flat on his back a few feet in front of the truck. He gets up, and I know he wants to let loose with some choice words. I know I would. Instead, he brushes himself off and continues down the road. Soon he reaches the bottom of the hill and turns and heads north to the shed.

While we're waiting, Cooper and I get out our phones. Why we decide to do that, who knows? Habit I suppose. We both fiddle with them for a minute and then Cooper says, "You have a signal?"

"No, none."

"I guess being on this side of the hill, we're blocked from any cell tower. It's like being back in the last century."

"Yes, it's all very primitive."

I get a smile for my attempt at humor.

I say, "At least we have a great view."

"We do. You know, we should be able to do something really good with this place."

"Coop, in my opinion there probably isn't anything better than this."

"This what?"

"Farming it, like Jim says."

"But that doesn't make us any money."

We're quiet for a moment, and then he adds, "Man, I should not have had that last cup of coffee."

"Yeah, I know. I was just regretting that too."

"I hate to think about having to go out here, but I don't think I can wait a half hour or whatever it's going to take to get us back to the shed."

"You go ahead and then I'll take my turn when you're done."

Cooper gets out of the truck and walks up the hill behind it. He heads across the road away from the mound and stands there with his back to me.

When he comes back, he says, "Your turn."

I hop out of the truck and go slightly uphill from where he just went. I'm not too excited about having to do this in the chilly air, for obvious reasons, but the need is too great.

When I walk back, Cooper is sitting on the driver's side.

"I'm guessing one of us will need to steer when Jim gets back, so I'm volunteering."

"I will let you do the honors."

Soon, we hear the perfect staccato sound of an old farm tractor coming up the hill toward us. Jim waves as he passes us, then finds an area behind us and backs close to Shania. He hops off the tractor, leaving it running and methodically attaches the chain to the tractor and then to the truck. Nothing much rattles Jim, and I think he has the kind of personality a guy needs to work on a farm.

When he finishes, he says, "Okay, Cooper, wait until I get you moving, then give it some gas. Dale, if you'd push, it might help, too."

"Got it."

Jim gets on the tractor and carefully eases it forward until there is tension on the towing chain, and then he revs it a little. Even with all the traction it can get, it still struggles to free us. He's working against gravity on a slick hillside. I'm pushing for all I'm worth, while wondering if I'm making any difference. Finally, we begin to feel the truck move, and when it does, Cooper puts it in reverse and gives it a little gas to help. Jim guides the tractor and Cooper steers the truck until we are safely on the road again. Jim signals to stop and gets off his tractor giving us a thumbs-up. He has the chain off the truck in seconds and wraps it around the tow bar on the tractor. I hop back in the truck.

He comes to the truck window and says, "I'll go up the hill a little to find a place to turn around. You think you can maneuver the truck down the hill from here?"

Cooper says, "Sure. I can. We'll see you when we reach the bottom of the hill."

Jim nods his head and hops on the tractor and heads uphill. Cooper puts Shania in gear and off we go. Soon we can hear Jim catching up with us. When we reach the valley floor, we proceed through the gap along the creek and into the southern valley, which is smaller and more bowl-shaped than its wider neighbor to the north. We get out of the truck and study the scene in front of us. Jim joins us as we do.

"I think this was a separate farm at some point, then the Walkers bought it."

I scan it and see no remnants of another house or barn. I look over at Cooper and I can tell some thought has entered his head.

"It's different than the other valley."

"It is. It's narrower, and the stream divides it instead of running along the hill."

"Yeah, and that kind of gives me some ideas. You know what I mean?"

I have this sense that I wouldn't like any of his ideas, and now is not the time for that conversation.

We study the valley a little longer, then Cooper says, "I don't know about you guys, but I'm getting cold. Let's go back to the shed and warm up."

We get back in the truck and Jim leads us down the main road back to where we started. When we get to the shed, Jim gets off the tractor and opens the garage door. He pulls the tractor in as far as he can and motions Cooper to follow with the truck, which he does. Jim gets off and shuts the shed door while we exit Shania, happy to be inside, and more than a little bit revved up by our adventure.

"Well, guys, you got a little more than you bargained for today."

"We did. Sorry again for causing you so much trouble, Jim. We should have turned around at the top of the hill."

"Oh, that's okay, I was fairly sure we'd make it. Don't worry about it."

"I want to come back and see this sometime, maybe when it thaws."

"Come back anytime, Dale. You're always welcome."

He looks at me, and I think he sees that I think like he does when it comes to Walker Farm.

Cooper says, "Well, we've wasted enough of your time, and we should get back to the office."

"It was good to see you again, and Dale, it was nice to meet you."

"And you, too. I will be back."

"Great."

"Oh, hey one last thing before we leave, have you let Cam Walker know that your farm deal fell through?"

"Not yet, I just found out. I'm going to call him later. At least we could get some crops out this spring while waiting to figure out what to do with the place right?"

"Yeah. I think that's a winning scenario. Cam will get some more money off the place, and it will buy us more time to figure out what we want to do. And you get some more time to think about what you want to do."

Jim likes the idea, but as I look at Cooper, I get a different read. Maybe he's worried that if Cam learns Jim isn't planning to leave now, at least for the foreseeable future, he might back off selling the place.

Jim says, "I'll call him today."

We say our good-byes and head back through the valley.

After we cross the bridge, Cooper looks at me and says, "Well, what do you think?"

"It was a good morning, and I enjoyed meeting Jim."

"Yeah, but what do you think about the property?"

"It holds snow well."

"Yeah, for sure, but what do you think about our *opportunity*."

"It has potential."

"I wish that Cam wasn't so set on not letting us develop it."

I say, "You mean, as in putting up a bunch of houses?"

"Yeah. Eventually the city is going to grow this way. It would be great to get out ahead of it and start subdividing the place and building homes on it."

"It's going to be a while before that happens don't you think?"

"I'm in sales. I mean I've *worked* in sales, and you don't wait for the opportunity. You make it happen."

"I don't know what I think at this point. I just saw the place. I'm willing to consider all options, but it seems like putting in a housing development is a non-starter, since Cam Walker won't sell it to us if that's our plan."

"Dale, here's what I think. We'll come up with something good, something we like and want to do, and then we'll sell that idea to Cam Walker. If it's a good one, he'll end up going for it, I'm sure."

"I tell you what. I have a busy couple of days ahead of me. Your dad has me set up to shadow some folks. Why don't we plan to meet on Friday, and begin to brainstorm some ideas?"

"Okay. But we need to figure out how to develop this place. It's a perfect fit for what we do, and we can make us some money."

Maybe because he's so adamant, or maybe because of something I've seen this morning, I think differently.

The rest of the ride is quiet. When we hit the interstate and head east, I get my phone out and check my messages. There's nothing much there, and I didn't really expect there would be, but checking my phone is a hard habit to break.

6

Wednesday, February 6

THE SUN HAS ALREADY SET by the time I pull in my driveway. I went to the gym after I left Morgan*Plus* today, did a light workout, then grabbed a sub at a local sub shop. Now I'm ready to get to work on it and settle in for a quiet evening.

My duplex has a single-car garage which sits next to the garage for the other side. It's a nice set up because the garages allow for privacy between the living areas. My new neighbor, Phyllis, is a fifty-five-year-old divorcee who also happens to be my landlady. She came over and introduced herself Saturday morning. I had moved in the night before and she was nice enough to give me some time to unpack and get settled before coming by to get acquainted.

I like Phyllis, and I think she'll be a good landlady. She's been through some tough times herself, losing her husband of twenty-five years to his younger office assistant. After the divorce, she bought the duplex and moved here, not wanting to have a large place to take care of, nor to live in the house she had shared with her ex.

As I wait for my garage door to open, I see Phyllis coming around the corner of her garage. It would be rude to go ahead and pull in, since she seems to be coming my way. I put my car in park, leave it running, open the door, and get out to talk with her.

"Hey, neighbor, how are you?"

"Great. How is the new job going?"

"It's been interesting so far; I'll say that. And how about you? How are things at the day care?"

"I'm having some staff issues, and we have lots of kids with sniffles. Just normal stuff for this time of year."

"I bet."

Phyllis smiles. "Dale, I have made a large pot of chili, and I'm thinking you probably could use some of it."

"I'd love that. I bought a sandwich, and your chili would be perfect with it."

"Well, I will give you some time and bring some over to you."

"Great. Give me fifteen minutes."

"Perfect. I'll bring you a bowl of soup and maybe something a little extra."

I am fairly sure she is still talking about food, so I tell her I can't wait.

I get my car parked, go in, and grab a quick shower, and change into jeans and a fleece. While pulling on my socks, I hear a knock at the door. I start to yell, "Come in," but remember the door's locked. I hurry to the door and open it for her. She is carrying a small basket.

"Come in, Phyllis. May I help you with that?"

"No, I've got it."

She heads to my small kitchen and sets the basket down on the counter.

"Seems like you might have a little more than soup, there."

"I brought you some extra soup. I thought you might enjoy some tomorrow night, too, or you could have it for lunch tomorrow."

"Well, that's thoughtful of you."

She uncovers the contents of the basket and pulls out a lidded container with soup, and another with some crackers and veggies. Then comes her surprise; she's also brought me some brownies and ice cream.

"Wow! Brownies and ice cream. I'm glad I worked out tonight."

"You're thin. This dessert isn't going to hurt you."

"Thanks for all of this. You didn't have to."

"It's okay. I wanted to welcome you, and this seemed like a good way. Go ahead and eat. I've already had mine."

She makes no move to leave, and it seems she'd like to stay and talk, so I pull out the other stool and ask her to have a seat at the island. She takes off her coat which I take from her and lay over a chair in the TV room; then I sit down and join her—one of us ready for chili and the other for conversation.

"I saw a nice-looking young man helping you unload on Friday. I'm assuming that was your brother."

"It was."

"Is he older or younger?"

"A year younger. He just turned twenty-four."

"So, you're both single?"

"Yes, you could say that, but he just got a divorce."

"Oh, I'm sorry. I know how that is."

"And he's got a little boy, five, named DJ."

"DJ?"

"Yes, Dave Junior."

"So, did he get custody?"

"Yes, full custody in fact."

"That says a lot."

"Yes, it does," I agree.

"And you said your new job is going okay?"

"I think so."

Phyllis eyes me. "That wasn't an overly enthusiastic answer."

"Well, you know. It takes a while to get settled in."

"So why, if you don't mind my asking, did you leave Philly and come to Missouri?"

I try to work in a spoonful of soup between answers, so she waits for me.

"This job, I guess."

"Just that?"

I take another sip of soup and a small bite of the sub I bought and hold up my index finger to signal that I need a moment.

"Oh, yes, please go ahead and eat. I'm so sorry I keep asking you questions."

"It's all right. To be honest, I wanted to think about my answer. I'm going to try to give you the short version, okay?"

"I have time for the longer one, if that's better."

"No, you don't have that kind of time!"

She laughs.

I have a little more soup and another bite of my sub, knowing it could be a while before I get another chance.

"Okay. I went to Philadelphia not too long after I graduated from Mizzou. I thought it would be good to go somewhere else and get a whole new experience. I'd spent my whole life in Missouri, and Philly seemed like as good a place as any, especially after I got accepted to work on my MBA there."

"So, did you finish your degree?"

"No, I didn't. I found that I was tired of college—burnt out really, so I took a position at a bank. I was working in consumer loans, helping people with remodeling projects and new cars. I liked it. I had a good boss, and I had good coworkers. Plus, there was another employee, a teller, that I was starting to go out with."

"So, what happened to change things?"

"In late October, my boss announced her retirement, so that was the first thing that took a bad turn. I respected her and liked working for her, but they replaced her with a guy from one of the branches, and he took an immediate dislike to my coworker, Matt, and me. Before long we felt the same about him. I had only been at the bank a couple of years, but I felt that even *I* would do a better job than that clown. Matt felt the same, and he got out of there right away. He got hired to work at another bank. Then there was Giselle, the coworker I liked; well, she broke things off at that same time and told me she was going back to New York to go to nursing school."

"So, this Giselle . . . did you see that going somewhere?"

"Yes, I did. Maybe I was getting ahead of myself, but I thought maybe she might possibly be the one."

Phyllis says, "I can tell that was a big blow."

"For sure, and that on top of the change at work was doubly tough."

46

"Oh, Dale, that was a lot to deal with. I could see why you'd want out of there."

I hesitate, knowing I can leave my explanation there, but decide to continue anyway. "Truth is, even with all that I was still determined to stay and fight my way through it."

"So, something else must have happened."

"It did. Right after I got back to Philadelphia after Thanksgiving break, my best friend Drew got killed in a car wreck."

"A car wreck! How awful!"

"It was, and to make matters worse I had a difficult time getting home. First, my new boss wasn't very cooperative in allowing me time off. I had to go over his head to HR. Then on the day I was to fly out, a snowstorm shut down every airport in the region except Dulles. I had to drive through the snow to get there."

"But you had to come home, didn't you?"

"I did. It was Drew and his family wanted me to speak at his service. While I was home, I realized with everything that had happened, it was time to move on from my job in Philly."

"And did you already have this job offer?"

"I did. Another story for another day, but I interviewed for it when I was back for Thanksgiving and things just fell into place."

"Sounds like it was meant to be."

"I guess that remains to be seen."

She looks at me and wants to ask another question but doesn't.

"Phyllis, I believe that ended up being the long version. I'm sorry."

47

"No. I'm glad you told me, and I hope you like this new job and I bet you find some girl here in Missouri."

"You've been talking to my mom on that last part."

She smiles. "I met her when she was getting this place ready for you. You know all us moms are alike. We want our kids to find someone special."

"The question is, though, if anyone will ever be special enough for a mother."

"In the case of my two daughters, I'd say yes to that. They both married great guys."

"I don't know if my mom would be as easy to please, but I guess if I wait long enough, she'll have to settle for just about anyone."

Phyllis laughs for quite a while at that.

"You won't have to settle, and neither will your mom. You're a nice-looking young man."

I smile and say, "I have this theory that *nice-looking* means not too painful to look at."

She laughs again and says she thinks I have a good sense of humor.

"Okay, I have to try this dessert you brought me."

"I'll let you do that, but I need to get back to my place. My favorite show is coming on."

"At least let me wash your containers and bring them to you."

"It's a deal."

"The soup was great, and I bet the brownies will be too."

"Thank you. I hope you like them."

She gets ready to leave, picks up and puts on her coat, and then turns to me and says, "Would you mind one more question?"

"No. Fire away."

"Your friend who died. Was he single?"

"No. He was married, and he left a wife and a little boy who's just about the same age as my nephew."

"Oh, that's so sad. How's his widow doing?"

"About as well as she could be I suppose. You know what? I haven't called her since I got here. I am going to do that right after you leave. I hope she's doing okay. Not that anyone deserves what happened to her, but she sure as heck didn't."

"No, no one does, and I can tell you think a lot of her."

"I do, and I need to call her. Thanks again for adding to my meager little sub. The soup was great."

"Talk to you soon."

She leaves and I go after the dessert. As I enjoy it, I pull up Sarah Marshall's number and click on it.

7

MY CALL GOES TO HER VOICEMAIL. There's a chance she hasn't stored my number among her contacts or she's busy with Alex. I leave a message and get back to work on the brownie and ice cream.

Soon, my phone rings and it's Sarah.

"Hello."

"Dale, I'm so sorry I didn't answer. I was trying to get Alex to take a bath. Dad's reading to him now, so I have a minute."

"How's Alex doing?"

"I think he's okay. I'm still not sure he understands what happened." She pauses for a second, "I'm not sure I do either, I guess."

"I know. It still seems unreal."

"So how are things in . . . oh my gosh you're back in Missouri, aren't you? I almost said Philadelphia."

"Yes, I'm back and I've started my new job."

"How is it?"

"It is different, that's for sure, but maybe that's just what I need."

"I hope so. I like knowing you're back. In some way it helps a little."

"How's school going?"

"School's fine."

"How many more semesters do you have?"

"I have this spring and then next year, but the exciting thing is I get to student teach next year at this time."

"Oh, that's great. What grade do you want to teach?"

"I think I would like third or fourth, maybe second. For sure not kindergarten or fifth grade though."

"That's pretty specific."

"I know, but I'll take whatever grade I get."

"You'll do great."

"That's kind of you, and it means a lot to hear it. So, tell me more about work, why is it so different?"

For whatever reason, I guess I need to talk through what has been going on. She listens, asking some questions here and there and when I finish, she says, "Well, you aren't wrong. That's different, for sure. I hope it all works out. I am concerned that they didn't follow through with their original plan for you."

"Yeah. I get that, but don't you think that's sort of our world now—compared to what our parents had? We'll have to be flexible for the rest of our lives."

"That's so true. As I get into my coursework, I realize that teaching is changing too, with technology and all the expectations now."

"My mom would agree. It's not the same job she had thirty years ago when she started."

"Wonder what the next thirty years will bring."

"No way to know, I guess. So, I don't know if I told you, but I live in Chesterfield."

"Oh my gosh, you're not that far from our house."

"That's right. You're at your parents! How's that going?"

"It's all right. Actually, I don't know what I'd do without them."

"You know Dave and DJ are living with our parents until he finds a new place."

"I do. I go up there about every weekend, and we've gotten the boys together a few times."

"Oh, that's great. I know the boys have to love that."

"They do. Alex is crazy about DJ. Even though they only see each other once a week or so, DJ is his best friend. And DJ may feel the same."

"Are you going up to Spring Mill this weekend?"

"I am on Saturday."

"Want me to come to Kirkwood and pick you and Alex up? We could ride together."

"I like the riding together part but let me pick you up. Your place is on our way."

"It's a deal. So, Saturday morning?"

"Yes. How about I pick you up at eight-thirty?"

"I'll text you my address."

"Great. Looking forward to it."

"So am I."

8

Thursday, February 7

IT'S THURSDAY, and it's already been a long week. I'm finishing my lunch and finalizing a few things for tomorrow's conversation with Cooper. I think he's been busy preparing as well. I'm supposed to spend the afternoon observing Paula, so I'm working through lunch. I'd like to get out of here on time today and go to the gym again. I still feel the need to work off those brownies.

As I close my document, I look up from my computer and see Paula waiting for me to finish.

"Well, are you ready to do this, Dale?"

"I think so. I've been told it will be the highlight of my first week."

"You may have gotten bad intel there, but I'll try to make it as interesting as possible."

"I'm sure I'll learn a lot, Paula."

"Mind if I sit down for a minute before we start?"

"No, please do."

She sits down, picks some lint that may be real or imagined off her blazer, then looks me in the eye.

"Would you mind a blunt question, Dale?"

"No. I prefer it when people say what they're thinking."

"Okay then, what's the deal with your being hired?"

"What do you mean?"

"Well, usually when new people come on board, they have clear job titles and descriptions. We were told you were being hired as Larry's special assistant, which seemed odd, because no one's ever held that position before. And then there's the whole Cooper thing. That was also out of the blue, and now we are hearing that he's working as your assistant. Add in the fact that he's the boss's son, and you have to understand it's got us all wondering what the heck is going on?"

"I totally understand that, and I'd be wondering, too, if I were in your position. In fact, I was in an uncomfortable spot about three months ago at my last job and I didn't like it much."

"Good. So, you can see our point."

"Let me add, though, that in my situation the guy they hired was a total idiot. He was self-important, rude, and not skilled in any of the areas he needed to be for his position. He was a terrible hire."

"Well, that couldn't have been good."

"It wasn't, and it was one of the reasons I left the bank. And Paula, I'd like to believe I'm not *that* guy, and that in time you and the others will see that I was, that I am the right guy for what Larry wants to do here."

"You needed to take a breath in the middle of that sentence, Dale."

"Yeah, maybe. Still, I hope I made my point."

"I *heard* your point. Whether or not I accept it, I guess time will tell, as they say."

"Give me a chance then?"

"What choice do I have?"

"You don't have to give me one, but I think you're smart, and I believe you're fair. Again, whether you accept me as a good addition . . . as you say, only time will tell."

"Well, since Larry named you as his special assistant, I would assume he has something in mind for you long-term."

"There's nothing set in stone, Paula."

"But there were some possibilities discussed, I'm sure. And I don't know what kinds of promises Larry Morgan made to you when he recruited you, but I'm betting those have been compromised by having his son join the firm."

"Paula, all I can do is my best and hope that it helps the business, and if it does, then I'll have put myself in a good position going forward."

"Well, no matter how well you do, you'll never be the boss's son. Just remember that."

She looks at me, and I think she's almost daring me to get upset. I do my best to maintain my cool. "Is that my first lesson this afternoon?"

"Yes, let's start with that. You ready to go to my office and get started?"

I should just say yes and follow her, but I'm still a little put off by what's just happened.

"I am, but before we do I have a question for you."

"Fire away."

"What's *your* deal here at Morgan*Plus*? Where do you see yourself in the next few years?"

She thinks a moment, then says, "I hope I can do a job that helps grow the business and that by doing so I'll have put myself in a good position going forward. Did I say it about right?"

"You did."

"But you'd have to understand that with recent developments, I'm not sure anything I do would ever be good enough."

"I see."

"Do you?"

"Paula, I think I do."

"Let's go start your training."

We walk down the hall to her office, and it occurs to me that Paula is essentially repeating what my mom has said. With Cooper on board, things may be very different than what I signed up for. Mom's concerns come from her love for me. Paula's come from seeing two new guys come on board, one of them the boss's son. One or both might be groomed to take over someday, and Paula has every right to feel she is more deserving.

9

Friday, February 8

WE'RE IN THE CONFERENCE ROOM and ready to start our conversation. We'd originally set an afternoon time to meet, but Cooper came in around nine o'clock and said he was good to go if I was. I asked for another hour, got a few things finished to my satisfaction, and here we are. I have my computer linked with the room's projection system so I can type our ideas as we go, and we can see them on the screen. I have a slide already up to get us started.

"I lifted some information from our folders to start with."

"Sounds good."

MorganPlus: Mortgages & More
Walker Farm Project
Possible Scenarios

Description of the property:

- The Walker farm has been owned by the family for at least three generations. It is approximately 480 acres, all of which lies in Warren County. Most of the acreage lies in two valleys separated by hills with the northernmost being 200 acres, more or less, and the southern valley being about 150 acres. The remaining acreage is made up of the hills that surround the two valleys. A stream runs along the hill in the northern valley then cuts through the hills into the southern valley where it meanders through the valley itself. The hills are forested with a few open areas of grassland.

- There are good fences around the property. There is a gravel road that runs along the east side of the upper valley to the southern valley. A second road leads past the house and buildings (see description below) and then to and around a small lake that is used primarily for recreation. This road reconnects with the main road at the opening of the second valley.

- The buildings consist of a shed for the farm's equipment, a barn which is in excellent condition, and a house that was originally built nearly 100 years ago with additions in the 1940s and 1970s. The interior of the house has been continually updated and it serves as a residence for the farm's caretaker. There is a small cabin by the lake, which is served by electricity but not by water nor sewer.

- The primary crops grown on the farm are soybeans and corn, which are grown in rotation. Occasionally the fields will be rested and planted in a cover crop. Some of the bottomland and some of the open land on the hills produces hay which is used for the animals on the farm and as a cash crop.

- The farm's equipment is well-used but also well-maintained. It is modest by today's standards but serves a farm of this size very well.

Cooper gives it a brief scan, looks at me, then back at the screen.

"That looks like something we'd say if we were trying to sell the place to another farmer."

"Nothing wrong with doing that."

"Unless we want to make some real money and expand our business operation."

"Okay, then. Let's brainstorm some ideas. I'll keep the farm on the back burner while you tell me what you're thinking. I'll type while you talk."

"When I looked at the farm on Tuesday, I knew what it was meant to be."

While he talks, I type *Cooper's Proposal* on the screen, and I look at him to see what he's going to say.

"Walker Farm would make a beautiful *golf* development."

I start to type, stop, then look at him for clarification.

"Golf course?"

"Yes, golf course, plus."

After I type *Golf Course*, I say, "But aren't there plenty of those already?"

"Don't we have plenty of farms?"

"Probably only about what we need, but go ahead."

"Golf's a popular sport and guys are always looking for a new place to play, especially if it's beautiful and challenging."

"We'd have a lot to learn about what's involved with putting in a golf course don't you think?"

"I've started doing a little research. I'll try to have more information the next time we meet."

"So, I'm going to type some things we should consider, such as *Cost Factors* and *Time Factors* here, okay?"

"Sounds fair."

"Okay. You said something about Golf Course *plus*. Plus, what?"

Cooper spends the next several minutes talking about golf courses that have homes adjacent. He mentions a couple in the area, so I go to the internet and pull up some images. The homes are larger and more expensive than you'd find in some neighborhoods. Cooper thinks that Cam might go for that. I add a few notes as we go and a couple of the images.

"I wonder if the people who could afford that kind of home would build this far out?"

"I think you market the heck out of it, and they will."

We talk for an hour, coming up with things that we might want to know before we present this idea. Cooper struggles with this a little as we do. He's a big picture guy, as most of us are, and details are not his thing. Making him think about them and that he will have to do some work to find answers is more fun for me than him.

"Anything else before I start with my ideas?"

"No. But I could stand to warm up my coffee. How 'bout you?"

"Yes, and I could use a bathroom break, too. You go get us

some coffee from downstairs, I'll hit the little boys' room, and then I'll pitch my idea when we get back."

Cooper goes to get us coffee, and I go to the restroom located just down the hall. I take care of business, wash my hands, and make it back to the conference room before Cooper returns. I sit down at my computer, cleaning up what I've typed during our meeting, when I hear someone enter the room. I look up, ready to take my cup from Cooper, but it's Larry, instead. He looks at what's on the screen and as he does, Cooper walks in with our coffee.

"You boys are making progress, I see. I like what you have so far."

Cooper sets my coffee down and says, "I thought you might, Dad."

I say, "Well, we'll have more than one proposal for you to consider."

"Looking forward to it, boys. I knew you two would do good work."

We say thanks, and he starts to leave us, then turns around.

"Guys, I just got a call from Cam Walker. Did you two know that Jim Lynch didn't get the farm he wanted?"

"Yeah, Dad. He told us Tuesday."

"Well, it appears that he will be staying on the farm and working it for the immediate future."

"That's good, isn't it?"

"I don't know that I agree, Dale."

"It buys us more time."

"That's not in our favor here. We have Cam on the verge of selling the place. We don't need him reconsidering."

Cooper asks, "How do we keep the pressure on?"

"I reminded Cam that Jim is most likely still looking around and that if and when he finds a place, we'll be back where we started, so it would be better to move ahead with our proposal. And he agreed."

"Well, we should get back to work then."

"Yes, you should. When you finish your meeting, come to my office and I'll treat you to lunch."

He leaves, and there's something I feel I need to say to Cooper, but I'm not sure how it will be received.

"I wish your dad hadn't come in here until we were finished."

"Why do you say that?"

"Well, he was looking at our work while it's still in progress. I would prefer that we discuss the next proposal, then polish what we have and give them to him in final form. That would be better, I think."

"Oh, I guess I don't see why exactly."

"It's just better, if for no other reason than it gives both ideas a fair reading without one having a head start."

"I don't think that'll be a problem."

"That's good, but let me ask you something. Does your dad play golf?"

"Oh, yeah, we both love the game, and he's not bad."

"Okay then. As the lead guy on this, I want to ask you to do something for me."

"Sure."

"He's seen your golf proposal, and he might bring it up with you. I think you should limit any conversation about our work until we are finished and ready to go."

"So, if Dad asks me about it, I should say I can't talk about it?"

"He shouldn't ask about it until we are ready."

"I guess, but if he does, it will put me in a tough spot. I mean it's Dad."

"Not so tough. Just say we want to wait until we have everything ready. He should respect that."

"Okay, I'll try. Now, go ahead and tell me what you're thinking about this farm."

For the next several minutes I talk about the fact that I think it should stay a farm. As I talk, I keep reminding him that the farm has been a money maker for Cam for the past several years. If it stays as is, we won't have to spend a lot of money or wait a few years before making money again as we might have to do with other proposals. But if making money is that important, there are ways we might look to enhance the income from Walker Farm. We could explore things like organic farming and pick-your-own farming.

He shows mild interest, but still has doubts that this is something Morgan*Plus* would want to get into, and if we did what would that role be? Would we basically replace Walker as the owner, and look for someone to hire to run it *a la* Jim Lynch? I admit I have not completely thought it through yet. I need to think long and hard about how to make this happen. If Cooper doesn't see it, chances are his dad won't. Oddly enough, I think Cam Walker might like the farm idea more than they do.

We talk a while longer, decide what we want to get done prior to getting together again, and set the date to meet. It's getting close to noon.

"I don't know about you, but I'm getting hungry. Dad said lunch is his treat. Want to go with us?"

"No thanks, I want to finish cleaning up our notes. I'll do that, then email you what I have."

"Okay. Want us to get you something?"

"Yes, that would be nice. Something healthy."

"Oh, man I know a place that has a great cheeseburger with bacon and ham. Want that?"

"Yeah . . . No. Not that."

He laughs. "I'll find something for you."

"I'll be interested and maybe a little worried until then."

"I'll treat you right."

10

Saturday, February 9

I'S BRIGHT AND EARLY at eight-thirty, and Sarah will be here soon; so I turn off my coffee maker, check to make sure everything is okay, grab my bags, and make my way to the front door to wait for her. Two minutes later, she pulls in the drive. As I walk towards her SUV, I meet Phyllis walking back with yesterday's mail.

"Hi, Dale. Where are you going today?"

"Going up to Spring Mill to see Dad and Mom."

"Great. Have a good time!"

By this time, Sarah has rolled down her window, so I take the opportunity to introduce them.

"Phyllis, this is my friend, Sarah, and her son, Alex. Sarah, this is my neighbor, Phyllis."

There is an exchange of 'nice-to-meet-you's.

Sarah opens the window so that Alex can say hi.

"Nice to meet you, Mr. Alex."

"I'm five."

"I bet you are."

Then, with the innocence and honesty of a child, Alex says, "My daddy isn't coming home."

The three of us are speechless for a second. Phyllis connects the dots from our conversation the other night and says, "I know, and I am so sorry."

She makes eye contact with Sarah and shares her sympathy. Sarah smiles at Phyllis and acknowledges her kindness.

Phyllis looks back at Alex. "So, what are you going to do in Spring Mill, Alex?"

"I'm going to see Papa and Gramma."

"Oh, that will be fun."

"And my friend, DJ."

"Then you are going to have fun, aren't you?"

"Yes. Sometimes we play at the park and one time we went sledding."

Phyllis smiles and gives the little guy nod of approval.

"Well, Phyllis, keep an eye on the place, okay? I'll be back Sunday. If you hear any wild parties on my side, you might want to check."

"Check? I might have to join them."

"Feel free!"

I get in the car and the three of us wave good-bye to Phyllis. Sarah backs out of the driveway. As we start down Piñata Court, Sarah looks over at me and then back at the street.

"She's seems really nice."

"Did I tell you she's my landlady?"

"You may have."

We get to a stop sign and stay there longer than needed. Sarah is staring ahead and not speaking.

"Are you okay?"

On the verge of tears, she says, "It's really hard. I mean I knew it would be hard, but this . . . this is . . . I don't know, Dale."

"I can't even imagine how hard it is for you. You do know we all care about you, and we'll do anything we can to help . . . right?"

"I do, and I appreciate it. My sister. My parents. The Marshalls. Your brother and you—you all mean so much to me, and that helps, and I'll get there. It's just so hard, Dale."

She starts the car moving again and seems a little more composed. From behind us comes a little voice, "How far is it, Mommy?"

"It's going to be while. Why don't you pull something up on your tablet? That will make it go faster." And soon the back seat is filled with the sounds of a children's show and Alex is quiet.

What my parents would have given for this technology twenty years ago. Dave and I made every trip of any length seem longer than it was. My dad used to joke that our family always took two-week vacations. When a friend said he didn't remember us ever being gone more than a week, Dad's comeback was that any time spent in a car with two boys is automatically doubled— "Kind of like dog years."

We're getting close to the ramp for I-64 westbound, and I decide to pick up the conversation.

"So, Alex and DJ have become buddies?"

"Yes, I guess it started in the kids' room at church. Whenever I attend service with the Marshalls, Alex goes there. He has fun and it allows the adults to enjoy the service. He met DJ there one Sunday and they became good friends. Anyway, I can't go to Spring Mill now without getting him together to play with DJ. The last couple of times, Dave has been there, too, and that's been a big help and lot of fun."

"Good, because people hardly ever say that about him."

She shakes her head and laughs. "You two are a lot alike, you know that?"

"Actually, I hear more often about how different we are."

"Well, that too, I guess."

It's quiet for a bit. I look over at Sarah and think how lucky Drew was to have someone like her.

She says, "You're quiet. What are you thinking?"

"I'm thinking how glad I am to be back home."

"I'm sure, and I know your parents are thrilled. Oh, before I forget it, would you mind if we started back a little earlier tomorrow?"

I'm thinking maybe she should have asked me this before we left, but I say, "I guess not. Why the change?"

"I just think it would be better for Alex if we did, and Mom and Dad want to have a little party with us and watch some of the game before Alex has to go to bed."

"Okay. So, what time do you want to pick me up?"

"Maybe three o'clock?"

"Sure."

"Your folks won't be mad?"

"They won't like it, but I'll remind them that I can come up any weekend now. That'll make it okay, I'm sure."

"Good. You know what? Since you'll be missing their party, why don't you come to our house and watch the game with us?"

I don't even have to think about my answer.

"That would be fun."

We soon pull into Spring Mill. Last Monday's snow has been cleared and piled at the sides of streets and parking lots. No longer pristine, it looks dreary and dingy, and certainly not a picture the Chamber would use in a brochure. Still, this is my hometown, and no other place, no matter how long I live there, will be home to me the way Spring Mill, Missouri is.

———————

Just before ten, we pull into my parents' driveway. DJ must have been waiting at the door, because he dashes out as soon as he sees Sarah's car. Caught off guard, my dad can't keep up and is a little irritated with him.

"DJ. Wait for Papa!"

I get out of the car and scoop the little guy up. "Papa's right, you have to be careful around cars."

I can tell the boy thinks he's in trouble. He hugs my neck and buries his head.

"It's okay buddy. We just don't want you to get hurt."

There are a couple of sniffles, then he sees Alex in the back seat, and all is well. He wants down, and as soon as he hits the ground, he opens the back door and crawls in beside his buddy.

I look around, and I don't see my brother's truck.

"Where's Dave?"

"Oh, he had to go help one of his techs on an emergency call. Someone's furnace wasn't working, and the tech was struggling, so Dave felt like he should help. He'll be back soon, I'm sure."

I get my things out of the car and say, "DJ, we need to let Alex go see his grandparents."

Reluctantly DJ gets out. He doesn't know that they'll be coming back after lunch. Sarah has asked for help from my mom on an assignment—writing a test for a science class. While they are doing that, Dave and I will take the boys bowling. It will be a surprise, because they'd make everyone crazy with their excitement and questions if we told them now.

Mom comes out to join us. As I look at her, I realize she's starting to show her age a little. She had her sixtieth birthday this year: an event she chose to celebrate quietly. I always think of her as younger than she is—more like forty maybe. And I'm not alone. People always compliment her on how young she looks, and she credits the elementary kids she taught all those years, "Kids keep you young."

Mom had me when she was thirty-five, after she and Dad had given up on ever having kids. I once overheard Dad tell a friend, probably after a couple of drinks, that I was a miracle and Dave was a mistake. The other guy laughed and said, "Really?" and Dad said, "No, not really. We're thankful for them both."

I tell Sarah thanks for the ride, then walk to where Mom is standing, knowing I'm about to receive the first hug of the weekend. I set down my bag and get the expected hug and it's accompanied by the first "I'm so glad you've moved back home," of the weekend. The smart money says there will be at least four more of each.

We walk inside and I start to take my bag from DJ who had picked it up and insisted on carrying it for me. Refusing my offer, he starts dragging it upstairs. I follow him up the steps and down the hall to my old room. He drags it the whole way.

I take my bag from him and throw it and my computer bag on the bed. DJ announces, "I sleep in this room now."

"You've taken over my old room, huh?"

"Yes. Daddy says I roll around too much and sometimes I kick him, so I get to sleep in my own bed now."

"Where do you want to sleep tonight, DJ?"

"Dad says I get to sleep with you!"

"Oh really! Well now, that will be fun. You and I will have us a sleep-over."

"What's a sleep-over?"

"It's what you and I will be doing tonight, sleeping here in my old bed. I just wish I had packed some rib pads."

"What are rib pads?"

I decide to bring this to a halt, and suggest we go back to see his Papa and Grandma. He bounds down the stairs, faster than he should, but who can slow down a hyped-up five-year-old?

"Have you had breakfast?"

"Oh, yes. I ate early."

"You hungry for anything? It's a while until lunch."

"Got some yogurt?"

"Yes. I believe we do. It's probably not the healthy kind you like."

"It'll be fine, Mom."

I start to open the door of the fridge when I see a couple of pieces of DJ's artwork on the front of it.

"I see you have a couple of your old magnets still in use."

"Yes. I boxed the others up when we got the new fridge. You and your brother will have to argue over who inherits them."

"We may need a mediator for that dispute."

I get a slight smile for my effort.

Mom is a charter member of the refrigerator magnet club. Our old fridge had an extensive magnet collection that held in place pictures of family vacations, calendars, and her two sons' poor attempts at art. When we were little, Mom had plastic letters she'd use to make words for us, hoping to improve our spelling skills. Those letters stayed on the fridge for years—well beyond their useful life. Then one day when Dave was in second or third grade, he searched for and found the letters *F*, *A*, *R*, and *T* and did what little boys will always do. The letters disappeared soon thereafter.

I take the two remaining magnets off and look at them. One has the words *Life is a journey, not a destination* in dark brown script on a lighter brown background, and the other shows a forest scene with diverging paths and the appropriate Robert Frost quote.

"So why keep these two?"

"Well, there is a little story there."

"I have time."

"When I went to college, I decorated my dorm room with posters. A couple of my favorites had those sayings. So, when I found these magnets, I had to have them. And I still like the sayings."

"Why?" I ask.

"I think they are two sides of the same coin and taken together they have an even larger meaning."

"What do they say to you?"

"I'm not going to say. You need to come up with your own answer."

Dad has been listening and has to chime in, "You can take the teacher out of the school, but you can't take the teacher out of the retiree."

Mom says, "This coming from my editor husband whose blood type is printer's ink."

I look at Dad and say, "Mom wins that point."

Dad agrees.

Mom, satisfied with her win, removes a faded flower from an arrangement that Dad bought for her. She throws it in the trash bin and carefully rearranges the ones that remain.

"Your brother should be getting back soon."

"I talked to him a lot about his work when he helped me move. Sounds like he's doing well."

"He's going to take over the business next year. The Thompsons are ready to retire."

"I'm thinking you and Dad are okay with this."

"We are now."

"Good."

My college-educated mom and dad weren't happy when Dave dropped out to get married. To them, college was the path to a good career and a happy life. It worried and disappointed them a little that he didn't go the same route I did. To his credit, he has stayed with his choice and he's doing well now, at least in that aspect of his life.

The TV in the family room suddenly gets very loud with the sounds of some Saturday morning cartoon. Dad heads in there to get the remote from DJ and correct the situation.

"DJ gets bigger every time I see him."

"He is growing so fast. He's such a cute kid."

"He looks like Dave."

Dad, returning to the kitchen after quieting the TV, says, "God help Dave if DJ acts anything like him."

Actually, I'm not sure Dad would mind if Dave got a taste of what he gave him and Mom. Not that he was a bad kid; my brother just pushed the envelope more than I did.

Dave was physically gifted in just about every sense of the word. He was active, he was fearless, he was curious, and he was, according to everyone, such a cute kid it was hard to stay angry with him. Now, I wasn't perfect by any means, but compared to my brother I was by far the easier of the two. My dad only needed to raise his voice with me or show the slightest displeasure, and I was remorseful. Dave was numb to just about everything, including Dad's hand on the one occasion he tried to spank him.

I say, "Isn't that every grandparent's wish?"

"What's that?"

"That their grandkids pay their moms and dads back for all the grief they caused.

"Yeah, we say that, but I don't know if we really believe it."

We talk until lunch, and Mom catches me up on the neighborhood. Just as we get ready to eat, Dave makes his appearance. He washes up and takes a seat at the table. We sit there for a second, and Mom asks him if would mind removing his ball cap. He does, then turns it around and puts it on DJ. The kid sits there for a moment, grinning from ear to ear, and then takes it off so he doesn't get in trouble.

As we eat, Dave tells us about his morning. We all know the man whose furnace needed attention. He's a local legend and known for being difficult. Everyone has stories about him, and even though we've heard them all before, we take turns retelling them and laughing as if they're new. It's nice, it's comfortable, it's home, and I like knowing there will be more times like this now that I live closer to my family.

11

"**B**OYS, THIS IS WHAT YOU CALL a bowling alley."

"Why do they call it that, Dad?"

"You know, I don't know why they do, DJ. Maybe Uncle Dale knows."

"I don't know boys, but I can tell you we are going to have some fun!"

Up to this point we've kept the boys in the dark as to what we were doing this afternoon. They have spent the ten minutes it took to get here, guessing. We pull into a parking space, get the boys out of their car seats and head inside. About half of the lanes are occupied, full of activity and noise. The boys take it all in.

DJ says, "So we get to roll those balls."

"Yes, and you are going to try to knock down those pins at the other end."

Alex thinks he'll knock them all down. DJ decides he will, too.

We walk up to the counter and a lady, who looks like she just got off the morning shift at a diner, greets us with a smoky "hello." The boys don't quite know what to make of her voice.

Smoky, as she will be known for the rest of the day, checks us out and says, "Oh you're the guys the young lady called about aren't ya?"

Dave and I look at each other, then, realizing that one of us needs to respond, I say, "We must be."

"Yes, she described you four perfectly. We got ya all set up on 17 and 18 there."

We check it out, and 17 already has bumpers set up for Alex and DJ. Neither Dave nor I thought to let anyone know we'd need the bumpers, so it must have been Sarah who alerted her.

"That's great. We'll need some shoes, and you'll have to point us to where the kids' bowling balls are."

Dave looks at me and, never missing a chance, says, "Oh I think you're ready for a grown-up ball now."

Smoky laughs at that and then launches into a thirty-second coughing spasm. The boys cringe and I step back in case there is some stray sputum.

"Sorry, about the cough there. I'm fighting a case of the bronchitis."

I'm thinking her bronchitis comes in packs of twenty.

"You'll find the kids' balls over there by lane 24, and there's all kinds of balls for you guys in the other racks. You'll just have to check them out 'til ya find one that works for ya."

She takes our shoe sizes and sets us up. We take the shoes and walk to where the kids' balls are, and the boys both like the first ball they pick up. I have no idea if the balls are appropriate for them, but they seem happy. We point them to our lanes and they both walk that way, struggling to carry the balls. I can't help but laugh, but also worry that one of them might drop his ball and, instead of an afternoon of bowling, we'll be sitting in the ER waiting for x-ray results.

After a couple more minutes, Dave and I find balls that work. I've selected a sixteen-pounder, hoping its weight will create some good pin action, while Dave picks a little lighter one for exactly the same reason.

We get set up on 18 and help the boys finish getting ready on 17. We'll alternate turns, with the two boys' bowling their frames, followed by Dave and me.

I decide to get even for the ball remark. "You sure you don't want to bowl with the boys? They've got bumpers."

"No, I'm good here, as you will soon see."

The boys are anxious to get started, so we finish with our shoes and decide to have Alex go first. He struggles with the ball, and I realize I'd better help him. There's no way he can bowl using any kind of a conventional delivery, so I take him to the foul line and have him set the ball down in the middle of the lane. Then I tell him to push it with both hands as hard as he can. He gives it a shove and the ball starts rolling slowly and drifting to the left as it does. If it weren't for the bumpers, it would have been a gutter ball already. It deflects back toward the middle of the lane, having lost some momentum, going even more slowly now, and drifting slightly to the right of the head pin. As it makes contact, it looks like the pins might reject the ball and send it back towards us, but then, miraculously, three pins fall. We have our first score of the day.

He starts to sit down but I say, "Alex, remember, you get another ball to try to get the rest of the pins."

"I do! I'm going to get them all this time!"

I remind him what to do, but from a distance this time, and he pushes the ball on another slow journey to the pins. It again veers left hitting the bumper farther down the alley this time, and the deflection kicks it into the pins on that side of the lane. His score doubles to a 6 and he's elated.

Dave repeats what I just did with his son. DJ puts a little more into it than Alex, but only ends up with a 5 for his frame. He knows enough to realize five is less than six, and he's disappointed to be losing already. Dave and I will need to employ some creative scorekeeping so that neither boy will lose today.

We start our game on lane 18. I took some lessons when I was in junior high, so I have some idea what I want to do—where I want to line up, what mark I want to hit—things like that. Dave has no idea. He just attacks the game, throwing the ball down the middle as hard as he can. There are a couple of times his approach works, but usually it doesn't. By the end of the game, experience has won out over raw athleticism.

Of course, the boys have to know who has won their game and ours. We tell them they have tied, which they may have. We've finagled the scoring so much, that there's no way to know. More important to the boys is knowing who has won our game. I wait for Dave to tell them.

"Uncle Dale lucked out and won that one, boys."

"Don't worry Daddy, you'll win the next one."

"I bet I will, Son."

I can't resist. I should, but I can't. "Want to make it interesting?"

78

"I do. How 'bout the loser buys ice cream for everyone?"

"Sounds like a deal."

The boys get into the bet and think they should have one, too.

Dave says, "Tell you what boys, if you knock down more pins this game than you did last game, we will make it a sundae at Cindy's.

Of course, the boys like that. They can pile on all the toppings they want at that place. There's no way I can't go along with it.

"Sounds like we have deal."

Dave and I have a silent understanding that DJ and Alex will do better this game, no matter how they do. We take turns on the scoresheet making sure that happens.

I bowl a little better during the second game, and Dave bowls much better. The game goes back and forth with each of us leading. The boys have decided to cheer for Dave. DJ, I can understand—Dave's his dad, but I think Alex should cheer for me. Then again, DJ is his buddy, so it makes sense.

We get to the final frame, and of course it's close. I have him by five pins. He goes first and gets a strike. That's big. He gets two more balls and the pins he knocks down will add extra to his score. By the time he finishes, his lead is fourteen pins. I just need a spare and five pins to beat him.

I line up to make my first shot, taking my time to relax and visualize my approach. I get ready to start when Dave says, "Sometime today would be nice." The boys giggle at that and repeat it.

"Sometime today would be nice."

I shake my head, regroup, and make my approach, the ball hits the mark, almost exactly, and I think maybe I have a strike coming, until a reluctant 10-pin refuses to fall. Of all the pins I don't want to stand, the 10-pin would be the one. Because I throw a big hook, I start on the left side and throw across the lane hoping the ball will curve back enough not to go in the gutter, but still make contact.

I make my approach and once again I feel I've hit my mark. The ball heads towards the right gutter, then bends back working its way along the edge. By the time it reaches the pin though, it has curved left just enough that it nicks the pin. It's not enough to knock it down and Dave has won.

There' some high-fiving among Dave and the boys.

"I can't wait for that sundae, Dale."

I smile at the guys, and say, "Well, then let's go have us a sundae."

"Do we get extra toppings?"

Dave assures them they do, and there are more high fives.

We change back into our regular shoes, return the balls to the rack and head to the counter. While I'm helping the boys with their shoes, Dave pays Smoky for our bowling. He turns to me, grins and says, "That was fun. Let's head to Cindy's."

12

CINDY'S HAS MOVED from the town square to a strip mall along the highway. I wasn't aware of the move until Dave told me on the way here. As we walk in, I see they've retained some of their old ice cream/soda shop décor, but they have made some changes. Now, the customer fills his cup with frozen yogurt, not ice cream, and then selects from a variety of toppings along a wall next to the counter. We don't tell the boys that it's not ice cream. With all their toppings, they will never notice, and frozen yogurt's not bad.

Dave helps DJ and I do the same for Alex, although neither boy wants much help. Our help is really guidance—suggestions ignored as much as followed.

After we've weighed our sundaes and paid for them, the boys ask if they can have their own table. Dave and I sit next to them; ready to spring into action if a sundae emergency should arise. The boys chatter excitedly about bowling and other topics of interest to pre-kindergartners. Each tries to out-do the other and they get a little noisy. I wonder if we should settle them down a bit, but there are only a few other customers, and Dave seems to be okay with it. More than that, their being so caught up in their conversation gives us a chance to talk.

Dave has a smile on his face as he watches and listens to them. He looks back at me, still grinning.

"It's good to have you home, Dale."

"It's good to be back; I won't lie. Thanks again for all of your help."

"It was no big deal."

"No, it really was. You had to leave work for the better part of a week to make the drive to Philly, help load my stuff, make the long drive to St. Louis, and then help me unload. On top of all that, you had to leave DJ for four days."

Dave shrugs. "He did fine with Mom and Dad. He always does."

"I bet they were glad to see you when you got home, though."

"Oh, yeah, for sure. A little boy his age can wear you out, but he did go to his day care every day, so that helped some."

We check out the boys again, and they're still going strong, talking and eating. By this point, chocolate, the main topping, is showing on their faces. Some cleaning-up will be in order when they finish.

"DJ looks like he's doing okay, Dave."

"I think so, but you never know. I hate it that my son is growing up with divorced parents. I just . . . it's something I don't want for my kid."

"You did everything you could to try to keep it from happening."

"I tried, but it takes more than one person working on it, and I was the only one."

"What do you hear from Brit? Is she doing okay now?"

"I guess so. She's on the road with that young guy most of the time," he mumbles.

"Young guy? You're only twenty-four."

"Almost twenty-five."

"Okay, almost twenty-five. How old is that guy?"

"Maybe twenty-one."

"Wow."

"Yep."

I try changing the subject. "Anyway, you're doing a good job with DJ."

He doesn't respond and instead looks at his phone.

"What are you doing?"

Dave grins at me. "Just wanted to note the time and date that you finally gave me a compliment."

"Okay. So, are you going out with anyone?"

"I am a little."

"With anyone I know?"

"Yeah, Kaitlyn Brown."

"Kaitlyn! From my class?"

"Yes."

"Wow, we all wanted to take her out back in high school. I thought she had gotten married and had a kid."

"Yes, to both, but she and her husband have separated, and the divorce is almost final. I ran into her one day and she still looks *really* good. We got talking and one thing led to another. We're going out the day after the divorce is finalized, to celebrate."

"Well, I guess I should wish you good luck."

He has a bite of sundae. "Luck will have nothing to do with it."

I have to laugh at that remark. Dave has never lacked for confidence in many areas of his life, and certainly not in that one.

"Do Mom and Dad know?"

"Why should they? I'm not seventeen."

"Yeah, I don't know why I said that."

Dave's eyes go to me. "Are you jealous I got to her first?"

"A little maybe. No, not really."

"Have you gone out with anyone since you've been back?"

"No. Not yet."

"Got any plans to?"

"Nothing too specific."

"Well, at least we won't be competing for the same girls when you get started."

"I guess not."

At this point, the boys have decided they want to sit with us, so we get up and move to their table; that being the easier and less messy option.

After we get settled again, Dave asks the boys if they are having a good time today and of course they are, *and* of course they want to do it again—tomorrow if possible.

"We will go bowling again boys, but not tomorrow, okay?"

They're disappointed, but Dave promises them we'll do it again soon, and that helps.

I look over at Dave and DJ and then at Alex now sitting at my side, and I think I'd be okay doing this again, too.

The boys finally finish their yogurt and for the most part they have done a good job of it. Still there is that chocolate situation to deal with.

Dave says, "Boys we need to get you cleaned up. And let's not mention the ice cream when we get home, okay?"

The boys nod yes while we wipe their faces.

"We had ice cream!"

"You had ice cream?"

"Yes, Uncle Dale bought it for us."

Sarah gives me a look and I shrug my shoulders with a guilty smile.

"He had to buy because Uncle Dave beat him."

Again, a look.

"We had a little wager on the second game, and I lost. I should have bet on the first one instead."

Sarah says, "It's okay Alex, but that was your sugar for the day. No dessert at Grandma Marshall's tonight."

Alex shows his disappointment. If you are a five-year-old boy, you will always give up the dessert you just had for the one you won't get because of it. He looks at his mom, but he knows there's no use bargaining with her.

Mom says, "So, bowling and ice cream. That sounds like fun."

Dave says, "We had a great time. We'll do it again soon."

"But not tomorrow."

"No, DJ, not tomorrow."

I ask Sarah, "How did you do on your homework?"

"Great. Your mom was so much help. I feel good about it now. Thanks again, Pat."

"You're more than welcome. It was fun to get my brain working again. I love retirement, but I miss teaching."

"I learned so much from you today."

"Anytime, Sarah."

Sarah picks up her things, preparing to leave. "Alex, we better get going. Say thank you to Uncle Dave and Uncle Dale."

He gives us a "thanks," and he and his mom head to the door.

As she gets ready to go to her car, Sarah says, "Will three o'clock still work for me to pick you up tomorrow, Dale?"

"Yes, that will work."

"See you then."

The front door closes behind them, and Mom looks at me and asks, "Three o'clock?"

"Yes, she wants to get back before it gets dark."

"But what about our Super Bowl party?"

"Mom, you'll just have to do without me."

"But we have friends coming, and they all want to see you."

"Mom, I'm home now. There will be other times."

"Well, I guess. What are you going to do when you get back to your place? You won't have anyone to watch the game with."

"I'll probably work some on a project, and maybe catch some of the game or watch a movie."

I should tell her I'm going to Sarah's, but I don't.

"That doesn't sound like much fun."

"Mom, it's okay."

"You should have driven your own car, so you could stay for the party."

"Mom, I like having some company on the drive. It's worth the trade off."

She studies me for a moment, and there's a question in her eyes she doesn't ask.

Dave is upstairs trying to get DJ to settle down and I can tell he's having no luck. The kid is excited to be bunking with me tonight and wants me to come to bed right now. I'd like to do a little work on my laptop before bedtime, and I hope Dave wins this battle. That said, I've got a good book that I can read if he doesn't.

It seems to be getting quiet when I hear an upset little guy again.

I yell upstairs, "Dave, you want me to come up?"

He says, "No, go ahead and work. We're going to read for a while longer."

I go back to work, and I hear my brother reading to my nephew in my old bed; a scene I never could have imagined a few years ago. Within a few minutes I hear nothing, so obviously Dave has succeeded. I find I'm getting tired, too, so, I shut things down, say goodnight to my parents and head upstairs. When I get there, I find Dave and DJ both asleep. I go to the bathroom brush my teeth, undress down to my boxers and t-shirt, and head to my old room. Quietly, I walk to my bed, trying not to wake DJ. I tap my brother on the shoulder. He stirs, realizes where he is and whispers, "All right, the night shift is here."

"Yep. Reporting for duty."

Dave gets up, and I take his place, trying to be as quiet as possible. As Dave opens the door, Duff, the family dog, comes in the room.

"Is it okay?" Dave whispers.

"Sure."

He closes the door.

Then there's a little voice, "Daddy?"

"No, it's Uncle Dale."

He says nothing for a moment, and I'm thinking he's already back to sleep. Instead, he turns until he's facing me and says, "Thanks for the ice cream."

"You're welcome. We had fun, didn't we?"

"We did. You beat Daddy in the first game, didn't you?"

"I believe I did."

"Then why did you have to buy the ice cream?"

"The bet was only on the second game."

"That doesn't seem fair."

"It's okay. I agreed to the rules and we both followed them, so that makes it fair."

"Yeah. Maybe you can win next time and Daddy can buy the ice cream."

"I'm planning on that."

Soon, he's asleep again. I try to join him, but Duff beats me to it, and starts making some sort of noise that I assume is a dog's version of snoring. Between that and my nephew's kicking and squirming, I may have a long night ahead of me.

Before I drift off, I think about bowling. I think about having yogurt with Dave and the boys. I think about going to Sarah's tomorrow, and then, of all things, I start thinking of Mom's refrigerator magnets and my mind gets busy on my "homework."

13

Sunday, February 10

"THANKS AGAIN, DALE."

"It's all right. If I'd stayed for the party, I wouldn't have gotten home until eleven. I need my sleep."

She looks my way for a second, then back at the road. Alex has his tablet going again and I would swear it's the same video he saw yesterday. No matter, though. He's content to watch and we can talk.

"You make this trip every weekend, I guess."

"Pretty much; yes. It's hard, but I think it helps Steve and Anne. They have lost Drew. They don't need to lose us, too."

"I'm not sure every daughter-in-law would do as much."

"Oh, they should. Besides, Alex loves his grandparents, and we get to see DJ and your family."

I ask her about the game tonight. Being a former athlete herself, she knows a little more about the teams than I do. She analyzes the teams and makes a prediction. I ask her if she misses playing a sport, and she says she does some. She asks me if I miss running distance and cross-country and I tell her that I still get to run, just not competitively.

We cross over I-70. Twenty-five minutes to my place now. She circles back to our conversation about making this trip every week.

"You have a good family, Dale. Your dad is such a smart man, I know you're proud of him, and your mom must have been a fantastic teacher."

"Mom enjoyed working with you yesterday. I know she misses the kids, and she misses working with the other teachers since she retired."

"And parents?"

"I don't think she misses them all that much."

"I've heard that parents are the worst thing about teaching other than working for a principal you don't get along with."

"I think she'd agree, although she never had the bad principal situation as far as I know."

"Well, that's good. I hope my luck is the same."

After a moment of quiet, punctuated only by the noise from the backseat, she looks at me again. "What are you thinking about?"

"Well, for some reason it just hit me that my mom worked in public education and Dad publishes a newspaper."

"You just figured out your parents' careers?"

"That came out wrong. I just realized that in their own ways they both have made careers of trying to help make people smarter and better."

"That's true. Did you ever think of doing what they do?"

"Some. There are times I've thought of being a teacher, and other times I've thought about what Dad does. I can tell you he'd love it if I took over the paper."

"Then, maybe you should."

"I'd be terrible at it."

She looks at me again and says, "I don't think so."

We are approaching the Missouri River Bridge and getting ready to enter the valley where Morgan*Plus* is located. I think about everything that's happening at work right now, and I wonder if running a paper wouldn't be better.

"I enjoyed watching you and Dave together," Sarah says.

"Yeah."

"It's funny. I love my sister, but our relationship—and we've always been close—but it's never been exactly what you two have."

"Yes."

I look over at her and can tell her mind is on something more than the road. I enjoy watching her and hate to interrupt her thoughts, but after a minute I have to know.

"Okay, what are you thinking about?"

"A couple of things involving you and Dave."

"Let me hear them."

She's a little embarrassed, something I don't think I've ever seen her be before, and it looks good on her. "Okay, first of all, that night six years ago, when you and Drew came to my house."

"You mean the night Drew took me there to help him out?"

"My mom really liked you."

"She liked me?"

"Yes, better than Drew actually."

I scoff. "You're kidding."

"No. She did. Although she could see why I had fallen for Drew and thought he was the one, she told Dad later that she liked you better."

"Other than my own mother, no one else has ever said that! Anyway, why do you think she felt that way?"

"You know how Drew was all energy and motion. He'd get caught up in something and everyone else would get swept along with him. She felt you were more steady and maybe more mature in some ways. She thought Drew was the kind of guy that girls love, but you were the kind of guy a girl would spend her life with."

"Ah, so the slow and steady turtle who wins the race."

"Sort of, I guess."

"But Drew was always going to win, and it never was a race. I was only there that night to provide him a buffer."

"He told me beforehand why he wanted you to come along, and I thought it would be okay. I knew my folks would like you, too."

"So, how does my brother fit into this?" I ask.

"Well, you and Dave were in our wedding party."

"Yes."

"Of course, everyone thought he was so cute."

"Yeah, he's always had that problem."

"I thought he was just a big kid, though."

"Well, he hadn't turned nineteen yet, so he was a kid."

"Well, he's not a kid anymore. He's had to change a lot, hasn't he?" She looks almost sad.

"He has. If you think about it, one year after your wedding he was getting married and had a kid on the way. That'll make you grow up."

"But he seems to be doing okay now."

"He is."

"He's really good with the boys."

"He's one of them, sometimes."

"Yes," she says, laughing.

"So, is there a common thread to all of this?"

"You are definitely the son of a teacher."

"Can't help it."

"There is, I guess. I just want to say once again how thankful I am to have friends like you and your brother. You two mean a lot to me. That's all."

I stare ahead for a moment, thinking about what to say, and it feels important to me for some reason that I say the right thing. Nothing I think of seems right.

A few minutes later we pull in my driveway.

"Well, here we are, Dale."

"Great. Let me get a few things done here, and I'll see you in a bit."

"Perfect. I know my parents will be glad to see you again."

"Me too. I haven't seen them since—"

I wish I hadn't started that sentence, because the last time was the day of Drew's funeral.

"I know."

I head to my front door. Phyllis has several cars parked in her driveway and out on the street, so I'm guessing she's having a little party, too. I'm glad that I won't be sitting in my place alone this evening while that's going on next door.

14

A T A LITTLE AFTER FIVE, I pull up in front of the Koulos's house in Kirkwood. This is my first time here since that night with Drew. The memory of it takes over.

We stop in front of the Koulos's home and Drew says, "Well, here we are, buddy."

I say, "It's a cute house. What's it like inside?"

"I don't know. I've never been here before."

"Wait. You've never been here? But you told me you and Sarah are about to get engaged."

"I know. It's all happened pretty fast, and I just haven't been here yet. We haven't said anything to anyone other than you, and maybe her sister."

"So, wait! I'm coming along on the first time you are to meet your future in-laws."

"Yes," Drew admits.

"And I'm guessing the purpose of my coming wasn't really to meet her sister, Nichole."

"No, that was part of it."

"But not the biggest part."

"Yeah. I just felt like maybe it would take some of the pressure off me if you came along."

"Because you would look so good by comparison?"

"No, dumbass." He finally breaks a smile. "Because I won't be the total focus, and, besides, you get along better with older people than any guy I know. It's like you're forty."

"Drew, you know they're going to like you. Everyone does."

"You think?"

"Pretty sure."

"Well, that helps."

"Still want me to come in with you, or should I just wait in the car?"

"You're coming with me."

I look at their house and picture the scene inside: Gus and Dee Koulos, Sarah, and little Alex, talking and probably having some appetizers while they wait for me.

And then, just for a second, I picture Drew there with them. He's smiling at something someone has said . . . and then he's gone.

A wave of something hits me. At first, it's grief, but it turns into something uglier and darker, and it becomes an anger I didn't know I could feel. I grip the steering wheel, and I have this urge to hit something. Instead, I yell at top of my lungs, and it's a sound I've never made before, and don't ever want to make again. When I'm done, I look around to make sure no one is on the sidewalk. I'm embarrassed and stunned a little by what just happened. Luckily, there's no one.

The front door of the Koulos' house is open though, and I see Sarah silhouetted in the light. She has her arms wrapped around her to keep herself warm as she begins to walk toward my car. When she gets here, she opens the door and gets in.

"Are you okay?"

"I'm sorry, Sarah. I just had an odd moment."

"We've *all* had that moment, Dale, and to be honest, we still do. It's okay."

"All of you?"

"Especially Dad. While he does great most of the time, there are times he is so angry with Drew for leaving us behind."

"Well, no dad would want to see his daughter hurt like you have been."

"No."

My eyes start to tear up, and now I am upset with myself. Sarah, seeing what's going on, slides over and hugs me. I fight it for a second, and then let go; weeping from the pain, but causing myself more pain as I do. She tells me it's okay; I need to do it. When I get myself together, I apologize again, and she puts her hand behind my head and pulls it next to hers. She whispers in my ear, "It's okay. You two were like brothers."

"We were."

We wait another minute. "You doing better?"

"I am. I'm sorry I put you through that."

"You've been so strong. You spoke at Drew's funeral, and you kept it together. It meant so much and it helped—it really did. You had to let go sometime."

"Okay. I'm better."

"Let's go inside. Mom's made a bunch of appetizers,

and Dad bought you some good beer. I know you don't like football, but let's go in and pretend you do."

"Let's."

We walk inside to find Gus, Dee, and Alex waiting for us. They're happy to see me, and that helps. There are appetizers on the counter—more than we could eat in one evening, and the pre-game is on. It's okay now.

The evening with Sarah and her family has been great, but it's now half time and the game has drug on for nearly two hours. Kansas City is leading, but if Dallas comes back to win, I don't want to be here to watch it.

Using the excuse that I have some things to get done for work tomorrow, I thank Mr. and Mrs. Koulos for having me over, tell everyone good-bye, and walk to my car accompanied by Sarah.

"You sure you don't want to see the half time show? It's Dr. Pop, Ernest James, and that twelve-year-old girl who won that talent show last year."

"Let me think. An aging rapper, a second-class country star and a child accordion player? It'll be a train wreck. How could it not be?"

"There will be plenty of lasers and fireworks. It'll be great, I'm sure."

"You'll have to tell me all about it the next time I see you."

"I'll do that."

"Let's get together for a cup of coffee sometime, Sarah. It might be good for both of us."

"Let me get through the next couple of weeks, okay?"

"Okay. I've got a few crazy days coming up too. I'll call you the week after next, okay?"

"Okay."

And with that she gives me a quick wave and turns around. I watch her walk back inside and admire how incredibly strong she is. I regret that I fell apart in the car earlier tonight, but I don't regret the moment of closeness with her that followed.

When I get back to my place, all the cars at Phyllis's are gone but one. It seems no one makes it past half-time of a Super Bowl. I park my car and go inside thinking I should spend some time doing what I told the Koulos family I needed to do. Then I reconsider. If there aren't too many interruptions the next couple of days, I should be able to get my work done in time for my meeting with Cooper.

As I brush my teeth, I have this thought that the car in front of Phyllis's house might be one of her daughters, or a close friend, or maybe Phyllis has an overnight guest! I chuckle at that last possibility as I spit into the sink.

15

Tuesday, February 12

"**R**EADY TO GO?"

"Sure, Cooper, come on in. I'm all set up."

Cooper and I are having a quick meeting to see what we've learned since last week and decide where we want to go from here.

"Do you want me to start?" Cooper asks.

"I'll have you go after me. I intend to switch it up today."

"All right. Fire away."

"Couple of housekeeping things first. We don't have a lot of time between today and when we present to your dad, so we need to start focusing on our best options. Right now, we have two different visions of what needs to happen. That said, we each need to support the other person's idea so that we can give your dad a good presentation. Make sense?"

He says, "I think so."

"Good."

"So whatcha got?"

99

"You made a statement the other day that I want to push back on a little bit."

"What was that?"

"First, you said something to the effect that we have enough farms."

Cooper squirms a little, looking a little like a kid about to get scolded. "Yes, I did."

"I thought about that, and I decided to do a little research. I could talk to you about all kinds of numbers related to farming, but I want to focus on just a few.

I pull up a slide for him.

- 2050 World Population Projection – 10 Billion people
- 2050 USA Population Projection – 438 Million people
- Total Agricultural Acreage – Decreasing by 3 acres per minute (Lost the equivalent of the State of Iowa in the past 20 years.)

I let Cooper look at the numbers for a minute. I can tell he's preparing a rebuttal even as he does.

"I see what you're saying, but would this one farm make all that much difference?"

"Okay. First, do you see the loss of farmland as a concern?"

"I get the point. I do! But in the grand scheme of things—"

I cut him off, "Cooper, we agree it's a concern. Here's why I want us to give careful consideration to a farm proposal. This is a big problem, but it might have a bunch of small answers. The solution might be found in a whole bunch of Walker Farms, but at least we'd be part of it."

"Thank you, professor."

"You are most welcome," I reply, relaxing a little under the influence of his humor. "I hope you took notes. There may be a quiz later."

"I am ready."

"Good."

Cooper pauses, then says, "Ok, so here's my concern, Dale. Dad wants to do something that carves a new niche for Morgan*Plus*. That's going to look more like property development than what you are proposing."

"I haven't told you my proposal."

"True. So back to my question. Whatcha got?"

"Here are our assets in this situation: We have an efficient, well-maintained farm with a great deal of productive acreage and a competent guy running the operation. I say we buy the farm and lock Jim Lynch in for five years to run the place."

I have caught him off guard. He knew I was thinking of an agricultural option, but he didn't have a clue I'd propose that it would involve Jim.

"I don't know how much return we get for that," Cooper says.

"We can sit down with Cam Walker and look at the numbers."

"What if it isn't enough of a return?"

"Then we take a good look at farms in the area and see what else they're doing to make money and if what they do is a fit for us. I mentioned a couple the other day."

I open up a slide that shows what I've just covered, and he stares at it for a bit.

"Okay. So that's your proposal?"

"In a nutshell, yes."

He looks at it again, thinks for a minute. I can tell he doesn't like the idea, and I'm about to hear why.

"I don't think this will excite Dad. In fact, I'm pretty sure it won't."

"But we will present it. We are going to support each other's idea, remember?"

"Okay. You're running this show."

"Good. Now you tell me what you have in mind."

He gets ready to start while I pull up items from the other day that I had told him to study.

- Golf Course:
- Planning and Development
- Cost Factors
- Time Factors

"Did you want me to go over those three, because that's not exactly how I've organized my proposal for you?"

"Go ahead. We'll just keep these up there. They have to be addressed."

"Okay. Well, here goes. You think farm—I think golf. What a great piece of land that farm is and what a beautiful golf course it would be! You have to admit."

I admit nothing at this point.

"So, what have you learned since last Thursday?"

I don't want to, but I've said we have to support each other, so I type as he talks.

"Okay. Well, an average golf course is around 120 acres or so. We have plenty of land out there. Heck there's enough land for two courses and you could put in a lake or two if you wanted, especially in that smaller valley to the south."

"Okay. Hold up and let me catch up with you."

I summarize what he's just said and nod at him; he continues.

"It could cost a couple of million dollars to do this."

I say, "At least."

"You think more than that?"

"Sure. The farm will cost a cool million, I think. Then you have to sod the fairways, put in greens and irrigation—which can be very expensive. Then you need to buy equipment to maintain it, and then buy golf carts and things like that to operate it. You'll have to build a clubhouse and buildings to store all your equipment. The list goes on, Cooper. It's probably five million or more, truth be told."

Cooper frowns. He is unhappy with me; probably because I took the time to think about all of this and to do a little research on my own. He knows five million is a whole different thing than two, and probably closer to the real cost.

I add, "And we haven't even talked about personnel expenses and marketing expenses. It's serious money."

"Sure, but it takes big money to make big money."

"And when does it start to pay off?"

"Three years, I would guess," he responds.

"That's very optimistic. I believe we should be conservative as we present this and think in terms of breaking even on an annual basis in *five* years, and then we start making money."

So, now I've added years and dollars to his estimates. He knows that makes his idea less attractive. Maybe now I have him rethinking my proposal. Instead, he says, "But Dad likes this idea."

"Excuse me? You mean when he said something about it when he saw it on the screen last Thursday?"

"No. He and I talked about it last weekend."

"You talked about it?" I work for an even tone.

"Yeah, we were at the driving range, and he brought it up."

"What do you mean, brought it up?"

Cooper is uncomfortable with this question. I can tell he's feeling like a witness who is incriminating himself at this point.

"He just said he thought a golf course might be a great project for the company."

"And you said . . . ?"

"I said I thought so too, and you had put me in charge of putting that part of the proposal together. That was all right, wasn't it?"

"Sure, if it stopped there. Did it?"

"Yeah, for the most part. He mentioned that he'd like us to think about putting in some high-end housing as part of the proposal. He thought it might help sway investors, and he really wants to get into property development."

I hardly consider that 'stopping there,' but I decide to try a different approach rather than contradict him. "Okay. Let me just stop right here and say this. I asked you the other day to hold off talking about this. It is inappropriate for you to be having conversations with anyone about what we are doing until we're ready to present."

"Wait. I can't talk to my own father?"

"He's our boss. And we are going to present to him. Do you not see the problem?" I ask.

"I see that you see one."

"Of course I do. I've been given the task of leading this, and the guy working with me on it has gone over my head to the boss—"

"His father."

"To the *boss* to talk about it. It's out of line."

He is angry with me. "I will make *sure* it doesn't happen again."

"Please do."

"If I can."

"You can and should. Okay?"

"I'll do my best, but I think you are overreacting."

I take a breath and think about what I want to say, then I remember what I said at the start. We're partners, and we need to help each other out. "Okay, we've beaten this to death, so let's move on."

"Good."

"I'm not sure we have the time between today and when we meet with your father to put together a full-fledged golf course proposal."

"Probably not."

In truth, there probably is time, but it would require someone who would be willing to spend hours on it doing extensive research and putting together a well-organized, visually appealing presentation. Cooper would never do that, and I'm not bailing him out.

"So, let's brainstorm what we can get done."

We spend the next several minutes exchanging ideas. I suggest some resources he might want to pursue to have more defined cost figures. He needs to get a list of people who design and install golf courses. He needs to find out where golfers are going to come from and then put together a list of our competition for those golfers. Those are all things he can get done.

"Let's confirm what day your dad wants to meet with us and then we'll set a time to meet and prepare," I say. "Shoot me any information you want included in our presentation and I'll get it set up. We can fine tune when we meet again."

"You've got it." Cooper pauses, then adds, "Hey, you know what, I'm so confident they'll go for the golf proposal, I'll make you a wager. If they choose the farm, I'll owe you a lunch at the place of your choosing, and if they choose golf, you'll owe me."

"You're on."

Cooper walks back to his office, and I have the room to myself. The fact that I think my option is the best combined with the fact that I really don't want to lose a bet to Cooper has me a little bit wired. I open the folder that Larry gave me on the first morning and thumb through it until I see a picture of Jim Lynch. Something clicks when I do. I get out my cell phone and punch in the number. I'm thinking I'll most likely leave a message, but he picks up.

"Hello."

"Hi. It's Dale Barnhart. I met you a few days ago. You have a few minutes to talk?"

"I do."

"Good."

16

Sunday, February 17

I'M ON I-70 about twenty miles east of Columbia, headed home after seeing my grandparents. I spent last night and this morning at the Lake with Dad's parents, and this afternoon with Gramma Spencer at the Senior Care Facility in Columbia.

My mind is jumping from thought to thought, thinking about my grandmother one minute and the meeting I'm about to have with Jim the next. I try to get some focus, but I can't.

My phone signals an incoming call and I'm almost relieved.

"Hi, Mom."

"Hi. Did you see your grandmother today? How was she?"

"She was doing pretty well, I think. The facility seems nice enough. Since it was my first visit, I had to be escorted by a staff member. When the lady told Gramma who I was, she said, 'I know who it is.'"

"She probably didn't at first, but that's Mom."

"Yeah, I think you're right. I asked her how she was doing, and she told me she thought she'd get to go home tomorrow."

"And what did you say to that?"

"I just said I hoped she would and changed the subject. She's really thin, Mom, and frail."

"I know."

"And her hair is pure white now, and there isn't much of it."

"I know. It breaks my heart. She always had such pretty hair, and it was so thick. Everyone envied her."

"Yet even with all that, she still looks like Gramma."

"So, what did you talk about?"

"We spent the day going through some pictures, and CDs and things like that. She remembered some things, and some she didn't. Overall, she did pretty well, but she got tired quickly. At one point, she fell asleep, so I woke her up to tell her I was going."

"What'd she say to that?"

"She said I was taller than she remembered."

"She might have thought you were Dad. He was tall, too."

"Yeah, she might."

"I told her I'd be back, and she said to let her know—she'd fix dinner next time. I hugged her a little and then I left."

"Thanks for doing that."

"We need to go back, Mom."

"We do, and your brother needs to go next time."

"Has he ever gone?"

"Once. He was so miserable the whole time he made me miserable."

"I bet."

"Are you getting close to home?"

"No. I'm still over an hour out, and I'm going to stop by and see Jim Lynch."

"Jim Lynch?"

"The guy who's taking care of the farm we're looking at."

"Oh yes. Well, call us when you get home."

"I'll text, Mom."

"Well, at least do that."

She hangs up and I find a station on satellite radio to keep me company. I see a sign that says that it's thirty miles to Warrenton. The turnoff to the Walker farm is not long after that, and Jim Lynch is expecting me.

As I turn on the road to the Walker farm, it looks different without the snow. I cross the bridge leading into the northern valley. Now, at the end of winter, with nothing growing, and not even the pure white blanket of snow from a couple of weeks ago, there is a still a simple beauty to the place. When I picture it with houses, and fairways and greens, I don't like those images. This is a farm, and I have made it my mission that it stay that way.

I should have called Jim from the road to let him know I was getting close, but he knows from our conversation the other day that I'll be stopping by today.

As I get closer to the house, he's standing next to a car in the drive. There's a young woman sitting in the driver's seat and Jim is leaning in the open window, talking to her. My guess is that Jim's girlfriend is preparing to leave after a weekend visit, and I feel bad for interrupting. She has parked in an area of the driveway that is wide enough for me to pass, and as I do, I stop and roll down my window.

"Hi, Jim. Sorry I didn't call today. Hope it's still okay for me to stop by."

"No problem. Dale, this is my girlfriend, Ginny. Ginny this is Dale. He's the guy I told you was coming out to talk to me."

"I'm so glad to meet you, and I hear you're with the company that might buy the farm."

"Yes, it's possible, but there's a lot to be considered."

"Don't ruin this place. It's too pretty."

"There's a lot of possibilities, Ginny. Nothing's off the table at this point."

Ginny's expression changes and she says, "Then, maybe I'd better be going so you two can talk."

"Don't hurry just because of me. I have plenty of time to hang around and talk to Jim."

"I need to be going. It's not a fun drive home and I might as well get it over with. Honey, I'll see you Friday."

"I can't wait."

Jim leans in and gives Ginny a kiss. She's quite pretty and I can see what he sees in her. I realize again that there's a gap in ages; that she's about my age while he's nearly fifteen years older. Seeing them together though makes the disparity seem less important.

After Jim watches Ginny pull away, he turns to me and says, "I have some overcooked coffee on if you'd like a cup."

"Sounds perfect."

I get out of my car and walk with Jim to the back door of the house. We enter an enclosed porch where we take off our shoes and hang up our coats before entering the kitchen.

It seems only appropriate that my first look at the inside the house is by way of the kitchen, which is always the heart of a farm home.

"I can't remember if you like sugar and cream or not," he says.

I take a sip. "Normally neither, but this might benefit from some half and half if you've got it."

"I believe I do, if it's still fresh."

He gets it out of the refrigerator, smells it, approves, and hands it to me. I pour some in my mug and stir it in with the spoon he hands me. I take another sip and it's still barely drinkable, but it'll do for now .

"So, Dale, you said you had some ideas about the farm that you wanted to discuss."

"Well, I've been tossing this place around in my mind ever since the day Cooper and I came out here. As I said earlier nothing's off the table at this point, but I feel if we don't have a plan, the firm might go the wrong direction. And by the wrong direction I mean its being anything but a farm."

Jim sips his coffee, looks at me with his blue eyes and then says, "You don't know how much hearing that means to me. I do love this place and I want it to be kept like it is, no matter who lives here next."

"What if that were you who'd be living here, if not forever at least for the next five years."

"How could it be me?"

I walk to the sink and pour my coffee out. "I think you need to make us a new pot of coffee, Jim."

———

Two cups of coffee later I am back on I-70 and headed home. My brain is buzzing from caffeine and excitement. Jim liked the idea of staying on until he can find his own place. Of course, it would be even better if this farm could belong to him. I let Jim know that Larry and Cooper are hell-bent on turning the farm into a golf course. It could be I've crossed a line in doing so. Have I just done something similar to what I've been upset with Cooper for doing? Maybe so, but that won't deter me. I think what I want done is right, and Jim's right there with me.

I'm in a 'go for it' mood right now, so I decide to dial Sarah.

I tell my Bluetooth to call her, and in a few seconds she answers.

"Hi, Dale."

"Hi, Sarah. How are you doing?"

"Great. Dave told me you went to see your grandparents this weekend."

"Yes. I saw my dad's parents, and Gramma Spencer."

"Dave said she isn't doing very well."

"No, she's not, but it was good to see her today, and I'll go back again soon. How was your weekend?"

"Fine. Your brother and I took the boys bowling again."

"Did they get ice cream again?"

"They got yogurt, and Dave bought it this time."

"Did you beat him?"

"Yes! And the boys made sure he bought."

"That's great." I pause, and then, "Hey, changing the subject, I was wondering if you wanted to meet me for coffee some night."

"Uh, sure. That would be nice. I'll be in your area on Tuesday afternoon. I'm meeting a teacher I'll be observing this semester. With luck she'll be the person I student teach with next year."

"So, we could get a bite to eat instead."

"We could do that. I'll text you when I'm finished and meet you wherever you choose."

"Great. Looking forward to it."

"How's work going?" she asks.

"I'll have to fill you in on Tuesday."

"Sounds interesting."

"Maybe even more than that."

"Okay then. I can't wait."

"Me neither."

We say our good-byes and hang up. It's been a good day.

17

Tuesday, February 19

"WELL. HERE WE ARE AGAIN."

"I have a *déjà vu* feeling, how about you, Dale?" Cooper smiles.

"A little. Thanks for sending me what you did. I've worked it into our presentation, and I think it's looking good."

"Let's see it."

I show him the presentation I've prepared based on my research and on what Cooper has sent me. I am going through the slides, starting with Cooper's ideas. It's not a lot different than what we've already discussed. I did a little research of my own and I've included the findings which show the number of golfers in the region and the options available to them. An unbiased observer would say that a new golf development might have a tough go, given all the places golfers can play.

Cooper says, "I don't think we need those tomorrow."

"Okay, I just thought they added some information that should be considered."

"Listen Dale, I've talked with Dad some more about the golf course idea, and I know he really likes it. He's not going to want to see those two slides you just showed me."

"You've talked with your dad about our work again?"

"Sure. It's hard not to. He brings it up, and what am I supposed to do, plead the fifth?"

"Hear me out on this, okay? Let's say our boss wasn't your father, just for the sake of conversation here. How do you think it would be, if you were going to the boss and discussing details with him about a project that I'm the lead on? Do you see why this bothers me?"

"Yes, I guess I do."

"Okay, then."

"I've told you why it's hard not to talk with him about it. I'm not trying to undermine you, Dale."

"Yet, that might be *exactly* what you are doing. And I will keep those slides available in case the information they contain becomes part of the discussion. Are we clear on that?"

"Yes."

"Good. Okay, so in the interest of time, let's move on."

I walk him through the rest of our presentation, much of which focuses on my proposal, and he shows little interest. I think this is due to the exchange we just had; and I would bet that it's also due to the fact he's sure the golf proposal is one Larry's will take to Cam—that it might be the only one. It's a little discouraging to me, but I think about my commitment to Jim Lynch, and I am determined to make sure Cooper's idea doesn't win out. Additionally, there's our lunch bet. It shouldn't be a big deal, but right now I don't like the thought of losing anything to Cooper Morgan.

We talk about how we'll proceed with our presentation tomorrow. I tell him what parts I want him to present and what parts I'll take. Being assigned part of the presentation renews his interest. As far as he's concerned, we're a team again.

When we finish, I go into my office and call Larry Morgan.

"Hello Dale. You two ready for tomorrow?"

"We are. What time do you want to meet with us?

"Let's go at ten. Do you want to come to my office?"

"Would you mind if we did it in the conference room? I've already got everything set up here."

"No problem. I'm looking forward to it."

"We are too."

I try to think about what I want to say next and how I want to say it. He senses I'm not finished.

"Is there something else?"

"Yes, there is, but I'd prefer to come to your office for that. Do you have minute?"

"I do. Come on down."

I make the walk down the hall thinking about how I want to voice my complaint to Larry. It's a legitimate grievance, and I want to make sure it doesn't come off as whining on my part.

His door is open, so I stick my head in and ask if he's ready for me. He says he is, so I walk in and take a seat.

"So, what's on your mind, Dale?"

"You put Cooper and me on this project and assigned me to be the lead."

"Yes, I did. And I think you two have been a great team."

"We have, with one exception."

"And what's that?"

"Well Cooper has told me that on a couple of occasions you and he have discussed our work even while it has been on-going."

"We have. Is that a problem?"

116

"I'd like to think that you'd see why an employee who's been assigned the lead on a project might feel undermined if one of the people working for him was having conversations with you, even while our work is in progress."

"I assume we're talking about the fact that Cooper and I have talked specifically about the golf proposal. Am I right?"

The fact that he goes straight to that tells me that he does know what's happened has been improper.

"You are correct."

"From what I saw on the screen the other day, it was obvious that golf was going to be one of the things we might pitch to Cam. And I was aware that was the proposal Cooper was working on. So, I guess I felt that a father and his son could have conversations about the son's work."

I hesitate, wondering if I really want to ask my next question, then go ahead, "What do you *really* want from all of this, Larry?"

It wasn't the question he thought I'd ask next, and it throws him for just a second.

"I've told you. I want to be able to go to my friend Cam Walker with an idea for his farm that he'd be interested in... uhhhm, that he'd be interested in partnering with us on or perhaps letting us handle."

"Okay, so if our goal is to find an idea he would like, aren't we better off if we go to him with at least two? And if so, are you open to all ideas, even those that aren't golf-related?"

"Dale, absolutely, and I'll be willing to go to him with everything we talk about tomorrow if that makes you feel better."

"Well, it's not about feeling better, necessarily. It's about feeling that I haven't wasted my time with what I think might be a good idea; one that maybe deserves as much consideration as the golf proposal."

"Then I can assure you that your work has not been wasted."

"Great. I appreciate your saying that," I say.

"Let me just say one more thing. I'm interested in this project, for sure, but my greater interest here has been to see how you work, and how Cooper fits in. That's more important to me than the Walker farm. I'm excited about the farm because I'd like to come up with something for my friend, Cam. I'm excited about it because I want to see if there are ways that we can expand our operation here, especially in the realm of property development. But I'm most interested in seeing what I have with you two. Intriguing opportunities will always be there, but getting the right people in place is what will ensure that my company lives on after my time here is done. And just to let you know how much I appreciate what you're doing, I have four tickets to the Cardinals Opening Day, and I'm giving them to you."

He reaches in his drawer and hands them to me. I don't know what I expected from this conversation, but it wasn't Cardinal tickets. I know I need to say something, and I go with a simple response.

"Thanks for taking time to talk with me, and thanks for the tickets. I can't wait for Opening Day, but right now I'm looking forward to tomorrow."

"I'm excited too. It's going to be good; I know."

I stand up, shake his hand, and leave his office with four Cardinal tickets and his assurance that I'll have a fair chance tomorrow.

18

"WOW! HE GAVE YOU TICKETS to Opening Day?" Sarah looks at me with a wide-eyed expression.

"He did. This may have been the first time that I felt I was talking to the guy I interviewed with in November."

"So, you're feeling better about things."

"I am. But I'm also aware that Cooper's all-in on the whole golf thing, and I think his dad will be sympathetic, so I'm not out of the woods yet. I feel like I'm operating from behind, since they've discussed golf extensively; but then again, Larry told me he's open to all ideas."

"What's your plan from here, then?"

"In a perfect world, I would have gone to talk with Cam Walker and told him that Jim Lynch, while he may not be family, is the next best thing. And if he doesn't want his farm to be something different from what it is right now, then he has his answer right there on the farm. And then I'd start working with him to make that happen."

"Why have you not done that?"

"Because then I'd be doing to Larry what I think Cooper has done to me."

"Well, that seems unfair to you. One of you is playing by the rules and one isn't."

"Right, but playing by the rules is how I'm wired."

"Even though you know you might *make* happen what you believe *needs* to happen if you worked around them?"

"Even then. I'm not ordinarily an ends-justifies-the-means kind of guy."

"Well, I admire that, but I feel you're putting yourself in a tough situation."

"I could be, I guess, but I have to be true to who I am."

She picks up her beer and takes a sip, pondering all we've just covered. I look at her and think she looks especially nice tonight; maybe she's done something with her hair, I don't know, but she looks great.

"So, do you think you might risk your future with the company if you pull this off?"

"Not based on the outcome *per se*, but on the way I go about it . . . yes."

"Wow! That makes my day dull by comparison."

"Sarah no, not at all. I'm so sorry. Please, you need to tell me all about it."

She starts, but just as she does our server arrives with our food.

"Does everything look okay?"

Sarah and I both say it does.

After we've had a few bites, I say, "Okay, tell me how your meeting went."

"It went okay."

"Just okay?"

"I'm really excited to get started teaching. The teacher I will work with, Marian Jones, is nearing the end of her career and it seems like she is thinking more about retirement than about her kids. She was nice but sort of detached. We didn't really click."

"That's too bad. Can you get a different match?"

"No. I'm going to do this. I've decided to accept it as a challenge and hope my enthusiasm will renew her somehow. I think she's been a good teacher, but something has worn her down. I know she has a lot to share, and I am determined to make this work."

"But what if she's so negative you don't feel you can try new things?"

"Dale. Before Drew's death, I might have backed off, but now I'm stronger and more resilient and more determined. I can do this."

"I think you can, and somehow I think Ms. Jones and her kids will benefit from you."

"And maybe that's why I've been given this assignment. Who knows?"

"I wouldn't bet against you."

"Nor I, you."

The rest of the meal passes with periods of quiet, interrupted by small talk about families and friends. It's great talking with her. Nothing against my parents, but it's nice to have a conversation with someone closer to my age; especially a female friend, who is attractive and easy to talk to.

"Sarah, I've enjoyed this. I hope you'd be open to doing it again sometime soon."

"Oh, I'm sure we can catch a cup of coffee, or a quick bite sometime, Dale."

"Great."

"I really appreciate your friendship, Dale."

"I feel the same about you, Sarah."

I realize at this moment that I might want more than friendship with her, and she seems to be reading me.

"Dale, getting together with friends for coffee or a beer or a quick bite is all I'm ready to do right now."

"Okay. How'd you know?"

"I could tell."

"You're good. I tell you what, I'll give you a couple of weeks, and then we'll grab a cup of coffee. Sound good?"

"Sounds great. By then we'll both have a lot more to talk about."

The server arrives with the check, and Sarah insists on splitting it.

We walk outside into the night air. There's a hint of warmer days coming, but sometimes a warm spell in winter is followed by snow. I hope not. We've had enough of that.

19

Wednesday, February 20

COOPER AND I ARE WAITING FOR LARRY. Our video presentation is queued and ready, with printed copies, too, in case technology should fail us.

Promptly at ten, Larry strides into the conference room, and to our surprise, he's accompanied by Paula and John.

"Hope you two don't mind, but I've taken the liberty of inviting these two folks to sit in on presentation. They'll bring good insights to our conversation today."

Paula gives me a look that says this wasn't her idea.

"No, we don't mind at all, Mr. Morgan."

Well, maybe just a little.

"They helped to put together the original packets I gave you, so they're quite familiar with the farm and I've brought them up to speed with what we're trying to get done."

John is expressionless, and Paula is as well, except for a brief moment when she looks my way and has a look that says good luck.

I decide it's time to start. "Great. We have a presentation for the three of you showing what Cooper and I believe to be a couple of good proposals to take to Cam Walker. There are three hard copies of this presentation, so Paula and John if you wouldn't mind sharing one, we're ready to go."

John says, "We'll be happy to share. Everything that's in here will also be on the screen, right?"

"Yes."

"We should be good then."

I pull up the first slide, which is the one describing the property and I start to summarize it.

"We all know this information, Dale, they did the folder remember, so go ahead with your proposals."

"Okay, then."

Is this the same Larry from yesterday?

"Cooper will go through the first set of ideas that we have for you."

Cooper won the coin toss to start today. I would have preferred it be me and am thinking I should have pulled rank. As he starts his presentation, his voice shows his nervousness—to me at least. I am sure he'd rather be showing a new Beemer right now.

We've set the slides up in such a way that the first one simply talks about the merits of the property as a location for golf. I go ahead and show the estimates of the number of golfers in the region. By itself, it doesn't tell the story, and I hope they ask the question that will provide more context.

Paula and John are smart enough to see what that is, and they ask how many other options local golfers have.

Cooper lists some of the other competitors in the immediate area, but not all. I hold my slide on that for now, waiting for the right question.

John says, "Okay, guys, you are going to get your golfers from the city for the most part, so what we really need to see is what other golf options are available in greater metropolitan area."

"Okay, Dale has that for you."

I scan the slide list and find that one. When I pull it up, John, Paula, and Larry study it for a minute while Cooper is quiet.

"So, there are a lot of golf options available already, according to your slide."

Cooper says, "Yes, John, that's right."

Paula says, "So how do you propose to get golfers to play at Walker farm when they have all of these other choices and have already established loyalty to them?"

Cooper returns to his planned presentation extolling the unique beauty and size of Walker Farm and arguing those assets will lure area golfers.

John says, "So primarily three things suggest using the property as a golf development. One, the novelty of a new place to play. Two, the property is very scenic, so it should become a pretty course if professionally designed. And three, you're thinking you might be able to have thirty-six holes so golfers would have several different options if they wanted to play eighteen holes?"

Larry says, "Paula and John, there are a lot of golfers in the area as you can see, and golf is a growing sport, so I have no doubt if we constructed an attractive, challenging course, we're going to get people to play there, and letting them design their own playing experience will excite them and keep them coming back, I believe."

His change from being an interested listener to being an advocate for this proposal tells me how this might go, so I have to hope Paula and John being here will work to my advantage.

Paula asks, "Have you researched how the sport of golf is doing right now, because I thought I'd read that there are a lot of courses closing."

I have prepared a slide that shows this, and I'm tempted to pull it up, but first I'll see how Larry and Cooper handle her question.

Cooper takes it. "You are correct on that, Paula. There was a course-building boom about twenty years ago partly due to the Tiger Woods phenomenon. Even though the sport was growing there was no way it could support all those new courses, so what we're seeing is a contraction, or maybe the word should be correction, right now. Basically, what that means is that fewer new courses are being built."

I step in here because I think the tide might turn if I do.

"I am sure you three will want to know what it costs to put in a golf course and how long it takes to start getting a good return on your investment."

I pull up a slide with those numbers and the three of them look at it. By his expression I can tell that Cooper isn't sold on my doing this right now.

John says, "So, it's probably five years before the course is in great shape for golf and starts making money."

"At the most, but I would hope we could get there in three; four tops," says Cooper.

"I think Coop's right. We could get this done quicker than five years," says Larry.

Paula wants to know if there are ways that we could generate income in the meantime. Her question is exactly the lead in Cooper needs for the next portion of his presentation. He's probably a little happier with me now. I'm hoping this next section will prove to be more of a deterrent to the idea than a selling point, so I let him go.

"We have an idea for additional income. We could sell lots in the one-to-three-acre range, which would lend themselves to higher-end housing.

I show a picture of a golf course lined with the kinds of houses that Cooper is describing.

"If you subdivide into larger lots and set up restrictive covenants regarding the types of homes, etcetera, that can be built on those lots, then your work is pretty much done except for laying out the streets and infrastructure. Then it's just a matter of selling the lots."

There is some more discussion and they come up with a few other ideas for Cooper's golf scenario when it is presented to Cam Walker.

"Cooper do you have anything else to add?"

"No, Dale. I think we've covered it pretty well."

I wait for other questions, while hoping for concerns or negative reactions. There are none. So, the idea is still on the table. Time for me to step up.

————————

Larry says, "I know you have another idea, so Dale, why don't you pitch it to us?"

I get ready to make my case and feel some of the same nervousness that Cooper felt.

I pull up some slides showing the farm at different times of the year. "Walker Farm, as noted in the introductory material, is prime agricultural land, so I wanted to propose an idea that might keep it that way. Once it is converted to any other use, it will be difficult, if not impossible, to restore it to what you see today."

I pull up a picture I've found of the Walker family when Cam was a youngster.

"The kid you see second from the left is Cam Walker. His family has owned this property for nearly a hundred years. I also want to respect that heritage as I make this presentation."

The next slide shows Jim Lynch. "Jim Lynch is the current caretaker of Walker Farm. He's been farming the property and taking care of the livestock, while maintaining and improving the buildings, fences, and equipment. As a result of his work, the farm has earned the Walkers a nice profit every year and provided Jim a small income and a place to live. Jim was looking at buying another property and leaving the Walker Farm, but that deal fell through. My first recommendation is that we see if he would be willing to stay on and continue working the place while we look at what might be done with the property."

Larry interrupts, "Actually, I got a message from Cam Walker and he and Jim have come to an agreement to continue their working relationship through this year at least, and through the next year if necessary."

Larry has unwittingly helped my cause, so I decide it's time to put up the slide with my proposal. The group studies it for a bit, and I study their expressions, looking for one that shows support. Seeing only non-committal looks at this point, I proceed.

"As you see on the slide, I think our best course for now is for us to purchase the property and sign an agreement with Jim Lynch to stay on for a period of three to five years. I prefer five, but if you feel three gives us and him more flexibility, I'd go along with it."

Larry, looking completely unexcited by this, puts his left hand under his chin and says, "So, we'd buy the farm and let Jim run it as he has. We'd pay him an annual salary, and then pocket any profits?"

"Yes. And the farm will appreciate during that time, so that we'd earn money on our investment, if we were to sell it in a few years."

"It's not a bad idea, don't get me wrong, but it's not all that different from what we have done in the past."

"So, you're saying it's an idea that is in our wheelhouse. But it has these two differences, Larry. We'd be the *owners*, not the lenders, and therefore have control over the future of the place."

"You say owners, actually we would have to put together a group of investors, so in a sense we would also be the borrowers on this."

"True, but we would be making money annually, where the golf proposal would offer *no* return to those same investors for several years."

Cooper adds, "Unless we get lots platted and start selling them."

Larry says, "I think we could do that."

"I would suggest that selling lots while we are actively developing a course might present some challenges, though," I say.

"We're always going to have to deal with challenges." Larry leans back in his seat, smiling. "That's what makes it fun, I think. Do you have anything else to present, Dale?"

"Just that I believe Cam might be very interested in keeping his family's place as the farm it has been. And wasn't that where we started—to make him happy?"

"Dale, this is interesting, and I appreciate having two ideas. Here is what I want to do, though. I want to go to Cam with a couple of clean ideas, so I'm going with the golf course as a stand-alone and the golf course with a high-end housing development."

I hesitate. "So, you're not taking the farm idea to him?"

"No. I want go with the two golf course options, and those two only."

Paula looks at me and then at Larry. "If we do that, could we keep the farm option as a backup, in case Cam Walker doesn't want to go the golf route?"

Reluctantly, Larry agrees. "Okay, as a backup, but we will not be presenting him that option when we meet with him on March first. If he doesn't like our proposal, we can re-group and re-work the farm idea and see if there is anything else in addition to it, then meet with him again to present what we have."

He looks at the four of us, and I wait, hoping someone will challenge him to let Walker hear the farm proposal on March 1 as well. No one does. Larry decides we're done. "I want to thank you two for a job well done, and John and Paula, thank you for your input. Dale, I'll need you to help me polish our presentation."

I want to tell him where to go. I want to tell him where to stick his Cardinals' tickets. Instead, I say, "Okay, Larry."

Everyone stands at this point, and Larry leaves with Cooper. They head to the other end of the hall. John and Paula stay for a minute longer.

"That was really well done, Dale."

"Thanks, Paula. I have to admit I'm a little disappointed that we won't be presenting Cam with the farm proposal,"

"Dale, here's the thing: Larry is thinking like a developer on this. He's picturing projects with big pieces of equipment. You know, big-boy toys."

"I guess."

"So, you weren't going to get anywhere pressing the issue today."

"Okay."

She looks at me, gets a slight smile on her face, and says, "But you're going to go ahead and work up your proposal anyway, aren't you?"

"Yes, Paula. Just in case Cam asks for other options."

"Great. But I would proceed with caution. Your partner is the boss's son, remember? And they are both all-in on the golf development."

"Well, as Larry says, that's what makes it fun."

Paula looks at John, who smiles, and then back at me. "Go for it. And by the way, this last conversation never happened."

"What conversation?" I ask, smiling back.

Paula says, "Exactly," and they leave me to think about my next steps.

———————

Cooper comes into my office an hour later. I assume he's been with his dad the whole time.

"Dad is very happy with what we got done today."

"Did it surprise you that he brought Paula and John to the meeting? Because it did me."

"Yeah, I asked him about that, and he said they'll be the ones to help him put together a bid for the farm, so they might as well be involved from the get-go."

"I see. I guess that makes sense. It would have been nice to have a heads-up, so that we could have prepared enough materials for everyone."

"I suppose."

He gets quiet for a second, then continues, "You know, when I sold cars, I was part of a team, but I was still an independent operator for the most part. I'm having to get used to working with a group of people on things. This is all new for me."

"Maybe that's one of the things your dad wanted us to get some experience with."

"How so?"

"Well, you know your dad is watching how you and I operate on this and trying to think about what happens next here?"

"I suppose so. I just think that if I'm ever in charge of a place like this, I'll tell my people what I want done, and then they'll figure out how to do it."

"That's part of leadership, but they say if you involve your people in making decisions about their work, they will be more committed to the work."

"Yes, I probably read that somewhere. You know I never did finish my degree. College wasn't for me . . . other than the social life that is."

"You enjoyed that, I take it."

"Yes, and that could possibly explain why I didn't finish."

"Possibly."

20

IT'S BEEN A LONG AND FRUSTRATING DAY, and I just want to go home, but I have to stop by a grocery store on my way. I'm in the produce section looking at the list on my phone when I hear a small child's voice. I look up and see the parents a few yards away. I think I might know the kid's mother from somewhere. As I'm trying to figure out who she might be, her husband turns towards me. We recognize each other simultaneously.

"Dale!"

"Hi, Phil. It's been a while."

"Yes, since our last year at Mizzou. Could it be that long? You remember Jess?"

"I do. Jess, I'm Dale. I think I met you at one of our parties."

"Oh yes. I remember that party, vaguely!"

"That's pretty much how all of us remember it. What's your little guy's name?"

"This is our one-year-old, Henry."

"Hi, Henry."

He gives me the once over, but no greeting.

"He's a little shy at first."

"He's a cute kid." Before Phil can thank me, I add, "So, who's the father?"

Phil shakes his head. "It's good to see you haven't changed."

"Not too much. So, do you live nearby?"

"Yes, we do. We live west of here in New Melle. And you?"

"I work near here and live in Chesterfield."

"Last time we talked, you told me you were heading out east somewhere to go to graduate school."

"I did. I moved to Philly, but after one semester I realized I was tired of school, so I took a position at a bank."

"And now you've moved back?"

"Yes."

"So how long have you been back?"

"Just a few weeks actually."

"It's good to see you."

"Thanks. You, too."

"Hey, you know what, we're having some friends over Friday night. Why don't you bring a date and join us?"

A date? Who could I ask? Wonder if Phyllis has plans!

"Sounds great. I'll see if I can get someone lined up. It's only a couple of days."

"Do your best. Come by yourself if necessary but come join us. We have a lot of catching up to do."

"I'll do that."

We exchange phone numbers, and as we do, Henry starts to get restless.

"I'll send you a text with our address and directions."

"Great. I'm so glad I stopped here today."

"Us too. It's great to see you again."

We head in opposite directions. I grab a few more things, go through the self-checkout, and take my bags to my car. As I pull out of my parking spot, I see the three of them come out. I give them a quick honk. They toss a wave my way, and as I look back at them in my mirror, Henry has decided to wave.

I make the short drive to my place and as I do, I debate whether to call Sarah. I'd love for her to go with me on Friday, but I think I need to make the invitation sound just right. It can't sound too date-like.

By the time I pull into my driveway, I decide to call her. I carry my groceries from the garage to the kitchen, unload and put them away, then go to my bedroom and put on my favorite jogging pants and long-sleeve T. After I make myself a salad, I think I know what I want to say to Sarah, so I make the call.

"Hi, Dale. How are you?"

"Great. And you?"

"Doing okay. What's going on?"

"Well, work is getting more interesting by the day."

"Yeah?"

I think she might be wondering why I have called her to talk about work, so I move to the real purpose of the call.

"Yes, but I didn't call to talk about that. I met a couple of friends from college, and they are having some friends over Friday night. I thought maybe you could use a break, so I wondered if you'd enjoy an evening out."

"So just a bunch of friends getting together?"

"Yes, and I think you may have met some of them one of the times when you and Drew came over to Columbia," I add.

"Oh?"

"I think so. Anyway, it's just getting together for pizza and beer. Nothing big. I bet your folks wouldn't mind watching Alex for a couple of hours."

"No, they wouldn't. I was thinking about going up to Spring Mill Friday night, but I guess I could delay and go up Saturday."

"Great. How 'bout I pick you up at six?"

"Where's this get-together going to be?"

"Oh, west of here about thirty minutes."

"Wouldn't it make more sense if I come to your place, and we go from there?"

She's right of course.

"It does. So, I'll see you then?"

"Yes, I'm looking forward to it. I definitely could use a break."

So, Sarah's going with me on Friday, and I'll get to see Jess and Phil again. All-in-all, not a bad ending to the day.

It started snowing when I pulled in my garage earlier, so I go to the front window and look out. The snow is coming down a little heavier now. The warm trend didn't last, after all.

After I finish my salad, I get my tablet out and open a blank document. Sometimes at the end of a day, I type whatever comes to mind. It helps me sort things out.

What do I need to do next?
- Work with Larry on the presentation for Cam.
- Need to confirm the date of the presentation.

• Need to figure out what's really happening here. Larry indicated his first priority was to see how Cooper and I work together. Yet he seems more interested in getting this golf course proposal done. What does he want? I know what I want. Will this be a problem for me, and if so, am I willing to go ahead anyway? Yes, I believe I am.

• Need to build on the fact that Cam and Jim have agreed to continue their partnership for the next couple years. This helps my cause.

• Need to figure out how I can do an end-run and get my proposal to Cam. I think he would be more receptive than Larry. Am I willing to risk my position to do that if need be?

And before I shut down, I type, "When you come to a fork in the road, take it." —Yogi Berra.

21

Thursday, February 21

I SEND LARRY AN EMAIL asking him to confirm the date of our presentation to Cam Walker. He responds that he'll check and get back to me. While I'm waiting, I look back at the presentation from yesterday and begin a new one focusing on the two golf course options. Separate from that, I'll continue to work on another presentation for the farm option. I decide that both will need a name, so I select *Walker Valley Golf Course* and *Walker Valley Golf Development* for the first two and *Petite Crique Farm* for my proposal. I think a French name sets it apart.

Although my heart is not in doing this, I need to make it look like I've given a good effort. Doing that means I need to enhance the presentation with additional images and information. I start going through an online search for images that fit and save some good ones in a file. The more I search, I realize I've taken this as far as I can go, and I wonder if there's someone in-house who can help me. I decide to check with Larry.

I check my email and see that he has responded. Walker still wants to meet on March 1 as originally planned, so I have just a little over a week. I email Larry back and ask him if he could recommend someone to help me with graphics, etcetera, and he directs me to Shelly downstairs. I pick up my office phone and dial her extension.

"Hi, Shelly, this is Dale, one of the new guys upstairs."

"Sure, I met you a few days ago. What can I do for you?"

For the next few minutes, I tell her what I'm working on, then ask her if she would be able to help. She says she would be happy to do that. I ask her if she'd mind meeting in my office today and she says she'll be right up.

Shelly walks into my office a few minutes later and takes a seat.

"Thanks so much for coming up immediately. I know this is short notice, but I have a bit of a time-crunch on this. Larry wants to pitch this to Cam Walker in a little over a week."

"It's okay. I'm familiar with this, since I was primarily responsible for putting together the folder that they gave you on your first day. I think I can get back up to speed on this and help you out."

I show her the images and information I already have. She interrupts me a few times with questions, making notes all the while. When I finish, she is quiet for a couple more minutes and continues to jot down some more thoughts.

When she's satisfied, she says, "I should be able to have something for you by Wednesday. Send me what you've just shown me, and I'll work on it and then send you an electronic file to review. I can also help you make a folder for the client when we get it where we want it."

"That's great. Having seen your work in the folder, I know you'll do a good job on this."

"This shouldn't be too hard, but I need you to go to bat with Larry and make sure that my calendar is cleared to do this."

"Consider it done. Oh, and Shelly—"

"Yes?"

"I'd like you to do one more thing, if time permits."

She gets a quizzical look on her face.

I spend the next few minutes showing her my farm presentation and talking about ways to improve it. She thinks she has some ideas and asks me to email her that file, too. She could be asking me why I just now brought this up, and why I didn't mention it as part of what Larry wanted. She studies me for a second and I think she figures it out. Shelly and Paula are two people I would definitely keep on board if I were put in charge of this place.

"Great. Well, if I'm going to turn this around in short order, I need to get started."

I like Shelly. She could have whined about this, but instead she just asked me to get her calendar cleared. After she leaves, I email Larry, and within minutes he replies.

I will make sure
Shelly has the time
and whatever else she
needs.

Great. I think
she'll do a good
job for us.

She always does.

And with that, I am now in sit-and-wait-mode for a few days. It'll be nice to take a break from this for a bit.

A few minutes later, I get a text from Phil with their address and directions. He tells me to come around six-thirty on Friday.

I tell him I will be bringing a friend.

What's his name? he replies.

And for a moment, we're back in college.

I realize I need to explain a couple of things to him, so I decide to call instead of text.

"Hey, Dale, got your text. Glad you're coming."

"I am too. I need to tell you a couple of things about the person who's coming with me.

"Okay."

I let him know about what's happened to Sarah: that she's lost Drew and is in a tough place right now. And I tell him that she's simply coming as my friend. I don't want people making her uncomfortable acting like we're a couple.

"Okay, I'm glad you gave me a head's up. I'll tell Jess what's going on and she can spread the word to the others."

I tell him thanks again for the invitation.

I want Friday to be perfect for Sarah, for her, and—selfishly—for me, too.

22

Friday, February 22

Sarah and I pull up in the driveway of Phil and Jess's place. My car lights show an old house that has a European look to it. Given that this area was settled by German immigrants in the 1800s, that is to be expected.

"Well, isn't this place cute?"

"It is. It's amazing that a few years ago we were all in college, and now Phil's married, got a kid, and from the best I can tell, owns a really neat house."

"Do you envy him a little?"

"No. I'm happy for him, but maybe I'm feeling a little behind."

"Would you trade what you've been through for what they have?"

"That's a good question."

"And the answer?"

"You know, I wouldn't. But I wouldn't mind being where Phil is in the not-too-distant future."

"If I've learned one thing, it's to be in whatever moment you're in right now, because you never know what's coming next."

I look at her again as she looks at me.

"So, I should stop worrying and just enjoy the moment?"

"Something like that."

"Then, let's go inside and have a good time."

I grab my beer, and we walk up a stone pathway to the front door. Phil must have been looking for us because he opens the door as we arrive.

"You found us! Come on in."

I introduce Sarah to Phil, and they realize they met before. As we reminisce about that weekend in Columbia, Phil tells Sarah what a great guy he thought Drew was, and how sorry he is for her loss. Sarah quietly thanks him.

"Let's go in and introduce you two to everyone."

We follow him through the house down a hallway to the kitchen where we find the rest of the group. Phil does the introductions. I was told once that repeating someone's name as you meet them is a way to better remember it. I'm not good at names, so I try it out. I get a couple of funny looks as I do, as if maybe I'm a little slow, but that's okay—I just might be.

After the introductions are completed, I give Jess a hug and hand her the beer I brought. She goes out to an enclosed back porch and puts it in a cooler. I study the kitchen while she does, and it looks great. One of the previous owners has done a great job. It could have been Phil, but I don't remember him being all that handy.

"You do all this, Phil?"

"I did. The appliances are new, obviously, and we took out the old cabinets."

Sarah goes to one of the cabinets and gives it a closer look, "These cabinets look like they belong here."

"They do, don't they. Jess and I know a guy who salvages windows and woodwork and cabinets and the like from old houses. The ones that were here weren't really salvageable, but he had these and I think they worked great."

"So, all of these were salvaged from another house?"

"Well, they aren't all old. Our friend is a genius at matching vintage wood. The island is new, I mean, after all, islands weren't really a thing in the early 1900s, and the cabinets to the left of the fridge are all new."

I tell him I think they look perfect.

"Yes, he and his guys did a fantastic job of matching them. don't you think?"

"Yes, I do. I mean if you hadn't told me, I wouldn't have guessed."

"Let me take you on a quick tour. The others have seen all of this before."

"Lead the way."

Phil shows us what they have done in the front room, and it is impressive. They've restored the flooring and woodwork and painted the room, and it looks great.

Sarah takes it all in and admires the work they have done. "Phil, this is beautiful. I think it might look much like it did when it was new."

"We're trying. Just after we bought the place, a descendent of the first owners stopped by and gave us some photos of the house from the late 1920s."

"Oh, that's neat."

"Yes, it gave the two of us something to go by, and that helped. Plus, the original flooring was still here under a layer of hardwood that was added in the 1950s, and the original molding and trim pieces were still here. We just had to strip some layers of paint off them."

Sarah has her eye on the fireplace. "This is beautiful. It has to be original."

"Yes, it is. Nice, huh?"

I say, "Buddy, you've done a good job here. Where did all these handy-man skills come from?"

"I can't tell you how many hours I've spent watching home improvement shows, and YouTube videos. But to be fair, what really helped is having a couple of friends who are good at this. I've traded labor on some of their projects for their expertise on mine. In fact, it's the guys you just met."

"Well, it's great."

"Thanks."

"You've done all this, gotten married, started a family. You've been busy compared to me."

"You'll get there."

"You think?"

He looks at me and I know he wants to say something like, "Well, not really, but you have a guest and I have to be nice." It kills him not to.

We walk into the kitchen where Jess is talking with the other two couples. They must have been taking about me because the guy named Greg asks me about Philly and why I decided to move back. I give him the condensed version.

When I finish a couple of minutes later, Greg says, "Why do I feel like there is quite a bit you left out?"

"Because I did, but I have a policy to not bore people the first time I meet them."

"The *first* time?"

Phil says, "Yeah. After that, all bets are off."

We decide it's a good time to hit the spread of appetizers that Phil and Jess have set out. As we do, the guys talk about work, sports, and things guys talk about. The women talk about their jobs and their kids, and they ask Sarah about school and her plans. The conversation is easy. The beer is good. The appetizers are great. The others make us feel like we have always been a part of their group; and to be honest, I like it a lot. I look at Sarah and it just feels good to see her looking like her old self tonight, even if it's just for just a couple of hours. While I'm looking at her, Phil is looking at me. I turn and I see the smile on his face.

"You need another beer, Dale?"

"I do. Let's go get one."

We walk out to his little porch to get our beers.

"She's really nice," Phil says.

"I know."

"And I think you would be okay if she was more than a friend."

I consider that, then admit, "I've always liked Sarah, and I hate what's happened to her. I feel like I want to help out somehow."

"Watch out."

"Why?"

"I think maybe it's getting to be more than that for you."

"You might be right. I care about her and there could come a point when I'd like it to be something more."

"Good luck, buddy."

I twist the top of my beer and take a sip, to find that it's a pale ale and maybe a little too hoppy, but I'm thinking about what Phil just said and not focusing too much on my drink.

We go back to the others, and by now everyone has regrouped, so the conversations go in new directions. The time goes by quickly and all too soon it's going on ten. The other couples decide it's time to bring the evening to a close. They have little ones who will be up early tomorrow, so no more late nights for them. Sarah is feeling like she needs to leave, as well. Everyone agrees we should get together again—maybe for a nice dinner somewhere.

I look at Sarah to see if she agrees, but I can't read her to tell for sure. I think she does, though.

Sarah and I get into my cold car. Luckily, the heater's good and we'll soon be warm. My car lights shine on the house, and once again we enjoy the view.

"That was nice."

"It was. Thanks for coming with me."

"Thanks for asking me. I didn't realize how much I needed a night out, and your friends are fun."

"Well, I really only knew Phil and Jess before tonight, but I figured we'd enjoy their friends."

"They were all nice."

As I drive, she talks about the other couples and tells me things she learned that I didn't know. Why is it that women are always better at this than guys? We talk about the house some more and she says she'd love a place like that someday. I say I'd love that, too, although I don't think I'd do as well as Phil has with the remodels and updates.

"You never know."

"Oh, I'm pretty sure on this one."

She laughs, and again, it feels good to hear her laugh.

"I'm glad you had fun tonight, Sarah."

"You may have said that once or twice already."

"I blame the pale ale."

"Was it good? I had the white wine."

"It wasn't bad. I'd give it one more try."

It's quiet for a bit, and I decide I want to follow up on the dinner invitation.

"When they meet for dinner, would you like to join them?"

"I enjoyed myself tonight. Give me some time though, okay?"

That throws me just a little, and all I can think to say is, "Okay?"

"Just give me time. It's only been three months. It was fun tonight, but as fun as it was, it was a little painful, too. One minute I'd be having a good time and it would feel like it used to feel, and then I'd think about Drew and realize he wasn't there. I just need some more time."

"I understand. Could I ask how much time you feel you need?"

"I don't know. Maybe June."

"June!"

"Yes, June."

"I understand. You need the time."

———————

After we get back to my place, I convince her to let her car warm up while I show her my side of the duplex. My place pales in comparison to Phil and Jess's house, but she realizes it's all I need right now and says all the right things.

Her car is warm when we finish the tour, so she gives me a hug and says goodnight.

I say, "Maybe coffee sometime soon again, okay?"

She says, "Perfect," and leaves me standing in my doorway, still a little confused as to the ground rules, but happy that coffee is still an option.

23

Friday, March 1

"YOU NEED TO HAVE YOUR DUCKS IN A ROW." As Cooper and I wait for Larry Morgan and Cam Walker to show, I'm remembering that old expression of my dad's and wondering if I'm ready for today's presentation—if I have everything lined up to get it where it needs to be.

Cam has encountered a problem at work and is running a little late. It's not a problem for us, because it gives Cooper and me one last chance to review our presentation strategy. Not that we really need it, since we spent time yesterday polishing and perfecting it. In fact, we are so prepared that I'm concerned that it may be too good, and Cam will like the golf course proposal. I want it to be good enough that Larry is impressed. On the other hand, I want Cam to think our proposal is okay but not be too excited about it, which would then allow me the opportunity to present my idea. It will be a delicate situation, to say the least, and I can only hope my ducks stay in line.

At precisely ten-thirty, we hear Larry and Cam coming down the hall. I've never met Cam and I'm looking forward to putting a face to the name. They enter the conference room, and we stand up to greet them.

"Cam, I want you to meet Dale Barnhart who has been working with Cooper on the presentation we have for you."

I shake hands with him. He's wearing a white shirt with a bright blue tie to go with his deep blue eyes and salt and pepper hair. I am positive his wife picked it out. Cam Walker is the shortest of the four of us, but he has the most presence of anyone in the room. I like the guy immediately. He gives me a quick once over and I hope I pass his inspection. His expression doesn't change, so I have no way of knowing.

Cooper and I have decided that the story of our getting stuck in the snow with Jim will be a good icebreaker. I get the story started and Cooper takes over. To his credit, he tells a good story.

When he finishes, and after we all enjoy a good laugh, I decide it's time to transition to our presentation. Our story has provided me with my opening.

"Even on that snowy day, Mr. Walker, we could tell the farm was a great place and we really wanted to respect that as we thought about its next chapter."

I begin to open our PowerPoint, but Larry steps in and asks Cam if there's anything he'd like to say first, since it's his property we're talking about today. So already there's a duckling out of line.

"Well, I didn't come prepared with remarks, Larry, and in some ways, I don't know if I want to say a lot today. To be honest, fellows, I could get a little emotional about this. This farm means a lot to me, and I'm a little sad that no one in the family wants to take it over. Since they don't, though, I want to make sure that the place is being treated right in that next chapter."

Larry says, "Then why don't you go ahead and start, Dale?"

I regroup and start again. "The Walker Farm has been around for three generations. Today we'd like to introduce you to the ideas of the Walker Valley Golf Course and the Walker Valley Golf Development."

For the next thirty minutes, I show him slides of golf courses which focus on their visual appeal. Then I show him some courses with nice homes beside them, and with more people and activity. Shelly has done a wonderful job with these images. Her choices are great; much better than I could have done.

As Cam takes in what we are showing him, I let Cooper talk about adding a lake or lakes to the project while I pull up the appropriate slides. Again, Shelly has done a good job of coming up with images to go with our presentation. We made a choice not to throw a lot of numbers at him at this point. Shelly felt it would be better to let him ask about those and then respond to them.

I can tell that Cam likes the look of what he is seeing, and I get a little worried that our presentation is so good that it's selling him on the idea.

When we finish, we turn to him for questions.

"Guys, I like this idea. Let me ask you a couple of questions, though. Are you sure your firm could make a go of this? I mean if you get five to ten years down the road, and the Walker Valley Golf Course isn't making any money, then you may be looking to unload the property and the very scenarios I want to avoid might end up happening after all."

Larry takes this question for us. "Cam, you and I know that there's no such thing as a 100 percent certainty, but I think we can easily get enough financial backing to pull this off, and I think we know the people who can help us design and build the course. And if we go with option two and sell some lots around the course, we'll have a stream of income that will keep us going while we get the golf course to the point that it's making money for us."

"Okay. Let me ask you this, then. Let's say you are trying to sell me a lot by a course that is still being developed. You'd be asking me to visualize what it might look like. Maybe I'd prefer to wait until the project is more complete so I can *see* what it will be. If other people think like that, then that stream of income might be a trickle at best."

"Oh, I have absolute confidence we can put together a professional sales pitch that will give buyers a clear idea of what our vision is for the place. We'll make it enticing and we'll create the impression that lots won't last long so they'd better get in while they can."

"I guess I wonder if the kind of person who would want to build there *and* would have the resources to do that . . . how do I want to say this? If that person won't have other options that are just as attractive, further along, and more importantly, closer to the city."

"We've considered all that. We'll just have to market the hell out of the place. Don't forget that we have some really good contacts with realtors, and we believe they will be a big help in getting buyers to pull the trigger."

"Do these realtors currently sell much property out near my farm?"

"They are comfortable with selling anywhere in the region; no problem."

That isn't an answer to Cam's question, and I hope he sees through it and sees how tenuous this is, instead he goes to his next question.

"Have you researched everything you'd need to do to get my farm zoned and permitted for this?"

"We are working on that right now, but there should be nothing we can't overcome."

"Overcome, yes, but in what kind of time frame?"

"That would be our worry, Cam."

"And mine, too if your plan doesn't work."

I am starting to get some hope now. Cam is sharp and I believe he sees the flaws.

Larry says, "My company is not going to let up on this until we make it work, Cam. You know that."

Cam is quiet and then, "I do, but you know the golf industry has slowed a little the past few years?"

I have slides that show this, and I want to pull them up. It would be heavy-handed, so I decide to simply tell him he's correct. "Our research does show that the development of new courses has slowed, and yes, some are closing."

Larry gives me a quick sideways glance, then returns to his sales pitch. "Yes, some have closed, but the places where they've done it right—those places are doing well. We're going to handle this the right way, and when we do, your farm will be one of the most beautiful courses, not just in the area, but in the region."

"I know you well enough to know that you wouldn't half-ass this, Larry. And I will say that it would be a spectacular golf course. It's not a farm, but it's not some crappy subdivision or a hog factory."

I think he has an unfinished thought, but as he hesitates, Larry sees an opportunity. "Then, let us do it."

We have reached a moment of truth, the moment at which I had hoped he would want to see other ideas. Cam gets quiet for a moment. Looking at him, I'm beginning to think he might just say yes. My heart sinks a little at the thought. If I lose this round without getting to present my idea, the game gets much harder. I try to think about how to head that off.

Cam says, "Okay, I tell you what. Have your staff draw up a Memorandum of Understanding."

"And what would you like us to put in there?"

"It would indicate that I will sell the property to you, at a price that will be determined by fair market value for a property of this quality, and that I will sell it to you for the sole and specific purpose of your converting the farm to a golf development, subject, of course, to my approval of the plans. Additionally, I want it specified that all legal and regulatory barriers be resolved to my satisfaction. And finally, it needs to specify that if for some reason you choose to relinquish the property in the next seven years, I and my heirs have the first right to re-purchase the property."

"So, may we include the high-end housing as part of the Memorandum of Understanding?"

"Yes, you may leave it as an option."

"We can draw that up."

"And you are going to have to figure out how to improve the road leading to the farm if you want to handle the traffic to your golf course and your new homes."

"Oh, that shouldn't be a problem, Cam."

"You're going to have to deal with Brotherton and Roberts, so it very well could be."

"I think we can convince them. We will ask them for easements to widen and improve the road and in return we will take over the care and maintenance of the road. I'm sure they will see the advantages of a wider and better-maintained road leading to their properties. I'm not worried about that at all."

Cam gives him a look that says maybe he should be.

"Okay, then. You've made the golf course an attractive idea, Larry. As I have said repeatedly, I wish someone in my family wanted to farm this place. It's still my preferred outcome, but that's doesn't appear likely, so let's explore this further—let's see where it goes."

They stand up and shake hands, then Cam shakes Cooper's hand and, finally, mine.

Cam says, "Good job on the presentation gentlemen."

Cooper says, "Thank you."

"I thought maybe I'd get to see more ideas, though."

"We showed you two."

"Well, they were basically two versions of the same concept. I thought you might have had something more."

I see a chance to show him my proposal, and I see Larry and Cooper eyeing me. While they know I have wanted to pitch the farm idea, they don't know I actually have that presentation ready. I need to figure out a way to get him to ask to see another proposal, so I say, "Oh, we had some other ideas, but it was decided to come to you with these first to see what you thought."

Larry and Cooper both look uncomfortable at my saying this.

Cam says, "Well I tell you what, we could always look at those ideas if the golf thing falls through."

Larry immediately jumps in and says, "Oh, it won't. The golf course and golf development were our best ideas. They are the ideas we could see ourselves having an interest in, and we will make sure the final plan will be successful."

"Okay, then. Let me know when you have the Memorandum of Understanding ready."

"Will do."

Larry says, "Let me take you back to my office to get your coat."

24

ONCE THEY LEAVE, COOPER SAYS, "Good job, Dale, but what was up with saying we had other ideas?"

"He said he was surprised we didn't have them. I don't think it hurt for him to know that we considered options and settled on the golf ideas for now. In fact, I think it helped."

"I don't see how it did, and it seems like you could have said something to the effect that we rejected all other ideas rather than we thought we'd show the golf ideas first. There's a difference, and he might have wanted to see what else we had."

Rather than being apologetic, I decide to throw it back at him. "He didn't though, am I right?"

"No, but it just seemed like an unnecessary comment after the deal was pretty much sealed. That's all."

"Let me ask you this. Was today's presentation not *good* enough?"

"No, it was great."

"Did you not receive the go-ahead to write up a Memorandum of Understanding to proceed on the golf course development?"

"Yeah, we did."

"Then why are we having this conversation?"

"You're right. You're right! It just seemed like we didn't need to bring up other ideas. It would only have complicated things."

"I'll just let the result of our meeting speak in my defense, then."

"Okay. We're good. We're good. Oh, by the way, I can't wait for my free lunch!"

"You've got it. You want it super-sized?"

He laughs at that. "Oh, it'll cost you a little more than that, I promise."

He can have his lunch, but this isn't over.

A few minutes later, Cooper and I are seated in Larry's office. He's asked us to join him for a debriefing.

"Guys, that presentation went about as well as it could go. I want to say thank you to both of you for all your good work. It was very well done."

Cooper says, "Thanks, Pop."

"I do have one question, Dale."

"Fire away."

"We had permission from Larry to proceed. We had what we wanted from the meeting. Why even bring up any other options at that point? There was absolutely no need, and it could have caused us a problem."

"Okay. Well, I'm sorry you feel that way, Larry. A couple of things I would say here. One, we did have other ideas. He wondered why we didn't, and as I just told Cooper, I thought it looked better if we did."

"Better, *how* may I ask?"

"Better, because we sorted through some ideas, came up with a couple, and as you said, we brought what we thought to be the best ones to him. I think if you step back and look at it, it strengthens your case, but that's just me."

"Okay, what was your second point?"

"I guess my second point was, what harm would have been done if we had made a second presentation?"

"Well, we want to do the golf course. We didn't need anything to complicate things."

"What do you mean by complicating things?"

"Well, what if he had preferred the farm idea?"

"Seems like if he did, that would have meant we would have developed a Memorandum of Understanding for that."

"Yeah, exactly!"

"And the problem is?"

"What's in it for us?"

At this point I really want to say something to the effect that I thought our original mission was to help Cam find something to do with his farm that would make *him* happy.

"Guess we were just looking at this from different perspectives then."

"What were you going to do if he asked what our other suggestions would have been?"

I open my folder and pull out the farm proposal. "I would have presented this to him."

Larry picks it up, looks at it for a minute, lays it back down, then looks at me.

"You did this?"

"Yes, sir."

"I instructed you to do the two versions of the golf proposal.

161

I don't think I directed you to do more than that."

"You instructed me to keep the other as a backup. I thought I'd go ahead and have it ready if needed."

"I'm trying to decide if you were showing initiative or going behind my back."

"I'd hope you would go with the initiative option. I mean there was absolutely no guarantee he would like either version of the golf proposal, and then what—we agree to meet again and present our other idea? Why not have it ready just in case."

"Okay. I'll grant you that for now."

He looks down at my proposal and gathers his thoughts.

"Boys, I want to discuss how things will be starting Monday. Now that we have secured Cam's approval to draft a Memorandum of Understanding, we'll be entering the next phase of this project, and I don't think I need both of you on it. Cooper, since this was originally your baby, I think it makes the most sense if you take the lead and work with the legal team to get the MOU done. You'll also need to start making contacts with people in the golf industry and with developers. Are you up for that?"

"Yessir! I can't wait."

So, I have been replaced. I wonder where I go from here.

"And Dale, it's time that we go back to our original plan and complete your training. I've delayed that for a month while we took care of the Walker Farm proposal. I've appreciated your willingness to dive into that for me, but we need to get back to where we were supposed to be a month ago."

"Okay, so where shall I start on Monday?"

"I want you to start with John and Paula. What they do is critical. If we don't have private investors, we can't handle all the business we get. I'll let you work with them for a week or so, then I'll want you to work with the folks who network with local realtors. They're also a critical piece, and I think those two together will give you a great introduction to the rest of the training."

"That sounds like a plan."

He gives me back my proposal and says, "Oh, and one last thing, Dale. I know you felt the best scenario for the farm was not the one that is going to happen, but you stayed professional except for one little lapse there at the end. Now, and I can't emphasize this enough, we are all-in on the golf course. No more farm talk."

"Okay, but since I'm not on the project now, that shouldn't be a problem, am I right?"

"True, and I want to thank you again for your help on Cooper's idea."

"Glad to do it."

Larry nods, then glances from me to Cooper. "Okay then, boys. Why don't you two take the rest of the day off. You've earned it."

Cooper says, "Great. And Dale, I will take a rain check on that lunch and go to the range and hit a few balls."

"Sounds good, Cooper. And thanks, Larry, it will be nice to start the weekend a little early."

"Got big plans?"

"I've always got a plan."

25

Saturday, March 2

ISTEP OFF THE ELLIPTICAL and towel off after a challenging work out. I check out the people around me. It's a small crowd on a Saturday morning, which is fine by me. There's a TV set in front of my machine, and for once it isn't on some news channel. Instead, it's a program about two people who have been dropped off in some remote, semi-tropical location with no clothing and very few supplies. I have two questions as I watch it: First, what is the target audience for this kind of show? And second, how is the person filming the episode equipped? I think if I were out there naked and starving and some fully clothed camera guy had a tent and a fully stocked ice chest, I'd probably lose my discipline the first day.

As I drive home after my workout, I appreciate the fact that I can take a shower when I get there, and that I can eat a breakfast that I don't have to trap or kill.

I get home and fix that breakfast, and while I'm eating, for no apparent reason, I think about Jack, my former neighbor and friend in Philly and realize I haven't spoken to that guy since he left for Ohio in January. I decide to it's time give him a call. I pull up his contact info and click on his cell.

"Morning Dale, or should I say Kyle?"

"You were right the first time, Jimbo."

For whatever reason, Jack could never get my name straight, so we began to play this little name game. Doing it today takes me back to Philly.

"Okay, we're even now. How's it going there in the Show-Me State?"

"Pretty well. I've been at my new job a couple of weeks, and it's been . . . interesting so far."

"Interesting, huh. What's that mean?"

"We don't have time for me to answer that. It is a story I need to tell you over a beer sometime."

"Let's make that soon."

"That would be fun. Maybe we could get together sometime next month, either here or there."

"You need to come my way, first. I'd love to show you around beautiful downtown Willmore, Ohio."

That, in a nutshell, is Jack: 'We need to get together whenever you can make it to where I am.' I let it pass and say, "Why don't you text me some weekends that would work for you, and I'll see if I can take a long weekend and make the drive."

"You gotta drive? They don't have air service out of St. Louis?"

"Yes, but it's probably expensive, especially if I do it last minute."

"Okay, right now, any weekend but the first weekend would work."

"Okay, Jack. I'll do my best to work something out and let you know. Tell me what you've been up to since we talked."

"As you know, I'm working with my brother, Sean. I've been handling sales and marketing for his company while he manages the day-to-day stuff. I've already generated enough new business for him that I'm earning my keep."

"How do you like living back home?"

"I like it okay. It's not 100 percent what I expected though."

"I bet you expected it to be just exactly the way you left it, didn't you?"

"I did."

"And it's not."

He nods agreement.

"I miss some things in Philly. Don't you, Jack?"

"I do. It was getting to the point that we had ourselves a nice little group to hang out with. I haven't quite gotten to that point here, but I'm working on it. Luckily, Sean knows a lot of people, and they're a lot like the gang back in Philly."

"My brother, Dave's an hour away, so he's not much help here. But like I said, it's getting better. I'm sure you've met some of the ladies in the area already."

"Yes, I have, but at times—and I can't believe I'm about to say this—at times it's a little boring."

"Boring? I have never known you to find women boring, or they you."

"Well, boring might not be exactly the right word, but it's just a little different. Maybe I'm ready for something more."

He gets quiet for a moment. I wait for him to speak, and then he says, "This is way too serious for us to be talking about when we haven't talked in two months. We need to have that beer."

"It did get just a little heavy, didn't it? Anyway, let me check at work and I'll let you know what weekend I can make it."

"Great. Sean and I will show you a great time. We'll send you back to Missouri with a smile on your face."

"Looking forward to it."

"Get plenty of rest and hydration before you make the trip."

"I'll do that. Talk to you soon."

"Glad you called."

I start to hang up, then stop. "Oh, Jack?"

"Yes."

"I'm glad you're okay. What happened to you at K&S was a bunch of crap."

"It was for sure."

I say, "I think I know what happened to you, but I'm never quite sure I have the whole story."

"Well, tell me what you know. I'll fill in the blanks."

"Okay, here's what I remember. Mick Kelleher and Truman Smith are the partners who started K&S Financial. Mick was your guru, and you were his heir apparent."

"Yeah, that might be overstating it, but you're close."

"Truman has his own guy, and you and Truman's guy were, for lack of a better word, rivals."

"Yes, we didn't care too much for each other. You've got that right."

"Mick went into semi-retirement and moved to Florida, but before he did, he designated you to effect a merger with another similarly-sized company."

"Yes, we were small players in Philly and both at risk of being taken over by one of the big national brands. He thought a merger would be the only way we could stay competitive and keep our identities. He worked hard to build that business and he didn't want to see it be swallowed up."

"While you're working diligently on that and making good progress, Truman and his guy are working on getting the firm taken over by one of those larger operations and they're working on getting themselves well-positioned when the take-over would happen."

"You have that exactly right."

"So Truman gets everything lined up and goes to Kelleher to tell him that he's about to make them both a lot of money. Kelleher wants to fight it, but his wife gets critically ill and that takes all the fight out of him. He can only wage so many battles at a time. The deal is done, and you are out on the streets within days of it's happening."

"Exactly. You know more about it than you think, Dale."

"Well, you got screwed, buddy."

"I did, but that's how the world works, and I've already come out ahead. I like working with my brother. I enjoy being back home. I'm okay."

26

I THINK ABOUT WHAT I'LL DO with my Saturday evening. I have no plans, so I decide to get in my car and start driving. I pass a strip mall and see a sports bar that says it has great wings and big screen TVs. Sounds good enough, so I pull in. There are enough cars in the lot that I think I'll be okay.

I park my car and head inside to see a place that except for its Cardinals and Blues paraphernalia, looks much like hundreds of other places around the country. I'll have a couple of beers and a burger and watch whatever's on their screens. It will kill some time, and the thought of being home alone and rattling around in my place with nothing to do doesn't appeal to me.

As I'm enjoying my beer and waiting on my burger, my phone rings. It's Jim Lynch.

"Hi, Jim."

"Hi, Dale. Wow you've got some background noise going on there. You at a party?"

169

"No, just grabbing beer and a bite at a bar. What's up?"

"Well, of course I've been wondering how yesterday went."

I should have called him. Of course, he wants to know how the meeting went!

"Not great, Jim."

"What's that mean exactly?"

"To my surprise, Cam actually liked the idea of the golf course development."

"Oh no. Did you not get to talk to him about the farm?"

"I didn't."

"So, my days at Walker Farm are numbered, I guess," Jim says.

"Well, not necessarily. Here's what they have to get done to make this fly. They have to put together the financing for the purchase. They'll have to get someone hired to design the course. They'll need to get the neighbors to agree to let them improve the road to the farm. Once that is done, they can then begin to plat out the land that will be used for the houses and lay out the course. I would assume the county zoning commission will have to give their go ahead, too. Only then can they begin the actual work. I can't see that being accomplished until the end of next year at the earliest."

"So, if the sale proceeds, will you all still keep me on while I figure things out?"

"We'd be stupid not to, and I think Cam will insist on it."

"Well, that buys me some more time."

"It does, and *none* of the things that need to happen are a slam dunk, Jim. A year and a half might be a conservative estimate as to how much time they'll need to get this going. There are any number of places where it could fall through. When that happens, then the farm is still the best option, and what you and I have discussed will still work out."

"But if I'm smart, I start looking around again."

"It's always smart to keep your options open. But Jim—"

"Yes?"

"I think we will win this thing yet."

"Easy for you to say, but we are in totally different situations here."

"We are," I admit, "but we both have the same goal. And I feel like something's going to break our way. It's bound to."

"Well then, I'll keep busting my ass to keep this place going until it does."

"Great."

I hear some commotion on his end, just barely above the noise here.

Jim says, "It's Ginny."

"Give her a hug for me."

"Probably do better than that."

"Talk to you soon, Jim, and I'll keep you posted."

"Please do," and with that he hangs up.

My food arrives, and I eat it without tasting a bite of it. It might be good, but I couldn't say. My mind is going a dozen different directions. I want to talk with Sarah or some of my friends in Philly or Giselle in New York, but for various reasons I call none of them.

There's a basketball game on ESPN that features a couple of small southern colleges. I like watching games like this. There are usually a couple of well-coached teams competing, so the basketball is good, and I prefer the announcers these games get. The guys who call the blue-bloods' games act as shills for those teams. These guys actually know a little bit about basketball and share what they know.

The game hits a media time-out, and it's as good as I hoped it would be, so I decide to sit here and watch it for a while longer. My second beer arrives, and I realize I need to nurse this one. I finished the first one too quickly. I look around and I see few single people here, but not a girl in the crowd who might be looking for someone new tonight. It's just me, my beer, and a good basketball game. It could be worse, I guess.

———

When I pull in my driveway, I see the same car in Phyllis's drive that was there the morning after the Super Bowl. Phyllis may have more going in her social life than I do tonight. If so, good for her.

27

Sunday, March 3

I'M ON MY WAY.

*Meeting us here or
at church?*

Meet you at the house.

Ok.

My parents always like it if I attend church with them,
so I figure it's the least I can do. I consider Dad and Mom to
be faithful rather than religious people. They quietly show
what they believe through the way they live their lives,
rather than citing scripture and claiming personal salvation.

173

I think many of the people who attend Spring Mill United Methodist are the same, and it's become a big part of who I am.

I pull in their drive a few minutes before time to leave, and they are in the car waiting for me. Dad and Dave are in front and Mom's in the back with DJ beside her in his kid's seat. I get out of my car and slide in beside him.

"Guess I shoulda called shotgun."

Dave says, "Yep. Beat you to it, but DJ wanted to sit by you anyway. We were beginning to worry that you would make us late and we'd have to sit in the front row."

Mom laughs at that, and Dad just shakes his head. Years ago, we were late for church service one Sunday, due to some problem caused by either me or Dave. When we got to church, our usual spot was taken by a new family and we had to sit in front, where no one ever wants to sit.

Dad was uncomfortable during the service because he thought every time the old minister mentioned a specific sin—and he preached a sermon that day that mentioned a *lot* of sins—he would look at us as if he knew Dad was guilty. It was long hour for Dad, and he made sure we were on time from then on. In fact, the next few Sundays he got us there earlier than usual to make sure our seats weren't taken. Dave and I were not the best at sitting through a long service anyway and adding a few minutes to our seat-time added to our misery. We eventually returned to our normal time, but it was not nearly soon enough for the Barnhart Boys.

"How's everybody?"

"Great; how was the drive today?"

"Pretty easy. Not much traffic."

We engage in some more small talk, and in a few minutes we pull into the church parking lot. Dad parks near a car I think belongs to the Marshalls.

"Is that Steve and Anne's car?"

"It is. Sarah and Alex are probably with them. They came up yesterday."

"Oh, yeah? How'd you know?"

Dave says, "She called me yesterday morning to see if we wanted to get the boys together. I had something to do at work, so I took DJ over to their house."

"Oh."

We get out of the car and head to the sanctuary. Dave takes DJ to the kid's room then returns to join us in our row.

The Marshalls are sitting a few rows behind us and to our right in the middle section. Sarah is with them. I look her way and she smiles at me. Steve Marshall does as well. Anne is looking straight ahead and deep in thought.

The new minister, Reverend Moseley, is a definite upgrade over the previous one. She is funny, personable, and does a good job of moving things along. Today's topic is something of a prelude to the Lenten season, and it has a lot of disparate elements for her to connect. She does her best but reads us well and can see it's not working. She realizes this is a good day to end the service five minutes early. I think the congregation will want her to stay at Spring Mill Methodist as long as possible.

She exits the church as the choir sings the final song and we soon follow her outside. The Reverend Moseley is one of the preachers who likes to stand outside, weather permitting and shake the hands of her congregation as they exit. When it's my turn, she says, "It's good to see you again, Dale."

"And you as well, Reverend Moseley. They gave you a rather tough assignment today."

"They did, and you should have seen the notes they sent me. If I'd have followed their suggestions, you all would have been asleep by eleven-forty."

"Then on behalf of your congregation, I'm glad you followed your better judgement."

She smiles. "So, how's the new job going?"

"It's very interesting."

Why do I keep using that word?

"Well, that could cover a multitude of situations, both good and bad."

"Yes, it could."

She turns to my parents. "Pat and Dale, it's good to see you two as usual. And I guess Dave has gone to retrieve his little guy."

Dad says, "He has."

"He is so cute."

"He is, but he can be a handful at times."

"And I hear from the girls who watch the kids that his buddy, Alex is a lively one, too."

Mom is concerned by this and says, "I hope they aren't too difficult."

"No, I don't think so. The girls think they are just active. Just like they should be at that age."

Dad says, "Active is a nice word for it. I'm glad I don't have to watch the two of them. DJ alone wears me out after a couple of hours."

"It's why young people have children, don't you think?" The Reverend smiles.

"Definitely."

Dave is coming out the door with DJ and he is shaking his head about something.

Dad says, "Everything okay?"

"DJ and Alex didn't behave themselves very well today. There was a new girl in there, and she couldn't get them to mind. She and the regular girl were both pretty upset."

Before any of us can say anything, Reverend Moseley says, "The new girl is my daughter. It's her first day. She'll learn."

Mom says, "Still, DJ should have behaved better. Right, DJ?"

The boy looks sad at this point, but tough little guy that he is, there are no tears. He simply nods his head yes.

Alex comes out with his mom, and it looks like he's shed enough tears for both boys. His sadness is exceeded only by his mother's quiet anger.

"Tell Reverend Moseley you're sorry, Alex."

He stammers out, "Sorry."

Mom says, "DJ, those girls back there are very nice to you and if you can't treat them nice, then maybe you need to sit between your granddad and me next week and not play with Alex."

DJ is not keen about this at all. "I won't do it again."

Dave has a funny expression. I think he knows that Mom's right in being upset, but maybe she should have left it for him to handle.

He says, "Okay. DJ is not going to do it again. Right?"

"Right."

"Now let's go home and have lunch."

We get in Dad's car and start to leave. I want to say something more to Sarah this morning, but there are too many of us and she is in no mood to talk.

On the way home Dave says, "Hey, Dale. The extended weather forecast for next Saturday looks good. Sarah and I talked about getting the bikes out. Why don't you bring yours up and we'll take the boys to Grant Park?

"Sounds like fun. I'll do it."

The ride sounds fun, and Sarah will be joining us. I'm not at all disappointed by that.

28

WHEN WE GOT HOME FROM CHURCH, Dave took DJ in the other room and had a little talk with him about his behavior. The little guy was quiet after that, and when Dave told him it might be a good day for him to take a nap, he didn't put up much of a fuss.

The nap gives the four of us a rare chance to sit around the table and talk. Everyone wants an update on my work situation, so we start with that. It's interesting watching their different reactions. I can tell Dad is the most supportive of my efforts to do right by the farm. Mom seems mildly encouraging, but I can see she doesn't want me to jeopardize any chances I might still have to move up at Morgan*Plus*. Dave thinks I'm wasting my time with the whole thing, and I need to let it go.

I turn the tables and ask him how things are going at his work.

"Well, since you've asked, I've had quite the week myself."

Everyone's interested at this point, and I'm glad the focus is no longer on me.

Dave proceeds to tell us about a customer who ordered and made a down payment on a new HVAC system. After Dave's crew installed it, the guy's neighbor convinced him that he'd been fleeced, so the customer said he wouldn't pay the balance due—that if they didn't lower the price they should just come and take it out.

"Take it out?"

"Yeah, Dad. Take the damn thing out!"

"What'd you do?"

"We asked him to bring his lawyer in and meet with us. We went through the whole agreement, showed them that we had installed exactly what they guy ordered, and the lawyer told his client he had no leg to stand on. So, get this—the guy fires his lawyer right in front of us."

Mom says, "Oh, good grief," which is almost cursing for her.

"Okay how'd you solve this?"

"I waited until the coldest day we'd had in a while, then sent the crew over to tell the guy we were taking out his furnace and AC as he had requested. He thought about it, then said he might keep it after all. I had told the guys that if he would write a check for the balance, we would add a year to the warranty so that he felt like he got something out of the deal. He agreed, paid us, and that was it."

I look at my brother with new admiration.

"Good job! Man, I don't think I could do what you do."

"And I couldn't work at Morgan*Plus*, so we're even.'

Mom and Dad exchange a glance, and my reading of it is that they think their two idiot sons are finally growing up. Or maybe not.

"Come on, Duff, let's go do the flowers."

The streets in our subdivision all have floral names, names like Rose and Iris and Gardenia and Sunflower. We live on Azalea. Around the time he turned twelve, Dave decided he hated the name Azalea. He thought it was too girlish. He complained to the point that one night at dinner, Dad announced he had bought a lot on a new street and that we would be building a house there. Dave and I were quite excited by this news.

Mom, however, knew the game Dad was playing so she asked Dad what the name of this new street was. Dad informed us that it would be Pansy Place. Dave dropped his fork and shouted, "No!" Dad said that if Dave would quit whining about Azalea Street, maybe he could cancel the deal and we could stay where we were. The whining stopped, and to my knowledge there never was a Pansy Place.

Walking the streets with Dave and me, Duff stops to sniff something, and I reach down to pet him. He's a great dog. My folks got him just before I moved out east, so I've not spent a lot of time with him. I think he knows I'm part of the family, though; perhaps because my scent is still in my old room, or maybe because he sees that they are comfortable around me. He does have that snoring issue.

I say, "You know, I think I could use a dog. That is, if I could figure out what to do with it while I'm at work."

"I had this same conversation with our receptionist a few days ago," Dave says. "She takes her dog to a doggie day care every day. She says it's great. He comes home worn out every night from playing with the other dogs."

"I guess I could do that. Wonder what kind of dog I should get?"

"You should get one that is a good match for you."

"And I'm sure you will tell me exactly what that is."

I already know that he's going to say something like poodle or Pomeranian.

"I think a Bassett Hound."

"A Bassett Hound!"

"Yeah, they're kind of mellow and easy-going. And it would be a great apartment dog."

"I don't live in an apartment."

"Duplex dog, then."

"Duplex Dog sounds like a rapper."

"It does." He grins.

"So, you've given me work advice and recommended a dog for me today."

"It's what I do."

I shake my head. "So, tell me, did you have your date with Kaitlyn?"

"I did in fact."

"Well?"

"Well, what?"

"How'd it go?"

He shrugs. "There were no complaints."

"Okay, so are you going to ask her out again?"

"No. I don't think she's what I'm looking for."

"Looking for . . . in a second date or a relationship?"

"Neither, really."

I pause then, "Well, it was your first time back out there after six years or so. Maybe you'll have better luck next time."

"Oh, my luck was okay. We just didn't mesh otherwise."

"Okay, then."

We walk quietly for a while, turn a corner and head into a chilly breeze.

"Hey, I haven't told you that I talked with Jack."

"The guy who lived next door to you?"

"Yes, and we're trying to get together for a long weekend in Ohio. You should come with me."

"I should?" He eyes me.

"Yes. You and I, and the two Nolan brothers. Ohio would never be the same."

"I might do that. Let me know when you're going."

"I will."

"Oh, and Dave. If we go to Ohio, maybe you will run into that bridesmaid again."

"If she's lucky."

Dave and I spent a night in Columbus, Ohio when he helped me move back from Philly. While we were checking in at our motel, there was a group of twenty-somethings getting ready to leave for a bachelorette party. One of the girls was particularly interested in Dave. Somehow, she figured out what room he was in, and encouraged by a night of partying with her friends, she knocked on his door around two in the morning. He had to spend some time getting her back to her room. The next morning at breakfast, he told me about his night. I asked him if he had any regrets, and he said he had a few.

We make it back to Azalea and soon reach the sidewalk to our front door.

"Well, let's get Duff inside and then I need to head out."

"You'll have to wait until DJ wakes up. He'll be upset if you leave while he's napping."

"Okay, then. Let's go in and see if he's up."

DJ is indeed up. He's sitting on the couch and not in the best of moods, so I go over to him and take a seat by him. At first, he pretends to hate it, but I soon have him laughing that hearty little laugh that always gets me laughing as well. I love this little guy, and someday, with any luck, I'll have one of my own.

I think I'll get the dog first, though.

29

Saturday, March 9

I PULL INTO MY PARENTS' DRIVEWAY at eight o'clock. I got up early and hit the road before seven so that Dave, Sarah and I can do our early morning ride with the boys. I haven't ridden much since I've been back, and I'm excited to do this today. The fact that Sarah will join us is a definite bonus.

I get out of my car. There's no one at the door to greet me and it has me wondering if they are still asleep. I take my bike off the carrier and lean it against the back bumper, grab my clothes, and head to the front door. When I get there, it's unlocked, so it appears someone is awake. No one greets me, but I hear conversation in the kitchen. I lay my stuff by the stairs. When I reach the kitchen, everyone's up and having breakfast.

"Hi, Dale. Have you eaten?" Mom asks.

"I ate before I left my place."

"Would you like some coffee while the guys finish?"

185

"No, I'm good. How's everyone doing?"

Dave says, "Three of us are fine and one of us is a little grumpy today."

"What's wrong with Dad?"

"I think maybe DJ is the grumpy one today," says Dad.

"I'm not grumpy."

The fact that DJ says it with a grumpy little voice makes me laugh.

"Aren't you excited to go bike riding?"

"I have to ride with training wheels. I don't need training wheels!"

His dad says, "Yes, you do, DJ. We don't need any anyone getting hurt."

This training wheel conversation makes me realize that three adults accompanied by two kids won't necessarily make for much of a workout. Still, it's better than nothing.

"What time are we meeting Sarah and Alex?"

"She just called and said they're almost ready to meet us."

"I'm going to change my clothes and I'll be ready."

Dave's not all that much into biking, and he wears the same outfit for just about everything non-work related. I know what's coming.

He says, "Don't tell me you're going to put on that spandex crap."

"I won't tell you."

"But you are."

"But I am."

"I don't know a single guy who looks good in that."

"But married guys are okay?"

"You know what I mean."

Mom says, "I kind of agree with your brother. I think they are a little too revealing."

"That's not a problem for Dale."

"Dave!"

He apologizes to Mom while Dad laughs so hard it makes me laugh. I grab my clothes and head upstairs. When I get changed, I feel the need to look in the mirror to check out how I look, thanks to my brother.

We reach Grant Park twenty minutes later and find Sarah and Alex already unloaded and on their bikes. Sarah has on biking attire, too, and she looks better in it than I do, for sure. Dave is wearing cargo shorts, a long sleeve T-shirt, a ball cap, and sunglasses, and of course he makes that look better than my getup.

As we take our bikes off Dave's truck, I think back to that Saturday after Thanksgiving; the last time the five of us were here at Grant Park. It had snowed the day before and we brought the boys sledding. It was a brilliant winter day, the kind you need to have at least once each year. Sarah let us know she had heard from Drew, who was on his annual ski trip with buddies, that they were heading up to a higher altitude resort to ski the following day. There was a terrible wreck on the way back to their lodge and none of them survived.

So much has changed since then.

Alex gets on his bike, and it doesn't have training wheels. That's going to be a problem, I can tell, and as soon as DJ sees it, my premonition is confirmed.

"See! Alex doesn't have training wheels! I want mine off, too!"

Dave can tell he's lost this battle, so he grabs a wrench out of his truck and quickly takes care of the situation. When, he's done, DJ is all smiles again.

We put the boys' helmets on, and Sarah and I follow suit with ours. Dave, of course doesn't have one. The boys want to know why they need to wear one if he doesn't.

"Boys, are we going to ride today or just sit here and whine?"

The boys opt for riding and we're off.

The trail runs along the top of the hill that marks the northern perimeter of the park. It runs west for the better part of a mile and then it joins another trail that circles the western edge of town. The first part of the trail is relatively quiet with only a couple of other bikers; an older couple walking two cute dogs, one of whom isn't too fond of bikes; and a younger couple walking with their kids. Sarah rides alongside Alex, and Dave does the same with DJ, leaving me to bring up the rear. I like the arrangement, because I get to see the whole comedy unfold in front of me. Alex is the better rider of the two. DJ is determined to keep up, but his route is a little erratic and he stops and puts his foot down on a number of occasions to maintain his balance. Luckily, the people on the trail are understanding. It would be hard for them to be upset with two boys who look so cute wearing bike helmets and peddling their little hearts out.

We ride for a few minutes and reach the point where the Grant Park trail joins the Burlington Northern trail. The BN trail is one of many rail-to-trail conversions in the state and it makes for a nice ride. As we reach it, Dave decides to turn around. The BN trail is busy today, so that combined with the fact that the boys might tire soon makes turning around a good choice.

"Let me take these two back to the park. You guys get a good ride in, and we'll meet you at the swings."

Dave has sweetened the deal for the boys, which was smart, and I don't at all mind that I have some time with Sarah.

"Great. We'll ride for a half hour and meet up with you."

Dave and the boys get ready to go back, but Alex wants some water first, so, of course DJ is also thirsty. Dave takes care of DJ and himself, while Sarah does the same for her and Alex. When they finish drinking, the trio heads back towards the park, and I can see that DJ is starting to do a little better.

"They're cute, aren't they?"

Sarah watches them and says, "Yes, they are."

I look at her and can I see a look on her face that I've only seen twice now since December. It makes me feel good to see it, and better to be part of it.

"So which way do you want to go?"

I say, "Let's go south past the quarry. We can turn around at Mill Road."

We start out at an easy pace. The ride to this point hasn't been much of a challenge and we need to warm up a little bit. We step up the pace now that the boys are no longer with us, but not so fast we can't talk.

"I can't believe how nice it is this morning. It's as if spring might actually be coming," she says.

"It has been a long winter, hasn't it?"

"In so many ways."

"Especially for you, Sarah."

We ride a little farther in silence, and I think I need to change the subject.

"How's school?"

"About the same. I did an observation with the teacher I told you about. It went okay. I'm still not sure she and I are a good match."

"But knowing you, you're still determined to make it work."

"I am."

"You know, Mom might know someone here in Spring Mill who could help out if you do change your mind. She's still pretty connected with the school district."

"Thanks. I know I can do this, but it's good to have a back-up plan."

We ride on, and our pace starts picking up. This part of the bike trail is busier, so we pay attention to the others on the trail and talk a little less. When we hit a slow spot, Sarah asks me how my job is going, and I give her the latest.

She digests what I've said, then asks, "Do you still have any hope for the farm?"

"Some. As I said, there are a lot of dots yet to be connected for this stupid golf idea to work."

"I still think you're going to get the right thing done."

"I appreciate the vote of confidence. I have a feeling that the game isn't over yet. The right thing might still happen."

"Is your feeling based on something specific?" Sarah asks.

"Yes. There's something they have not paid nearly enough attention to, which is Rolling Hills Road. There are a lot of unresolved issues with it, and if they aren't resolved it could kill the golf course proposal."

"Good. I hope you're right. I admire you for fighting for it, and I'm sure the guy who lives there appreciates what you're doing."

"Thanks. He might, but right now I'd say he's probably thinking I've let him down."

"Then he doesn't know you."

190

Hearing that feels great. It energizes me and makes me step up the pace. We're going by the old quarry now and our turn-around point isn't too far away. Without saying anything Sarah matches my pace. There's a group of riders ahead of us coming our way. They shift to a single-file line, and I let Sarah take the lead. This provides her with an opening, and she takes off. I step it up and get on her back tire. We ride like this for another five minutes until we see the sign for Mill Road. We decelerate in preparation for the turn-around. When we get there, we pull off and take a second before we start back.

"You set a good pace there, Sarah. I had to work to keep up."

"We're only half-way. Let's see what you've got left in your tank."

"Challenge accepted."

We make the U-turn on Mill Road and start back. Within a quarter mile, she's really moving. She maneuvers around traffic, and I do as well. It's not exactly protocol to be going this fast on the path today, but the competition is on and neither of us wants to let up. I've not seen this side of her before. I knew it was there from her soccer days, but it's my first time experiencing it, and I'm loving it.

We keep it up until we get to the intersection of the Grant Park trail where we make the turn. We use the distance back to the park as a cool-down ride.

"Sarah. I needed that. I'm a little out of shape."

"Have you ridden any since your move?"

"Oh, a time or two. The weather hasn't exactly cooperated."

"Then I'd say you did all right."

"Well, I've ridden stationary bikes, but you know it's not the same."

"Close though."

"Yep, but not nearly as much fun as this."

"You're right," she agrees. "Something about riding outdoors in the sun and fresh air."

"And real scenery. And good company."

We circle the park back to the lot where we started, and as we get there, we can see the playground south of us. Dave is alternating back and forth between the swings, pushing the boys. They're challenging him to push them higher. Each of them wanting to outdo the other. Dave has a rhythm going. He's caught the eyes of a couple of the young moms who are at the park with their kids. I know my brother well enough to know he sees them and is enjoying putting on a show.

We pull up and Alex sees us first. "Hi, Mommy!"

"Hi, Alex. Are you having fun?"

"Yes. We've been on all the equipment."

"Where did you learn that word, Alex?"

Dave says, "I taught it to them, and they've been using it continually since I did. They love it all, but we keep coming back to the swings."

"How are *you* doing, Dave?" I ask.

"Good. Really good. Getting my cardio in. How was the ride?"

"It was great. Sarah just about wore me out. She's tough."

"You need to remember that you're not a kid anymore," Dave teases.

"Says the guy who's fifteen months younger."

I take a seat at a picnic table and take a long slow drink from my water bottle while Sarah and Dave push the boys. Every few swings, they ask the boys if they've had enough, and the answer is always a resounding no. While they're doing that, I check my phone and see that I have a text from Giselle. I text her that I'm busy but will get back to her.

The boys, persuaded by the promise of lunch at their favorite fast-food place, finally decide they've had enough. We head back to our cars and agree to meet at our parents' house in forty-five minutes. We're sure Mom will have started something for lunch, so Dave assigns me the task of letting her know of our change in plans.

I text her and invite her and Dad to join us. She texts back that they will do that, and the meal she's been working on will now be dinner. So, the plan has come together.

While we're driving back, Dave quizzes me about my ride with Sarah. How busy was the trail? What did we talk about? I tell him that we talked a lot about him, to which he says, "Well, at least you had an interesting conversation."

"Actually, we talked about my work and her school. You know, the usual conversation topics with us."

He looks at me and then back at the road.

"You looked like you were having fun with the boys." I comment.

"I was. They're both great kids."

"Did you see the two moms checking you out?"

"I did. I don't know if you remember me saying one time that I was worried that having a kid might be a problem with the ladies."

"I remember that."

"I was wrong. It's exactly the opposite, I think."

"Oh, really?"

"Yeah. Maybe we should rent you a kid. You need all the help you can get."

"And here we go."

He looks at me and grins.

"How's work, for you, Dave? Did you get things settled with that customer you were telling us about?"

"I did. He actually came in and apologized a couple of days ago."

"What did you say to him when he did?"

"I told him thanks, and that we would follow through on the maintenance agreement we had with him, and that I would hope he would come directly to me with any concerns in the future. He said he would and walked away happy."

For the rest of the drive, I fill him in on my week at work. When we pull in the driveway, he turns to me and says, "Like I said, I wouldn't trade places with you, Dale."

"Well, like I said, I'd be terrible doing what you do, so I guess it's all working out okay."

"Do you feel a little uncomfortable that you're trying to undo what your boss wants done?"

"I should maybe, but I don't."

We look back and see that DJ is fast asleep. Dave quietly gets out of the truck and open his door. The boy immediately wakes up and wants to know when we're going to Chick-fil-A.

"We need to get cleaned up and then we'll go."

The little guy, who was grumpy to start the day, is all smiles now.

30

Sunday, March 10

MY PHONE RINGS. I look at the car's display and it's Giselle. "Well, this is a nice surprise!"

"Hey, I keep sending you texts, and you never respond. Are you okay?"

"I'm fine. I've meant to get back to you and I just haven't. I'm sorry."

"That's okay. Is now a good time to talk?"

"It's a great time. I'm driving and I have some time. How are things in New York?"

"Oh, everything's fine. Not a lot new to report. My classes are much harder than I thought they would be. A couple of people have dropped out already. I think they are trying to weed out the ones who aren't too committed, maybe to save those folks a lot of time and money. At least that's my theory."

"Glad you're hanging in there."

"What are you doing today?"

"I've been to my parents this weekend and I'm headed back to my place."

"How's work?"

"It's . . ."

I try not to say interesting.

"It's been going okay."

"Okay, huh?'

"Better than that. It's not what I expected, and we don't have time for that today. In fact, let me send you an email when I get home to fill you in. It'll be an interesting read."

I just can't help myself.

"I can't wait."

"How're things going for you, Giselle? You know, outside of school stuff?"

"It's going well, but I am guessing you're asking me about my social life?"

"I'm pretty transparent, huh?"

"You are, and no, I'm not really seeing anyone. I've gone out with an old friend a couple of times just to catch up. School is keeping me too busy to have much of a social life."

"How're your mother and sister and brother doing?"

"They're all great. Have I told you that Karen is getting married this summer?"

"No, I don't think you have. That's great."

"I really like the guy a lot. He's super nice and has a great sense of humor—kind of like you, Dale."

"Oh, no! Poor Karen. I hope she's not settling after all these years."

Laughing, she says, "No, not in the least. You'd like him."

I start to say I can't wait to meet him, but then there's no plan for me to see Giselle anytime soon.

And then, as if she's reading my mind, she says, "Are you coming out east this summer?"

"I think so."

"Are you going to do your annual beach week with your friends?"

"I think that's the plan."

"Why don't you come see me while you're that close?"

"I might do that."

"Please do. I miss you."

"I miss you, too, Giselle."

"So come see me then!"

I know in that moment I will be changing plans and adding some days in Upstate New York to my itinerary.

"I will."

"Great! Well, I'd better let you go. Are you getting close to your place?"

"I'm taking the exit ramp to get to my subdivision as we speak. Good guess."

"Great talking with you."

"You, too, Giselle. Thanks for calling. I've missed talking to you, and I'm sorry I haven't texted you back. I will do better."

"It's your turn to call me then. Okay?"

"You've got a deal."

It was great to hear from Giselle. There was a time I thought she and I were right there at the beginning of something special. I think she may have, too, but she had a chance to fulfill her dream of being a nurse and that was that. It was hard to let go. Maybe that's why I'm not good at getting back to her.

197

31

Friday, March 15

COOPER WALKS INTO MY OFFICE and says, "Dad just called, and he wants us to meet him in his office."

"Like, right now?"

"Right now."

I stop what I'm working on and walk with Cooper down the hall to Larry's office. I want to ask Cooper if he has an idea what's going on, but there are a couple of doors open and I doubt he would want to share anything, if he even knows anything more than that his dad wants to see us.

Larry is waiting at his door and waves us in. As we enter, I see Cam Walker.

We exchange handshakes and 'nice-to-see-you's and Larry tells us to take a seat.

"Cam has come in with some news that I want you two to hear, so I'll let him fill you in."

"Guys, there's been a development out at the farm since we last talked. I don't know how much it changes things, but

198

I know that it could. My guy, Jim Lynch, had a conversation with Ben Roberts yesterday and called me as soon as it was over."

"Ben Roberts owns the farm to the west of your place, right?"

"Yes, he does. At least for a little while. You see, Roberts and Rusty Brotherton have reached an agreement for Brotherton to buy the Roberts farm. Roberts will keep his house and a small acreage around it, but Brotherton gets the farm."

Cooper whistles, "Whew. That's a wrinkle we hadn't considered."

"Yes, it is. My farm will be an island now nearly surrounded by Brotherton property."

We're all quiet for a second, and then I ask, "Tell me, what are your biggest concerns about this, Mr. Walker?"

"Rusty Brotherton has been trying to buy my place for years now. Somehow I think one of the reasons he is buying Roberts out is that he thinks he can put the squeeze on me."

Cooper asks, "How does his owning the Roberts farm put a squeeze on you?"

"Well, I can't say for sure, but I know it will. I know Rusty, and he's got a plan in mind."

I think I can see what that plan might be, but I'm going to let the others figure it out. This might help Jim.

Cam continues, "Okay, for one thing the road into my place now runs through Brotherton property, where before it ran along the boundary between the two farms. I think you can see how that might change things. Will you be able to improve the road now that it will lie totally within his property? I don't know. It will be something for your attorneys to look at."

So at least Cam sees it.

Larry says, "We're going to have to clear up the right of way situation for Rolling Hills Road before we move ahead, for sure."

"Yes, and there's one more thing I need to tell you. When Ben Roberts and Jim were talking, Ben said that he bet that Brotherton would make another offer on my place, and Jim said . . . and I have no idea why he let this slip, but anyway Jim told Ben that I was already working on an offer. Ben pressed him for details, and all Jim told him was that it is going to be sold to a company that is looking to do something with it. Ben wanted to know if that meant it wouldn't be a farm anymore, and Jim tried to finesse the conversation and said he wasn't sure."

I say, "So Roberts knows you might sell. Are you worried he'll tell Brotherton?"

"No, I'm sure he'll tell Rusty Brotherton, and Brotherton will try to figure out a way to screw with our deal so that I'll end up selling to him."

"So, your thought is that Brotherton will play hardball to get you to sell, and he'll use the access road to your farm as his leverage."

"Yes, and he'll probably lower his offer when he tries to buy it again."

Larry says, "Cam, why don't you just go ahead and sell it to us now. We'll figure it out."

My anxiety goes up at this point. Larry has actually made a good play here, and Cam, frustrated with the whole situation may just be ready to void the MOU and sell without conditions.

"No, I want to stay with our agreement. I need to be absolutely sure you can pull this off."

"Okay then. Guys, we've got some work to do."

"Larry?"

"Yes, Dale."

"Is there some concern this legal situation could drag out and maybe scare off some of our potential investors?"

"That might be a worry, yes."

Cooper says, "Then let's get to work."

"Let's," I agree.

Larry says, "Boys, you got any more questions for Cam?"

We have none for Cam, but I ask Larry, "What would you like us to do first?"

"Well, Cooper is heading this up, so I want him to keep working with the golf people to get the course laid out. We at least can get that done while we're dealing with the legal questions. Dale, I'll let Cooper tell you what he needs from you. Cam will be talking with his attorneys, and I'll be calling mine as soon as you two leave."

Cooper and I stand up and shake Cam's hands again before we go.

As we walk down the hall, I know Cooper wants to talk, but again, he is going to hold off until we reach our offices. Paula is coming out of the women's restroom. She looks at us, and she's sharp enough to figure out that something big has just happened.

"Dale, I need to meet with you later. Would two o'clock work for you?"

"Sure, Paula."

"Great."

When we reach my office, we walk in, and Cooper shuts the door.

"Well, this is a hell of a deal!"

"It is, isn't it?"

201

"Why the heck didn't Jim just keep his mouth shut? Roberts has probably already talked with Brotherton, and I'll bet you he's already looking into ways to cause us problems."

"Ways?"

"Well, zoning permits and the like, and that whole road access thing. I'm still steamed with Jim Lynch. Why would he do that?"

Probably because he's sharp enough to know an opportunity when he sees one.

"He was probably just responding to Ben Roberts and didn't consider the ramifications."

"I guess. Well, I need to go make some calls and set up some meetings."

"Let me know what you need from me."

"I will. I'll probably have something for you after I talk with my golf guys. Anyway, it sounds like Paula needs you to work on something with her."

"Yes, it does."

Cooper leaves my office, and I pick up my cell phone. I pull up Jim Lynch's number and send him a text.

Cam Walker was just in our office.
Seems like your conversation with
Roberts has stirred things up.

Smiley face in return

Maybe the tide is turning.

Jim sends me a thumbs-up emoji.

32

"AND THAT'S WHAT WE LEARNED TODAY."

Paula says, "Well, that's huge. You know how this might change things don't you?"

"I have no idea what you might be thinking, Paula."

"I'm sure you don't. You know, there's a little more to you than I thought."

"I usually make a poor first impression."

"And then?"

"Then things usually take a turn for the worse."

She grins and says, "I could see that."

"So, what do you have for me today?"

"Oh, there are a couple of other things for us to look at if you're ready for a change of pace."

"I'm ready. There's nothing else I can do right now. I just need to let things play out at this point."

She laughs, then pulls up a file for us to look at.

All the while I'm thinking about what I've learned today and trying to figure out how to leverage it to my advantage.

Normally by this time of night, I'd be getting sleepy and ready to call it day. Not tonight though. My mind is spinning, and I need some way to get it to slow down. I get out my laptop, open up a blank page and type.

The road's the thing. Cam tried to warn us that day he gave the go-ahead on the proposal. None of us saw it at the time, but then none of us could know that Rusty would buy Roberts' farm and have the potential to make life more difficult for us.

The question is, what should I do from here?

I spend the next half hour laying out different scenarios. I decide to keep my options open and make my move when I see an opening.

I save what I've typed, then just before I close it down, I add: *The ball is in our court.*

I've operated from behind on this since day one. It's fun to be on top for a change. Tonight, I feel more strongly than ever that I'll win this thing in the end, and I like that feeling a lot.

33

Tuesday, April 9

IT'S A PERFECT APRIL AFTERNOON, and I'm sitting here in the seats that Larry gave me, getting ready to watch the Cardinals' home opener. A parade of cars full of players from the past has just finished circling the stadium to a continuous ovation. Now, this year's roster is being introduced. Each player is cheered by the fans as he comes out of the dugout, with Yadi and Waino and Matt getting the loudest and longest ovations. It's a long ceremony, but we love it. Winter is over. Spring and summer stretch out ahead of us, and baseball is about to start. The field is perfectly green, the sky's a shade of blue it can only be in April and sandwiched in between the two is a sea of fans in red. Every club in baseball thinks they do opening-day right. No one does it better than the Cardinals.

Dave, Sarah and Alex are with me and taking it all in.

DJ and Dad were supposed to be here, but they came down with a 24-hour bug yesterday, so Dave suggested Sarah and Alex as last-minute replacements. When I first heard Dad and DJ couldn't make it, I thought I should invite someone from the office, but I didn't really want to do that. A couple of people might be moderately happy, while the rest of the office might be upset for not being asked.

Dave made his suggestion, and I agreed and said I'd give them a call. He told me he'd already invited them, and they were excited to go. To be honest, I was little surprised he had done it without first asking me, but not at all disappointed to have Sarah join us.

Alex is sitting between me and his mother and he has a million questions about what's going on: Who's in each car? What's the big red bird's name? And when do they start playing? I love how into it he is. All the while, he also has his eye on a guy about my age sitting to my left who's wearing a blue Duke basketball shirt. Finally, the little guy whispers to me, "Why is that man wearing a blue shirt? You're supposed to wear red."

"I don't know Alex. Maybe he didn't get the memo."

He's quiet while he thinks about that, then asks, "What's a memo?"

I come up with the best and shortest answer I can, and that seems to satisfy him, but I think he feels bad for the guy who didn't get the memo. The guy in the shirt is red-haired with fair skin. Although it's early April, the sun is bright today, and he's in trouble if he didn't wear sunblock.

Finally, the ceremonies are over, and the game gets going. After an inning I can no longer resist striking up a conversation with my neighbor. I have to ask him about the shirt.

"Hi, I'm Dale. I couldn't help noticing that you're about the only guy here wearing blue."

"Hi, I'm Chad. Yeah, I guess I shoulda worn red, but I like this shirt. I'm a Duke fan."

"Did you go to school there?"

"Oh no. I'm from Minnesota and went to a small college south of the Twin Cities. I've just always liked Duke."

"I thought I heard a little Minnesota or Wisconsin in your voice. So, you live in St. Louis now?"

"Yes, I just moved here. My friend, Tyler, here had an extra ticket and invited me. He thought, as a newbie, it would be good for me to see Opening Day."

The guy next to him leans forward and extends his hand to me.

"Nice to meet you. I'm Tyler."

"And I'm Dale. Nice to meet you, too. Looks like we have some work to do on your buddy, here."

"Starting today, right?"

"Right."

Chad smiles and says, "I'll try, guys."

I say, "Well, Chad, you have to admit this is pretty impressive."

"It is. Not being into baseball, I didn't know much about the Cardinals. You can tell this city loves them though, and the franchise has a lot of history."

It hits me that I had lived in Philadelphia for more than two years and never purchased a single Phillies, Eagles, Flyers, or Sixers shirt or cap—nothing. So maybe I can't be too hard on the guy.

———

The game has moved to the top of the second inning, and Atlanta scores a run to take a lead. We get out of the inning but don't do much in our half. Neither team scores in the third, and then the Cardinals score two in the bottom of the fourth to go ahead 2-1. Alex decides he wants a box of popcorn, so Dave and I go for popcorn and sodas. We get our refreshments and make our way back to our seats only to find that the Braves have scored two in the fifth.

"Well, Sarah, we leave you for ten minutes and you let the Braves take the lead."

"I know. I failed. Next time, I'll go, and you can see if you do any better."

I look at Alex, and he seems upset that we're losing.

"Hey, buddy, it's okay. There's still a long way to go in this game. We can still come back and win."

Then, to prove me right, the Cards score three of their own in the bottom of the inning. Alex is beaming as we head to the sixth inning. I show him the bullpens where both teams have relief pitchers warming up.

He takes it in, and then a minute later asks me what a relief pitcher is. I try to make my explanation short and clear but fail on both counts.

I look over to see Duke-Shirt texting someone, probably a friend or family member back in Minnesota. Having spent a couple of years away from my family and friends I know how he's feeling.

The score holds until the Cardinals tack on a couple more in the bottom of the seventh. We'll get a look at the Cards' eighth and ninth inning guys and see if they can hold this lead.

"I need to go to the bathroom," Alex says.

Never should have given him that soda.

"Come on, Alex. Let's take you to the bathroom, and while we're down there, we'll buy you a Cards' hat."

By the time we find a restroom, I can tell Alex is really needing to go, and now so am I. We finish our jobs, wash our hands, and go out to find a cap. There's a vendor close by, and Alex tries on a few until we decide on one that we both like. I cinch it up so that it nearly fits, but it still wants to slide down and sit on his ears. There's nothing cuter than a kid with an oversized ballcap. I buy two more caps like his, and we head back to our seats. By the time we return, It's the bottom of the eighth, still 7-3, so our eighth inning guy did his job.

When we approach our seats, Sarah looks at Alex and smiles when she sees his new cap. She notices that I have a bag, "Looks like you got one too."

"Nope. Just watch." I tap Chad on the shoulder, he looks at me, and I hand him one of the two caps. "Here, and welcome to St. Louis."

He looks at the cap and says, "Really? You didn't have to do that."

"You needed to wear something red today, and it looks like the sun's starting to get to you. So, here you go."

He puts it on, looks at me with an appreciative smile, and his buddy reaches around and gives me a fist bump. Sarah and Dave both nod their approval, as well. I hand Dave the bag and say, "And here's one for DJ."

"Great! He'll love it."

When we turn our attention back to baseball, the top of the ninth inning is getting tense. Our closer started off okay. He got two quick outs, loaded the bases with walks, then a double which cut the lead to one, and they still have the runner on second. The batter works our guy for a full count and fouls off two of his best pitches. The crowd stands, hoping to help out our struggling closer. No one is very confident in our guy, though. He was a starter until a couple of years ago, when an injury sidelined him. Now, he's trying to make a comeback. His stuff is good, but his mind . . . well that's always been another matter. He keeps trying to work the corners, but the batter keeps fighting off his best pitches. I am feeling like he might throw him some meat here and we'll find ourselves behind, when, finally, after two more foul balls, he induces the batter to chase a slider low and away. The crowd roars, and that, as they say, is a winner.

After two good series on the road to open the year, our record is 5 and 2, and it looks like the season might hold some promise for the Birds. Some people leave, but most of the crowd stays around to see the post-game fireworks display. Alex is ecstatic and Chad reaches past me to give the boy a high five—two new converts it would appear.

After the fireworks, we make the slow exit from the stadium, walk to my car, get everyone buckled in, and set out for Sarah's house. Progress is slow, because the game traffic is compounded by the craziness of rush hour. As we make our way to the highway, Alex falls asleep in his car seat with his ball cap down over his eyes. I look at him and Sarah in my rear-view mirror and she smiles at me and whispers, "Thanks."

I mouth, "You're welcome."

I look over at Dave and see him looking at the two in the back seat and smiling as well. The four of us have had a great afternoon.

When we pull into the Koulos's driveway, Alex wakes up, pulls his cap off, looks at it, and puts it back on cockeyed, of course. Sarah invites us in, saying that she can throw something together for us before we go. I'm okay with it, but Dave wants to get home to rescue Mom and Dad. Sarah understands and says she'd do the same thing if it were Alex.

She leans into the car and says to Dave, "I'll be back up in Spring Mill later this week. Why don't we get the boys together again?"

Dave says, "Sure. Let's do that. DJ will love it."

I remind Sarah that she and I have talked about taking Alex to the City Museum sometime. Dave says he thinks DJ would like that, too, if we wouldn't mind them coming along. Sarah assures him we wouldn't, and I have to agree, although I would have preferred it just be Sarah and me with Alex.

We watch the two of them go in the front door, and then start the trip to my place. Dave and I don't talk too much on the way there. The traffic is heavy and I'm locked in. Dave calls home and checks up on DJ and Dad. Mom says they are doing better, and she'll have dinner for him when he gets home.

After he hangs up, I ask if he's heard from his ex-wife. He tells me yes and that things are still the same there. She's still happy with her new life and the freedom she feels now that the divorce is final. He asks me about my friends back east and I fill him in on the latest, and remind him of the invitation from Jack for the two of us to come see him and his brother, Sean in Ohio.

"That would be kind of cool, wouldn't it? Let me know a specific weekend, and I'll see if Mom and Dad will watch DJ. What about your friend Giselle, have you talked with her?"

"Yes. She called me once a couple of weeks ago. Sounds like she's busy but liking school."

"You need to go see her sometime."

"Maybe."

I get ready to say something when a car two lanes to my left cuts across traffic so he can make an exit.

"Jesus Christ!"

"Really. What a dumbass."

We're quiet for the next couple of minutes, and then I say, "Dave?"

"What?"

"I had a great time today. I think I'll call Sarah after I get you on the road and see if she might move up her June date."

"Her June date?"

"It's a date she set for when she might start seeing guys again."

"Do you have something special in mind?"

"Yeah, I do. A group of friends are getting together this weekend to go out to eat. She knows them and I think it would be fun for her."

"You like Sarah, I take it?"

"I do."

"Well, I think you should honor her wish and wait. It's not that much longer."

"You're probably right."

I think about it some more. "No! You know what? Screw it! I'm going to call her."

"She'll probably still be trying to get Alex to settle down, don't you think?"

I look over at my brother, who's staring straight ahead and maybe frowning a little. It seems like Dave is more concerned about this than he should be.

"Dave?"

"Yeah?"

"May I ask you something?"

"Sure. What is it?"

"Do you care for Sarah more than you're letting on?"

"Why do you say that?"

"You keep throwing out things like I should wait, like you really don't want me to ask her out."

"No, not at all, I like her a great deal. Sarah's the kind of girl a guy could get serious about, if he wanted to get serious. I don't want that right now. I've got a little making up for lost time to do. Sarah's great to talk to and the boys have fun together. She's gotten to be a really good friend, Dale. That's it. If it were more than that, you'd be the first to know. I promise."

"Okay. So, I'm going to call her."

Dave turns towards me and studies me for a moment. We pull into the driveway, and he heads towards his truck.

"Well, I'd better get home. Mom is probably ready for a break. Great time today, Dale. Thanks for inviting me."

"And thanks for thinking about Sarah and Alex. That worked out great."

"Yeah, it did."

I watch my brother drive off and head inside. I think about it for a few minutes, then pick up my phone and select Sarah's number from my contacts.

"Hi, Dale. What's going on?"

"Hi Sarah. I just wanted to tell you that I had a great time today."

"We did, too."

"Sarah, I wanted to ask you something."

"Okay."

"Remember the couples we met a few weeks ago?"

"Yes."

"And remember they said something about going out to eat?"

"Yes."

"Well, I heard from Phil today and they are going out Saturday night. I wanted to ask one more time if you would enjoy going with them."

"Oh, Dale. It sounds fun, but I just can't."

"Why not? I'm sure your folks wouldn't mind watching Alex again. It would do you good."

"Dale, I'm not ready for that yet."

"I know, but you already know them, and you liked them, and it's just eight people going out to eat, have a drink, and enjoy some conversation. It doesn't have to be anything more than that."

"I'm not ready."

I have to let her do this her way.

"Okay. I can respect that."

"Sorry."

"No, it's okay. But you can be sure, I will be calling you in June, Sarah. I'm ready for something more than a cup of coffee or a beer."

"I know, and thanks for asking me, and more than that, thanks for understanding why I just can't do it yet."

The Brothers Barnhart

I'm conflicted to be honest. I respect that she needs time, but I'm ready now.

Just before bedtime, I get a text from Dave.

> *How'd it go with Sarah?*

She still wants to wait, so I will wait.

> *I had a great time today.*

Me too.

34

Thursday, May 15

I HAVEN'T SPOKEN MUCH TO JIM for the last month. I've been keeping eyes and ears open for any opportunity to advance our cause. Tonight, I think I have an idea that might work.

"Hey Jim, you got time to talk?"

"I do. I just stepped into the shed for a minute. What's on your mind?"

"Well, I hadn't spoken with you for a while, and I was wondering how you are doing?"

"It's all right. Been a difficult spring getting everything planted what with all the rain, but there's still a little time left to get it done, and we should be okay."

"Too *much* rain?"

"Yeah, it's been too wet some days to get out in the fields and plant, but we've had a few dry days and a few windy days in between. We're getting caught up."

"Good."

"Dale, I've almost called you a couple of times. Not hearing from you for like a month had me worried. I hope you've called with some good news."

"Jim, I have no reason to say this other than a gut feeling I have, but it's been ten weeks since Cam said he'd be interested in the golf course proposal, and the longer this thing drags out, the less interest I think Cam might have in it. I think he knows that Brotherton and his attorneys can tie it up for a long time. They've already let us know they won't agree to anything being done with the road, which means to get what we want we'll have to take it to court. That will tie things up for several months if not longer, and if we *don't* get permission to widen and improve the road, then it would make it very difficult to construct a golf course and almost impossible to build homes on the Walker place."

"Okay. I think I follow all of that, and I like the sound of it. So, Dale, I've been thinking about this, too, and I have a question for you. What if Cam does get tired of it, but instead of calling it off, he decides to just go ahead and sell to your group and let you all deal with the headaches?"

"That won't happen. He wants things to be resolved before he sells."

"Okay, so what does that mean for us?"

"I think it's time for us to make our move. Let me propose what I think that should be."

"I'm interested."

"Meet with Cam Walker; tell him you want the farm; tell him you know you don't have the financial wherewithal to purchase it outright; but make a case for how well the farm has been doing under your management. Tell him how much you care for the place and how you want to see

217

it continue to be what it has been. Tug at his heartstrings a little, then see if he would be interested in working with you along the lines of your present arrangement, but with an eye to using a portion of the profit as a mortgage payment on the place."

"Okay, but it would take forever to get the place paid off."

"Yes, it would be slow, but maybe he'd be okay with that if it meant his place would still be farmed and taken care of like you would do."

"And if he was okay with the idea but wanted the place paid off sooner?"

"If he wanted the timetable to be accelerated, we could go back to some of the research I did when I was working on my proposal. Maybe some of the things I was considering could bring in more money."

"Okay. You'd have to remind me of the specifics of those ideas, but I'd be willing to consider them if they would help me pay it off. Maybe you're right on him liking the thought that I'd be taking good care of his family's place."

"I'm just throwing stuff out there. I think as your starting point, you don't bring up the other ideas. You hold onto them in case one becomes a card you need to play. Remember the one thing Walker doesn't want is for Rusty Brotherton to get his farm, and that's always our ace in the hole."

"Okay. As it turns out, Cam's coming out here later today to check on spring planting. If I get a chance, I'll start the conversation then."

"Great, but don't wait for the chance. Go for it."

"I'll do it! I'm fired up to be doing something other than just waiting to see what happens with Brotherton."

"I thought you might be. I feel the same."

"I'll call you tonight and tell you how the conversation goes."

"I'll be waiting for your call."

As soon as we hang up, I call Sarah. She left a message while Jim and I were talking.

"Hi, Sarah. Sorry, I was on a call."

"Dale, a bunch of us are getting together tomorrow for an end-of-semester celebration. There will be people there you'd enjoy meeting. Why don't you join us?"

"Great. I'll do that."

She's inviting me for a change, and June's coming. That can't be a bad thing.

"I called your brother to see if he'd like to come, too. He's going to try."

"Well, I'll try to represent the whole clan if he can't."

Dave too. Well, that makes my invite a little less special, but watching my brother go to work on all of Sarah's single friends should be fun.

I've got my fridge door open trying to decide if there's anything worth eating when my phone rings. It's Jim Lynch.

"Jim! I've been waiting to hear from you. Did Cam come out? Did you talk with him?"

"Dale, yes he did. He came out to tell me that Rusty Brotherton has made a very attractive offer for his farm, and for the first time he's considering it. He said the agreement he signed with you folks will be easy to get out of, so he's free to do what he wants, and at least the place would still be a farm."

"Did you tell him what we discussed?"

"I did. It almost seemed like he was feeling me out to see if I had any ideas. I told him I loved his farm, that no one would take better care of it than I would, that all I needed was some help from him to buy it. I told him he'd never regret it if I got the place."

"That was perfect. How'd he react?"

"I think he was pretty interested, to be honest. He said he was glad to have another offer to consider."

"Was that all?"

"He said he'd think about it and get back to me. Oh yes, and this is big, he said the golf course thing is dead in the water as far as he's concerned. He's going to let Larry know tomorrow."

"Oh boy," I chuckle, "this is about to get good."

"Be ready, Dale. They might connect the dots back to you."

"I'll be prepared in case they do."

"Good to be prepared."

"Always. And Jim—"

"Yes."

"We're getting closer. I think we might pull this off after all."

"I kind of feel the same way." I can hear him smiling. "By the way, in other good news, Ginny and I are engaged."

"Great!"

"And she's ready to start a family."

"Oh wow! Are you?"

"I'm forty."

"Are you ready though?"

"Is anyone?"

"Good point. You'll be a great husband, and dad, if it happens. I can just see your new place crawling with little Lynches."

"You make us sound like vermin."

"Yeah, I guess that didn't come out right."

35

Friday, May 16

IGET TO WORK EARLY. I have a feeling a storm might be brewing, and I want to get a front row seat. Until things break loose, I try to busy myself with a project, but my mind's not in it.

Cooper walks in at nine-thirty and says, "Dad needs to see us."

I have this momentary flutter in my stomach. I'm more nervous about this than I thought I would be, but excited too.

We walk in and Larry motions for us to take a seat.

"Boys, it's been quite a morning. I just got a call from Cam Walker, and he is no longer interested in our golf proposals."

"What! After all the time and effort I've put into this."

"Son, I understand and I'm right where you are."

I have to be careful not to show how much I enjoy this—to act like it's news to me.

"Why the change of heart, Larry?"

"Well, it appears that Brotherton wants to buy Cam's place and he's made a good offer."

"Call him back, Dad."

"And do what?"

"Tell him we will match the offer. No, tell him whatever Brotherton offers we'll go 5 percent more. We can't let this get away from us."

Larry sighs and, in the voice that dads use to calm their upset kids, he says, "Cooper, it's over."

"It doesn't have to be. Call him!"

"The game changed when Roberts and Brotherton reached a deal, and the farm road became part of Brotherton property. We should have seen access to the farm was always going to be a problem. Hell, Cam tried to warn us it could be, and we didn't listen. It's over, Son."

I know there's more to this that Larry hasn't said yet. I ask, "So, he's going to sell after all?"

"Maybe not."

"What do you mean maybe not?"

"Cam says that he and Jim Lynch are discussing a deal that would turn the farm over to Jim."

"He doesn't have that kind of money!"

"No, he doesn't, Son. I don't know what he's thinking." Larry looks at me as he says this as if to read my reaction.

Cooper is still angry—enough so that he can't even talk at this point.

I say, "Larry, so the two options Cam is considering are accepting a bid from his neighbor or working out a deal to sell it to Jim Lynch?"

"Yes."

Cooper regains control and says, "Wait, what about our MOU? Can't we hold that over his head?"

"There are so many conditions to be met, it will be easy for Cam to get out of it. It's of no help to us."

"He's your friend and he's screwing you over, Dad."

"He's a businessman, too, and he's played this as he should. I can't begrudge him that."

The two of them go quiet, one still steaming and one realizing the game is over. I enjoy the moment, then seize my chance. "I have a thought."

"Let's hear it."

"We went into this with a goal of helping Cam Walker, right?"

"Yes."

"And we went into this hoping to make a little money?"

"Yes."

"Well, what if we helped Cam with the sale of the farm to Jim Lynch? It might not be as exciting as a new golf course or new housing development, but we would still make the kind of money we would normally make on a mortgage, and Cam would be ecstatic that Jim got the farm and not Rusty Brotherton. Think about that for a second."

"That's quite an idea you just came up with, Dale."

"Well, I am just trying to think of a way you and Cooper wouldn't have wasted your time on this."

"Okay."

"Let me add one more thing to the conversation."

"Go ahead."

"The idea of the golf property doesn't have to be specific to the Walker property, am I right?"

"I guess not. So, what are you suggesting?"

"Maybe we could find another property that would lend itself to that use—one that would be equally attractive and have better access."

"You seem to have given this some thought."

"It was always possible this would fall through, and it became a greater possibility when Roberts agreed to sell."

Larry takes a long, slow breath, then reluctantly says, "Okay. I think that's the way we will go. I'll get some people working out an arrangement with Cam and Jim. I'm sure we can help with that. For one thing, Cam owns the place, so he could carry the mortgage on it."

"Sounds good."

"Okay guys, I'll call Cam. Cooper, tomorrow you start looking for a new piece of property."

We stand up to leave, but as we do, Larry says, "Dale, would you stay minute?"

"Sure."

Cooper leaves and Larry closes the door. "You're pretty smooth, aren't you?"

"Oh, I don't think I'm smooth. I prefer agile."

"I'm not thrilled with this, and I don't know exactly how you have pulled it off, but I do respect the fact that you have."

"I'm not sure what you mean by 'pulled it off.' Your friend Cam wanted a good outcome for his farm. If Jim Lynch gets it, the farm will be in good hands for at least twenty more years, and I'll bet you twenty dollars that Cooper and I will find you a property to develop into a top-drawer golf venue. I don't think anyone lost here today, Mr. Morgan."

Normally he would remind me to call him Larry. Today, he just smiles. I smile back, wish him a good day, and head down the hall. I catch Paula's eye as I walk by her office. I give her a wink and she returns it with a smile. I refuse to feel bad about this, even though my future at Morgan*Plus* has most likely taken a turn today. When I get to my office, I get out my phone and text Jim.

I think you are about to become a landowner.

Really?

Yep.

That's awesome! What happened?

I'll call you this weekend, but you may hear from Cam before that.

Great.

226

36

By THE TIME I MAKE IT TO SARAH'S PARTY it's well underway and everyone at Southwest Brewing is having a great time. I look around and find her at a table with one of her friends. She sees me and gestures me to come over.

"Hi Dale, this is my friend, Allie. Allie—Dale."

Allie and I exchange 'nice to meet you's, and I learn that she's from Pennsylvania, so we'll have something in common if needed at any point.

Sarah says, "Have you heard from your brother? Is he on his way?

I tell her that Dave called me on my way over. He has an impending deadline on a big contract and it's all hands on deck."

"Oh, I'm sorry he can't make it."

"Yes, he is too, and when I tell him about all the single women here tonight, he'll really regret missing it."

Sarah looks at me and says, "There are a lot of us. You need a beer, Dale. Allie and I need another refill, so I'll go do that while you two get acquainted."

"Sure, that would be nice, and pick out a good one."

"I'll get you what we're having. I think you'll like it."

Sarah leaves and goes to what looks to be a very busy bar. I can tell it is going to take her a bit to get our beers.

By the time she has our beers, Allie and I have exhausted everything we could possibly have in common. My next topic was going to be favorite book genres, I don't know who is more relieved to see Sarah—Allie or me.

"So did you two have a lot to talk about?"

Allie says, "We did. I know the area where he lived in Philly. I had a few college friends who lived near there. I know a lot of the places he and his friends hung out."

"Great. I knew you two would hit it off. So, Dale, what's new with work?"

I spend the next several minutes catching her up with what's been happening at Morgan*Plus*. She's impressed, but poor Allie is confused. I try to fill in the blanks for and if she doesn't get it or if I am boring her, she doesn't show it.

Having told my story, I feel the need to change the subject, so I ask the two of them about their summer plans. Allie is going to take a couple of classes, while Sarah is going to play some co-ed rec softball and watch her son play tee-ball. She is also considering taking one class if it's available. Otherwise, she's just going to take it easy for a couple of months.

Sarah says, "What about you, Dale. Did I hear you might be going to see some friends out east?"

"I am in late July. How'd you hear that?"

"Dave told me. That sounds like fun."

"It will be."

Allie wants to know my itinerary, so I tell her that I have some friends to see in Philly first, then some of us will be going to the shore, and I might end up going to see a friend in upstate New York. She shows interest, but I don't think my itinerary impresses her all that much.

A couple of girls come over and say a group of them are going to get some Thai food. They ask if we want to join them. Allie is up for it, and I think it sounds good.

Sarah says, "I think I'll take a rain check on that. I need to go and help my parents get Alex ready for bed. He's going through a spell right now where if I'm not around at bedtime, he gets anxious."

I say, "Poor kid. Give him a hug for me."

"I will. Bye you two. Hope the food's good."

She goes around the room and says good-bye to the rest of her friends then goes to the door, ready to go to her car. I tell Allie that I'll be right back and hurry to catch up with Sarah.

"This was fun. Thanks for inviting me."

"I knew you'd have a good time. I wish your brother could have made it."

"I'll be sure to tell him all about it."

"Are you going to talk to him tonight?"

"I don't know."

"Are you going up there tomorrow?"

"I don't think so. Larry Morgan has us all involved in a charity benefit tomorrow."

"Oh, okay. Well goodnight, and thanks again for coming to help us celebrate. Have a good time with Allie. She's nice."

"Okay. Wish you could have Thai food with us, but I understand."

She leaves. I wish I had reminded her that June is coming, but I am sure she is aware and there's no need to be pushy. Just a couple more weeks now. I know I'm ready for it.

By the time I get back inside I learn that the Thai food crowd has grown by several people, which is fine. It should be fun, and it will feel a little less like Allie and I have been paired off. I don't think she has any expectations, but it could get awkward.

———————————

A couple of hours later, I'm on my way home. As luck would have it, another guy was more interested in Allie than I was and they left together, so that worked out okay. Now all I need to do is get home and have some Tums and remind myself not to get menu item #7 next time.

My phone rings and I know from the ringtone it's my brother.

"Dave. What's up?"

"How was it?"

"It was fun."

"Did you talk with Sarah?"

"Quite a bit, yes."

He's quiet as if waiting for me to say more.

I say, "How's the job going?"

"I think we are in for a long weekend. Are you coming up?"

"No, I don't think so."

"Oh."

"Was there some reason you wanted me to come up?"

"Oh, uhh, I've found a house I might want to buy, and I wanted you to see it. Sarah saw it last weekend and she liked it."

"Great."

"Yeah, too bad you didn't come up when she did. We could have looked at it together."

"Sorry I missed that, but Phil and I were prepping for a Memorial Day 5-K run."

"So, can you come up Memorial Day Weekend, then?"

"Well, we have a company barbeque I should probably attend on Saturday, and then the race on Monday, so it would only be Sunday for the day if I did."

"Try to. I'd really like to talk to you about this house."

"Sure. But if not that weekend, then I'll be there the next one for sure."

"Okay, that could work."

"Well, I've made it home, Dave. Talk to you later."

"Yeah. Good night."

37

Saturday, May 17

MY TABLET SIGNALS that I'm getting a webchat request. I check, and it's Jack. I accept the request and wait for his face to appear on my screen. When it does, I see he is sitting at a table in the kitchen of what appears to be an old farmhouse. I'll have to ask him about that before we finish.

"Jack, what's up, man?"

"Hey, Dale. I think this might be the first time we've ever done this."

"I believe so. It must be a special occasion."

"Well, not special necessarily, but I wanted to talk with you in person rather than by text."

"Uh-oh, sounds serious."

"No, not really. I just wanted to let you know that I need to take a rain check on getting together. Is that okay? You haven't bought a plane ticket yet, have you?"

"You know, I've been so busy I never got around to it. What's going on?"

"Nothing bad. I'm going back to Philadelphia for a few days, so I need to reschedule."

"Have you cleared this with your boss?"

"Yes, I have. Sean's a tough negotiator, but when I reminded him that our mom doesn't know everything he did when we were younger, he decided to let me have a few days off."

"So, what's with the Philly trip, if you don't mind my asking?"

"Something has come up at K&S, and there's a couple of people I want to see while I'm in Philly."

"Any of the female persuasion?"

"Definitely. At least one of them is for sure."

"May I ask what is going on at K&S?"

"It's big. Truman fired his golden boy. Apparently he was sexually harassing a couple of the employees and they had to let him go. And here's the big news. They want me to come there and talk to them about coming back on board."

"No!"

"Yes."

"Are you going to do that?"

"No."

"You can't just tell them that over the phone?"

"And miss the opportunity to stick it to them? No way. I will always regret it if I don't go there and turn them down in person. I'm not going to be an ass about it, but I am going to tell them no, then get up and leave that place forever."

"Okay, then about this someone or some ones you'd like to see there…"

"Yeah, I want to catch up with the old group, including Kylie. They're good people."

"Yes, they are."

"So Dale, can you reschedule your trip here until later this summer?" he asks me.

"I might be able to. It depends on some things at work. I'm in the middle of something there, plus I've got something of a personal nature going on. How those things go may decide if I want to or even can come that way."

"That's a little vague," Jack says, sounding amused.

"Just be satisfied with that explanation for now, okay?"

"Okay."

"The full explanation would take too long."

"When would you know for sure?"

"First part of June, I think."

"That doesn't give you a lot of time to work things out for a summer trip."

"No."

"Well, I tell you what. Call me as soon as you know."

"Sounds like a deal."

38

Monday, June 2

I LEFT RIGHT AFTER WORK and made the drive to Kirkwood to see Sarah. I probably should have called her first, but all the romantic movies I've been forced to watch have convinced me that women love to be surprised.

She was in Spring Mill over the weekend, but I didn't make it. Mom and Dad had to go to Columbia to see Gramma. The care center called to let them know she had fallen and suffered a minor wrist fracture. They went over to see how she was doing and to meet my Aunt Teresa to talk about things that needed to be discussed.

When I pull up in front of the Koulos's house I don't see her car. I assume she'll be back soon. I came here on impulse tonight, which is something I rarely do. At work today, I looked at my calendar and realized it's June. I'm not trying to rush Sarah. If she needs more time that's fine, but it is a date she bookmarked for her getting back out there, and I just want to sit down with her and have a talk about that. I want to see if I can be part of it.

I ring their doorbell and Gus comes to answer it.

"Well hi there, Dale. This is a surprise."

"Yes. I just finished looking at a property in the area and thought I'd stop by to see Sarah. I haven't talked to her in a couple of weeks and thought she might want to go out and have a beer or a cup of coffee and catch up."

"Sorry, you just missed her. She's gone to a tee-ball game with Alex."

"Oh, okay. What time will she be back?"

"Hard to say. The game starts at six, but they usually get started late. It could be over around seven-thirty, but the parents sometimes take the boys out for ice cream. You know Alex and ice cream!"

"I do. Well, I guess I will catch up with her another night."

"Okay. Good to see you."

I start to go to my car but get an idea. "Where's the game being played? I might go watch Alex."

"Oh, it's over at the park, not too far from here."

"Okay, I think I'll head over there and catch a little bit of the action. Good to see you, Mr. Koulos."

"Nice to see you, Dale."

Dee comes to join him, and I can see them have a brief conversation then look at me. I get a wave from Dee.

———————

Ten minutes later I arrive at the park. After some searching, I find Sarah.

"What a surprise. How'd you find us?"

"I stopped by your house and your dad told me that you two were here. I thought it would be fun to see Alex play ball."

"He'll love it."

Sure enough, Alex comes over to me and he's thrilled his Uncle Dale is here to watch.

The game gets going, and I had forgotten what a hoot tee-ball can be. We've got kids running to the wrong bases, kids hitting the tee squarely below the ball with the ball dropping straight down and the kid staring at it, not knowing what to do next. We've got kids throwing the ball at the base runners to try to get them out *a la* dodgeball, and a few outfielders who discover an interesting-looking plant species that merits close inspection. A person would be hard-pressed to top this for entertainment on a Monday night.

Alex comes over after the game demanding to know who won. He's upset the coaches told them that no one is keeping score, because he's sure his team has won.

Sarah says, "Alex, you might have scored more runs, but it doesn't matter. We're out here for fun, okay?"

"Okay."

I say, "Alex, you did a good job. Someone has been working with you I think."

Sarah tells me that she has, but that he also has been taking his ball glove up to Spring Mill and playing catch with DJ who is also in tee-ball, and with his Uncle Dave.

Another little player comes over and invites Alex to go with his family to get ice cream.

"Can I go, Mom?"

"Sure, but get a cup, remember? You don't need to get ice cream all over your uniform or your friend's car."

The boys take off, leaving Sarah with me.

"You want to go get something, Sarah?"

"I should get home, Dale."

"Could we talk for a minute?"

She looks at me and her expression is neither encouraging nor discouraging.

"Sure. There's a nice walking trail here. Want to get in a few steps?"

"Okay, sounds great."

For the first part of our walk, she tells me about her summer to date. She did enroll in a class. She is on a softball team and she's loving that and finding that she's been missing the competition. She and Alex have joined a swim club and that's been fun, too. She wants to know what's new with me. I fill her in on a few rather boring items from work, telling her I'm trying to keep a low profile for obvious reasons.

"Sarah, could we talk about the fact that it's June?"

"Okay."

"I'm not trying to rush anything and if you aren't ready, that's fine, but I think I am ready, and I want to see if you'd like to get back out there with me and start going out for something more than a beer now and then."

"Oh, Dale. I don't know."

"It's okay, and I may regret what I'm about to say, but I'm gonna go ahead and say it."

She stops and looks at me, starts to say something then it looks like she changes her mind, and she lets me continue.

"Okay here goes. Over the past couple of weeks, since I saw you at your party, you are all I can think about. I think about how great you are. I think about how much I enjoy being with you and how much I care about Alex. Tonight has been awesome. I loved sitting with you and watching him play. Someday I want to be in that picture in a much bigger way."

"Wait, Dale. That almost sounds like you are proposing."

"I know it does and I don't mean it exactly that way."

"How do you mean it?"

"I think there is a day when I might very well propose. I just wanted to ask you tonight if you're ready to move ahead with me, to put aside your grieving and to start living again."

"Dale."

"Yes."

"I've already done that."

"How? What do you mean?"

"There is someone I am ready to do that with." She takes my hands in hers and looks directly at me. I search her face for affection—for a sign that it's me she's talking about, but I don't see it.

"I can tell by your expression it's not me."

"No, it's not."

"Please don't tell me it's Dave."

"Why do you say that?"

"Well, first of all because he once told me he didn't think of you that way, and that he'd let me know if things ever changed. If it's Dave, then he's been lying to me. And the other thing is that if it's Dave, then I feel like you've been a little unfair to me. I respected your need to wait. There were times I wanted to push it some, but I didn't. You needed time. But if it's Dave, it seems like he didn't have to wait like I did.

"Okay, here's a bench—can we sit down to do this?"

"Sure. So, tell me. Is it my brother?"

"It is."

"Dave! What the hell? Does he feel the same?"

"Yes, he does."

A couple come by pushing a baby in a stroller with an older brother propelling himself on scooter. If that weren't enough, they also have a small dog on a leash. The dog seems taken with Sarah and comes over to check her out.

Sarah tells them, "Your dog is sweet. What's its name?"

The guy says, "Bruno."

"Well, that's quite a name for a little Yorkie or whatever it is."

"It's a Yorkie mix. We aren't sure what the rest is, Maltese maybe."

"Well, Bruno's cute."

I chime in, "He is. And how old are your kids?"

"We have a four-year-old and a six-month old."

The boy makes sure we know he's the four-year-old and his sister is the younger one.

We talk for a few more minutes and they resume their walk.

Sarah watches them walk away and says, "Cute family."

"They are."

She looks at me again and tries to pick up where we left off. "Dale I'm sorry about this. I didn't want to be the one to tell you."

"I know that. All the while those people were talking to us, I was trying to picture how all of this went down."

"It just happened, Dale. Don't overthink it."

"Let me see if I have it about right. You two get the boys together every week. They have a good time, and you talk. Then my brother starts calling you to plan the next week and then the phone calls become more frequent and then at some

240

point you talk about how you feel about each other. Do I have it about right?"

She has a look of incredulity. "It is. How'd you know?"

"It just about had to be that way. So when did you both realize that there was something more than being friends going on?"

"It was the week before my party, actually. Your brother called me one night and told me he was looking at a couple of houses and he wanted my opinion on them. I agreed to do that, and when I came up that weekend, we walked around the houses. As we did, we talked about what could be done with each of them and what it would be like to live there."

"When I got home on Sunday, I was telling my mom about it and she looked at me and said, "You know why he asked you to look at them don't you?" I realized that I did and then she asked me how I felt about Dave. I told her I wasn't sure. Mom looked at me and told me that she could tell he was special to me, because of the way I'd light up when we talked, and how excited I was about the houses. I realized she was right and called your brother. I wanted to make sure he felt the same. We talked for a long time, and I felt something with him that I've only felt one other time, Dale."

"And never with me."

"No. I'm sorry. I think the world of you, but I don't think of you the way I do your brother. When you find the right person, there's a spark, Dale. I'm so sorry that I don't feel that way with you. I really am."

"So why didn't one of you, especially my brother, call me after that?"

"We decided we'd tell you at my party the next week, then Dave couldn't make it, so that plan fell through."

"I see. But he never did call me. He could have, you know."

"He should have. I'm upset with him that he didn't. He put all of us in a bad spot."

"I guess I should have rented a kid so I could have competed."

"This was never a competition, Dale."

"I can tell you that my brother will think it is, and he will think he's won."

"You are making him sound shallow. There's a lot more to Dave than that. He can be very sweet, and very sensitive. He's a good dad to DJ, and Alex adores him."

"That's good, because I don't care too much for him right now."

"You two need to talk."

"We can do that, but it doesn't change the fact that he could have called me before now. He should have, don't you think?"

"He didn't think that was a conversation a guy should have with his brother by phone."

"Okay. Sounds like an excuse, but okay."

"We thought you would see each other at your mom and dad's before now. And we sure didn't think about this happening the way it has tonight."

"Yeah, I'm an idiot."

"Why are you an idiot?"

"First of all, for putting you in this position. Second for not seeing what was going on behind my back and right in front of my face apparently. I still can't believe Dave did this and didn't tell me what was going on."

"Talk to him, Dale."

"Okay, I will."

39

Tuesday, June 3

AFTER I TALKED WITH SARAH last night, I called Dave and told him we needed to talk. He let me know he had just spoken with Sarah and was expecting my call. I started to talk about it with him, but he asked if we could talk face to face. He said he'd be waiting at Dad and Mom's when I got there.

Work was rough. It was hard to focus, and I couldn't wait for the day to be done, so I left work an hour early. I've calmed down from last night and I am at a point that all I want to do is to talk to Dave and work things out. I want him to own up to what he has and hasn't done, and to admit that I deserve better from him. I know my brother well enough to know if I come on too strong, he'll bull up and we'll get nowhere.

When I get to Mom and Dad's, I get out of my car and walk inside. I don't hear anyone, so I yell out, "Anyone here?"

Dave answers, "I'm in the kitchen."

I walk down the hall and turn the corner to see him sitting at the island checking something out on his tablet.

"Where is everyone?"

"Mom and Dad took DJ out to get a bite. They should be back soon."

"So, we've got a minute to talk before they get back?"

"Yeah, sit down. Let's talk."

"How are things going, Dave?"

"Going all right. Thanks for coming up here tonight. I think it will help."

"I hope it will."

"Sarah was upset with me that I hadn't called you. You got me in a lot of trouble. We need to get this figured out."

"We need to get it figured out so that you won't be in trouble?"

"Yes."

"And what about how I'm feeling about all of this?"

"Well, that too."

"So let me ask you Dave. How do you think I'm feeling right now?"

"Well, I guess you're upset. After all you made the drive up here on a Tuesday night, so that would indicate you're upset."

"So you get that. Why do you think I'm upset?"

"Sarah says it's because I should have called you earlier."

"And do you agree or disagree with her on that?"

"I feel like you've got me on a witness stand here."

"You're right. I'm coming at this the wrong way. Let me just phrase it in a way that you and I have always talked to each other. I am upset with you, and I'd like to know if you understand why and if you do understand, then what you are going to do to make it right."

"Okay. There's a lot in there. Let me start. I think you are upset because you care about Sarah and when you went over there to talk to her, you found out she doesn't feel the same. And I think that hurt your feelings."

"That's a little bit of it, to be sure, but what else?"

"Obviously it has to do with the fact that she and I are starting what you wanted to start with her. I know that I'd be upset if someone I liked a lot picked you over me. That's only natural. No one likes to lose."

"Okay, again, part of it, but there's more. Keep trying."

"And you think when I found out that she felt the same way that I felt about her, I should have driven down to see you or called you or something."

"Bingo. Now we're getting there."

"Okay, first of all this thing between Sarah and me hasn't been a thing for very long. She told you that, right?"

"Yes."

"So there hasn't been a lot of time to tell you."

"There's been way more than enough time Dave. That's a very poor excuse."

He doesn't like that. I can see I'm doing what I did not set out to do.

"Dave, that was a bad choice of words. I just think there was time for a brother to have that conversation with his brother."

"But that's just it. You are my brother. I'm not going to pick up the phone and say, 'Hey that girl that you like, well, I like her too and she likes me, so . . . sorry.'"

"I think maybe you could have managed that conversation better than that, but I see your point. I would have wanted to do it person."

245

"And you never came up."

"I would have if I'd known there was something this important for us to talk about. Hell, Dave, I'm here tonight!"

"Well, we could have still had time if you hadn't gone over to see her and tried to propose."

"That's not exactly what happened, and you know it!"

"Sounds like it was from what I hear. And what guy doesn't even have a date with a girl and then tells he wants to get married?"

"Again, that's *not* what I did, but let's put that aside. You say that we didn't go out. That's right. We didn't. She wanted to wait until June to start doing that, so I waited."

"No self-respecting guy does that. If you see something you want, you go for it. You don't sit around twiddling your thumbs."

"No, Dave, apparently what you do is arrange little get-togethers with your boys, and sweet little phone calls in between to make your move behind my back."

We both stand up and he pokes me in the chest as he talks, "That is not what I was trying to do."

"Get your hand off me, and I'm sorry but I don't believe you for a minute."

He keeps his finger there, and I brush it away. I think he's about ready to hit me at this point.

Mom, Dad and DJ come in the kitchen door and find us face to face.

Dad assesses the situation and says, "DJ, why don't you go watch one of your TV shows. DJ gives me a little wave as he goes by, and I return it.

"What's the deal here, boys? We leave you alone for a bit to work things out, and we come home to find you squared off here in our kitchen."

246

Dave says, "Nothing's happening Dad, we're just having ourselves a nice little conversation."

"It doesn't feel like it's all that nice to me, Son. What's going on?"

"Your oldest son here seems to be a little sore that Sarah chose me over him. He's not coming right out and saying it, but I think he came here to tell me we need to break it off."

Dad gives me a questioning look.

"No, that's not at all what I've been saying, and it's not why I came tonight! Here's what you need to know about this. I've told Dave on more than one occasion that I care a lot for Sarah and that I was waiting for June when she would be ready to start going out. One time when I told Dave about how I felt, his response was to tell me to hold off. I thought that was odd, so I asked him if he had feelings for Sarah. He said he didn't, but if he ever did, he'd let me know."

"Is that true, Dave?"

"Well, he thinks it is, so let's say yes."

"You absolutely said it!"

"And you didn't tell him what was going on, Dave?"

"He went to Sarah's and asked her to marry him before I could tell him! Can you believe that? And of course, she turned him down. She told him about her and me, and so now he's mad at *me*."

"Don't you see why, Dave? You could have told him. You *should* have told him."

"He didn't give me a chance."

"I don't know what he means by a chance, but he had any number of times he could have said something to me, Dad."

"I wanted to tell you in person, and I was waiting until you came here, so I could tell you."

Dad says, "Okay. Okay. You've both made your points. Can't we just get past this now. What's done is done. Dale, it's obvious that your brother and Sarah are at the beginning of something. And Dave, you really should have told your brother before he found out from Sarah. You owed him that. You should have found the time."

"I don't think that would have made any difference, Dad. I still think he'd be mad at me just because she chose me instead of him. He can say all he wants, but that's *really* what's happening here."

I look at my parents again to see if they'll challenge Dave on this. They have to know that's not the situation. I know they're caught in the middle and trying hard to help us work through this. Maybe they think Dave will come around and apologize for not letting me know like he should have. More likely they are thinking I'll calm down and get over it. I've always been the brother who's made things right.

I look at the three of them. I hear the TV in the family room and I'm glad little DJ went in there rather than stay in the kitchen and hear what's being said. I feel drained, and I lack the energy and the will to go on with this. Dave leaves me with our parents while he goes to check on his son.

"Okay, I think maybe I wasted my trip here tonight. I'm going to go back to my place."

I give Mom a hug and turn to walk out the door.

"Honey, stay and eat something before you go. I'm sure we have something in the fridge we can make into a salad or a sandwich. Please."

"Food won't solve this one, Mom, but thanks for the offer."

I take the kitchen door because it's the closest and gets me away from them the soonest. I hear the door open and shut behind me as Dad follows me down the driveway.

"Please stay. I'll bet your brother will calm down and he'll get to where he needs to be."

"And if he doesn't?"

"He will."

"I'm not as confident about that as you are."

"Dale, you can't fight love. It has a funny way of happening when it's least expected, and when a guy falls, he doesn't always think clearly. Your brother will eventually come around."

"Okay, Dad. If you say so."

"And I know you're disappointed about Sarah. I can tell you cared about her, too, but there is someone out there for you. Someone who is as great as you deserve. You will find someone who feels the same about you as you feel about her."

I look at Dad. He's one of the smartest and fairest men around. I'm lucky to have him and Mom as my parents. Yet even as fair and smart as he is, he's also a practical guy. He's the kind of guy who doesn't spend a lot of time talking about why or how a problem has come up. He doesn't have time for processing feelings. He's more interested in finding a solution. This is one time I have things I need to sort through, and I need to get away to do that.

"We'll talk to you in a day or two. Drive safe."

"Okay, Dad. Love you."

"You, too. It's going to be okay. I promise."

It's not up to him though. I hope there will be some sort of apology, and hopefully a sincere one from Dave in the next few days, and I'm sure I'll be okay with it when and if it comes. It will make things better, and then Dad will have the solution he wants. But without Dave's apology there will be no solution.

40

Wednesday, June 10

I STILL HAVEN'T HEARD FROM MY FAMILY. I am amazed, to be honest. It seems they still think this is something I need to get past. I'm sitting here at my counter eating dinner and considering whether I should just go ahead and make the next move. My phone rings. It's Sarah.

"Hi Sarah."

"Hi Dale."

I wait for her to continue. She's made the call, and I'm not up for small talk tonight.

"Dale, I talked with Dave and he said you went to Spring Mill and things didn't go well."

"I think that's a pretty good description."

"Well, I don't like this. First of all, I want you to know that I'm sorry I've upset you, and that I've caused a problem in your family."

"Sarah, I appreciate that, because I *am* upset, and it *is* a problem."

250

"I didn't set out with the idea that things would end up this way. This is something I just realized was happening within the past few weeks. I never intended for there to be something between your brother and me."

"It helps to hear that, because I feel that I did as you asked, and Dave didn't. I can't think of a better way to say this, Sarah, it just feels like there was one set of rules for him, or better yet there were no rules for him but a clear set of rules for me."

"It was never intentional on anyone's part, Dale. I promise you that. It just happened."

"Even with all of that, Sarah, it wouldn't be a problem if he'd step up and man up."

"Man up?"

"Yes. Apologize for not being as open with me as I have been with him."

"I see."

"He needs to do that to make this right."

"Well, here's why I called you, Dale. When Dave was telling me what had happened with you two, I told him that until you work this out, he and I don't need to see each other. I don't want to be a problem in your family."

I pause, think about my reply, then say, "I hope that gets Dave to do what he should. I really do."

"I know. I just wanted to tell you, so that you and Dave . . . so that you and your family can heal from this problem I've created."

"You didn't create it. Dave did more than you. And it says something that you are the one, and right now the *only* one, who is trying to make it right."

She's quiet, and I think she might be crying now.

251

"Sarah, I'm sorry. You really weren't the cause of this. It was—it is Dave."

"I just hope you can work things out now that I'm out of the picture."

"Sarah, you're a good person to try to make things better. Dave should understand he needs to make the next move."

"Okay. I better go. I can hear Alex calling me."

"Goodnight, Sarah."

"Goodnight, Dale."

After we hang up, I replay our conversation in my head. I guess I should feel better, but I really don't. I sit down and think about things. My issue isn't with their seeing each other, although I am unhappy about it. My issue is with what happened between my brother and me, and that isn't going to be resolved by Dave's not seeing Sarah.

And then there are the boys. Those two little guys have been through a lot of changes in their lives. If Dave and Sarah don't get together, then the boys will lose getting to see each other. I don't want that. I think about it for a little longer and decide there is only one way to solve this problem. I call Sarah back.

"Hello, Dale."

"Sarah. I don't want you or Alex to be unhappy because of me. I don't care how Dave feels, but I do care about you and the boys. Please let the boys get together. If that means you and Dave are together too, then so be it. I'll make sure I get things back on track with Mom and Dad, and maybe eventually, I'll figure it out with Dave."

I wait to hear her say something, but she won't or can't yet.

I continue, "If you *don't* see him, there's a whole bunch of unhappy people, and if you *do*, there's only me—so, several unhappy people versus one. When you get down to it, it's a numbers thing. Go ahead and let the boys have fun. I understand that you and Dave will most likely see each other outside of getting the boys together. I know that will be part of the deal."

"Are you sure?"

"Yeah, it's the right thing to do."

"And you'll try to patch things up with your brother?"

"I don't know another way to say this, Sarah. At this point, I don't think I've done anything that needs patching up. I think he needs to do that. I've done all I can. I may be the only one who thinks that, but in my heart, I know I'm right."

A couple of hours later, my phone rings. It's Dad.

"Hi, Dad."

"Hi, Dale."

"How's it going down there?"

"It's going all right."

"Sarah called Dave and he told us about your call. We're glad everything is back to normal."

"But it isn't, Dad. And I'll bet Sarah told Dave that it wasn't. He just conveniently forgot to tell you."

"Maybe we should come down and see you this weekend?"

"You and Mom?"

"Yes."

"Sure. I don't have much planned at this point. Will you be coming on Saturday?"

"Yes. You need to find us someplace good to eat."

"I'll do it."

"Your Mom will be happy."

"I'm glad she will, but everything's not okay, Dad, so don't oversell it."

"I won't, but it will be nice to see you, and it feels like things are going to be okay."

"Time will tell, Dad. See you soon."

We hang up. I look forward to seeing my parents. I don't have any desire for them to be caught in the middle of this thing while I wait for Dave to do what I feel he needs to do.

41

Tuesday, July 15

"YOU NERVOUS?"
"Yes, a little. I've never done this before. You'd think at my age I would have bought a house by now, but for whatever reason, I haven't."

Five minutes from now at ten o'clock, Jim, Ginny, and I will make the walk to the conference room downstairs to handle the closing. Today, Walker Farm will officially be theirs.

"Well, it's a great day, Jim, and I promise to make it go smoothly for you two."

Ginny is quiet. Smiling. Almost serene. Maybe the moment is so big, she's not sure how to act and she's retreated to some quiet, happy place until it's over.

Jim is nervous and fidgety. Playing with his fingers, checking his phone for messages or the time, and making small talk with me. We talk about how everything's looking at the farm, and I tell him I'd enjoy seeing it again.

"Come out tonight."

"Tonight?"

Ginny joins in, "Oh, yes. We're throwing a little celebration. We should have invited you already. You have to come."

"Okay. I'll do it."

"Come when you can, but we're starting at five."

"I might need to go home and change first."

"Leave work early then."

"I might just do that."

Jim checks his phone and looks at me. It's time.

"Well, let's go buy you a farm."

We take the short walk to the stairs and head down to the conference room that we use for closings. When we arrive, Cooper and our closing officer are waiting for us. Our closing officer is here because she's done several of these and she'll help me make sure I do it right. I suppose Cooper is here to observe a closing as part of his training, but I would bet he's here hoping for some last-minute snag. We take our seats and Jane, our CO, opens the folder with the paperwork.

I say, "Jim, it's an honor to be the guy who handles your closing."

"It's only right. I wouldn't be doing this if not for you."

That gets me a look from Cooper. I shoot him a big smile and fight the urge to say something to him. There'll be a better time for that.

Yesterday, Cam Walker sat with us in this same office to sign his portion of the paperwork. Since he was both the seller and the mortgage holder, it took a little longer than normal. I think the experience was a little bittersweet for Cam. He's selling the farm but doing so to the best guy he could find outside of his own family. For that reason, Cam has been generous to Jim. He is demanding a modest interest rate and requiring minimal payments. Based on Jim's history, he'll pay more than the minimum and have the place paid off well before the end-date of the loan.

Before he left yesterday, Cam told us that he was extremely happy how this had all turned out and he thanked us for helping make it happen. Cooper and Larry put on a little show as if it were their plan all along. It would have been funny if it weren't so pathetic, and if I didn't know how miffed they still are.

Today, Ginny is sitting by Jim's side; watching as the Walker farm becomes their place. She and Jim just announced they are going to be getting married in August. No word yet on future Lynches.

After forty-five minutes of explanations and signatures, we finally near the end.

"Jim, here's the last piece of paper that needs your signature, and you are done."

"Great. Let me at it."

I hand him the document and the closing officer explains it to him. He studies it a second, knowing that everything will be official with this last signature; then he signs it with a flourish and a big smile.

"Congratulations, Jim."

"Thanks, Dale. And thanks to you, Cooper, and your expert staff." He acknowledges the closing officer as she gathers her copies and leaves.

He hugs Ginny, and I think they both have tears in their eyes. I'm thrilled for them: happy how this all came out.

The five of us stand up and shake hands. Ginny gives me a hug and thanks me for everything I've done to help Jim. I tell her it has been my pleasure. They gather up their things and head out the door to begin their new lives together, but before they do, Jim reminds me that I am invited to the farm later today. After they leave, Jane congratulates me on my handling of the process and leaves me alone with Cooper Morgan.

"Well, Dale, Dad was right."

"Right how?"

"You are slick."

"Well, thank you Cooper, but I think your dad called me smooth."

"I prefer slick."

"Well, say whatever you want. This is done. No sense wasting time rehashing what's happened. You and I need to keep looking for that property for your dad's golf course."

"Okay, but it better be good. The Walker farm was perfect."

"As a piece of land, yes. As it sat in relation to the properties around it and with its access complications, not so much. We can and we will do better."

"Dad and I will hold you to that."

I look him straight in the eyes, challenging him to look at me the same way. "And if I'm true to my word and we find a suitable property?"

"Yes?"

"Then no more talk of this situation, unless it's to say that everything happened for the best, okay?"

"Deal."

"Cooper, I still owe you lunch."

"Do you now? I think you won the bet."

"Let me buy today. I'm feeling good about how this turned out."

"Deal."

We're at a nice little place near the office and having a good conversation. Cooper seems to be taking this well.

Cooper says, "Dale, it looks like I'm going to be joining you."

"Joining me?"

"Yeah, in training."

"Oh, I hadn't heard. Great."

"Yeah. Great. While you're gone on vacation, they are going to get me caught up with you and then we'll start working together when you get back."

There's a question I have for Cooper. I consider if this is the right time, then decide to go for it.

"Cooper?"

"Yes."

"If I ask you a point-blank question, will you give me a straight answer?"

"I'll do my best."

"Back in December, when your dad hired me, the idea was I'd get trained in the different aspects of the business, then when I was up to speed, I'd start running things for your dad so that he could ease into retirement."

"Yes, I know that."

"So. Here's my question for you. Has that changed?"

"What do you mean?"

"You weren't here at the time I was hired, and my understanding was you weren't all that interested in working here and certainly not interested in taking over for your dad. Then on my first day, here you are, and everything has been different since then. And now you're telling me you're going to train with me. So, I have to wonder if plans have changed, and you and your father are thinking you'll be in charge someday."

"I would be lying to you if I said I hadn't started thinking about that, Dale."

"Then you know that changes things for me, right?"

"I do. I mean, I can see why you think it does, but I'm not speaking for Dad."

"Well, I would imagine he'd like it if you were the next Morgan in charge."

"I suppose he would."

"You *suppose*. You don't know?"

"Okay, this will surprise you, but we haven't talked about that yet."

"Yet."

"If and when we do, Dad needs to be the one to bring it up. That way I will know he thinks it's a good idea."

"Well, you know when he does bring it up and you *do* have that conversation, I'll probably need to move on."

"I would try to sweeten the deal for you so that you wouldn't want to. You're smart and you have a different way of looking at things. I think we'd make a good team."

"I'd do the same for you, Cooper, if I took over for your dad."

"Great. Let's see how it plays out, then."

Even with that, I'm thinking his dad knows Cooper's interested, and most dads, Larry for sure, would be excited at the possibility of having their sons take over. If I didn't know it before, I know it now: there's a number on my days at Morgan*Plus*, and it's up to me to decide how big that number is.

———————

An hour later, I walk back to my office and, as I make it to the top of the stairs, I see Paula standing in the hallway. I remember a conversation with her in February. She tried to warn me then that whatever situation I thought I was walking into at Morgan*Plus* had changed the day Larry brought Cooper on board. I may have been in denial at the time, but eventually I saw what was happening.

I've often thought about the Walker property and why it was so important to me that it stay a farm. I want to believe that I fought for it because it was the right thing to do. I wonder though, if getting back at Larry Morgan for bringing Cooper on board might also have been part of my motivation.

"How'd the morning go?"

"It's done."

"You happy with it?"

"Delighted."

"Do you feel like you won the battle but lost the war?"

"No, I feel like the battle was the war, and by the way I just learned at lunch today, Cooper's going to join me in learning everything there is to know about Morgan*Plus*.

"You know, back in February, I wanted to warn you to keep your eyes and ears open. Based on the way I feel I've been treated; I had this suspicion they might mistreat you too.

"It's okay, Paula."

"You gonna stay on?"

"For a while."

"Yeah. I wouldn't stay a day after I found a better opportunity."

"You talking about you or me?"

"Yes."

42

I TOOK OFF AT FOUR TO GO TO MY PLACE and change into something more suitable for the farm, and now I'm on my way to the party. It's been a good day—one of the few good ones since that night with Dave six weeks ago.

I'm looking forward to my evening. That snowy day in February when Cooper and I came to check out the farm, I made a vow I'd return to see it in summer. Tonight, I'll get my chance.

It doesn't hurt my mood that I'm leaving for my vacation this weekend. It will be nice to have some time off. I'll fly to Philly, spend a day or two there, then go to the ocean with Mariah and some of our mutual grad school friends. From there I plan to do a quick trip to Upstate New York to see Giselle, then end the trip spending some time with Jack in Ohio. It all sounds so much better than another week at Morgan*Plus*.

I cross the old bridge and see the Walker Farm sign. I hope Jim leaves it. It would be a nice touch to keep the name. As I drive through the valley, everything that was white that day is various shades of green and gold now. The cattle are in a pasture west of that great old barn. The calves that I saw that first day have grown, and they've been joined by ones born later. Beyond the barn there's a field of corn that looks to be as high as my chest. It's a perfect scene, and even more so because, as of today, it belongs to Jim and Ginny.

There are cars parked in the road by the barn and near the shed as well, so I search for a place to park. I continue until I see a spot in front of the house. I pass a pick-up truck that has the Brotherton Farms logo on its door. I'm a little surprised that Brotherton was invited and even more surprised he accepted. As I get out of my car, I hear the celebration, but it's not by the house, where I had expected it to be. Instead, it is up the hill by the lake. It's a bit of a walk to get there, and I think about getting back in my car and driving but decide I could use the exercise.

I make the trek up the hill and, as I do, I see several large round bales of hay on the hill just below the dam. They draw my eyes past the hill and across the little valley, where I see the outcropping of rock that presented us such a challenge that snowy day. I smile at the memory.

I make it up the hill and past the dam to my right. I circle west of the sky-blue lake and take in the scene in front of me. The swimming dock is anchored in the middle of the lake with a few people waiting for a chance to go off the diving board. On opposite side, there's the sand beach that was covered in snow just a few months earlier, and I see beach towels there and a couple of folks talking and sharing a drink. To the right there is a couple who have gotten the canoe out and are paddling around the lake. It's another great scene. An artist would have a lot to work with at Walker Farm this evening.

I keep walking until I make it to the cabin at the west end of the lake, where, in the middle of a small crowd of people, I see Jim. He greets me, insists on pouring me a beer, then starts introducing me to everyone, and I'm thanked repeatedly for helping him get the place.

I spend some time talking with the group, then Jim takes me to another group that includes Ginny and a couple I'd guess to be her parents. It also includes a girl that looks like a slightly older version of Ginny. We are introduced, and Ginny's parents can't stop shaking my hand and patting my back. If I had the smallest doubt that I had done the right thing, it's gone now.

Ginny's older sister, whose name is Jean-Anne and who appears to be a few drinks ahead of everyone else, keeps going on about how excited she is that Jim and Ginny are going to get married and live here. She finally gets so worked up, she grabs both sides of my face and pulls me down so that she can plant a wet, sloppy kiss on me. Her dad tells her that maybe she should have warned me before the kiss. She said she likes to surprise people. I think ambush might be a better word.

We talk for a few minutes, then we keep moving so that Jim can introduce me to his parents who are standing close to the beach. As we walk toward them, he tells me that Jean-Anne has two kids by two different men, and she is looking for her Charm.

"Her Charm, huh?"

"Yep, third time and all that . . ."

"Well, I don't think I would be interested in signing up for that."

He chuckles and says, "I don't blame you."

Even before I am introduced to him, I immediately know which man is Jim's dad. He looks like he could be Jim's older brother. The Lynch men age well. Jim's mom is standing beside him. She's tall, thin, and not unattractive. They are talking to a guy who has grey hair and a grey beard to match. He is big and burly and wearing an NRA cap. Jim and I join the three of them.

"Dale I'd like to introduce you to my dad, Daryl Lynch and my mom, Carlene. Mom and Dad, this is Dale Barnhart, the guy I've been telling you about."

We shake hands and they, too, share how ecstatic they are about what's happened. I'm a little embarrassed at how good all this gratitude tonight has made me feel. I feel both contented and energized—ready to do something special again, and soon.

Next Jim introduces me to Rusty Brotherton, the burly, grey-haired guy in the cap. He and I exchange handshakes. Rusty has been listening during the conversation and adds his congratulations. I can tell that he's sincere, and that he likes Jim. It's apparent too, as we talk, that he's not displeased at how things have turned out. Because of that, and in spite of the ball cap he's wearing, I end up liking the guy.

We talk about the farm and for some reason, the conversation turns to the old bridge that leads to Jim's new place. I don't know if it's the celebratory mood of the people, my personal satisfaction for helping make this evening happen, or the second beer I've been handed, but whatever the cause I feel bolder than usual.

"You know something, Mr. Brotherton . . ."

"Rusty."

"Rusty. You know what we should do? Why don't you turn that old bridge over to Jim, and while you're at it, turn Walker Farm Road over to him, too."

"Why should I do that?"

"He can take them over and handle the upkeep. They wouldn't be your problems anymore."

"What would you give me for it?"

"Well, since Jim would be assuming all the costs of the maintenance, I'd say a dollar would be just about right."

"A dollar?"

"Yes, I think that would be about right."

He laughs at my idea, and as he does, I pull a dollar out of my wallet and hold it out to him. He looks at it; looks at me; then grabs the dollar and tells me to draw up an agreement for him to sign.

Emboldened, I say, "While we're at it, we should add some language regarding the road that leads through your farm to Walker Farm Road."

"And I'm sure you have some good reason for suggesting that."

"I think we should make sure we know how the road will be used to protect the interests of all sides, you, Roberts and Jim here—something that would remove any possibility of there ever being a disagreement about it."

"Okay, have your people add that to the mix. We'll get something signed. I like the idea of everything being spelled out."

I tell him I'll get on it tomorrow.

Jim and his dad are both wide-eyed at that point. This little exchange removes a possible bone of contention and puts a capper on a good day for Jim. After I shake Brotherton's hand, they do the same.

I'll waste no time tomorrow morning getting our people to work on the agreement. I think of how Cooper and his father will react when they learn about my coup, since access to the farm sealed the fate of their golf course. They won't be happy, and I will love every minute of it.

This evening has been a great one for me. This whole day has been. I'm sure that when I return from vacation there will be plenty of things to deal with. That's for later. Tonight, it's all good. Tonight, I don't have a care.

43

Saturday, July 25

"THANKS FOR THE COFFEE, Mrs. Hunter. I need it this morning."

"How long did you two stay up after I went to bed?"

"Not long. I think I fell asleep soon after you called it a day. Giselle woke me up and told me I should go to bed. There may have been snoring involved."

"Well, I'm sure you were tired. You've had a big week."

"I have."

"You've put in some miles, and still have some to go today."

"I do."

"Ready for breakfast?"

"I believe I am. I should go out and run, though. I haven't done much of that this week, but breakfast sounds good."

"You can run next week. You're on vacation."

Giselle's mother sets a plate of bagels and fruit in front of me, then joins me at the breakfast nook.

"This is perfect! Thanks, Mrs. Hunter."

"G told me what you like."

She gives me a look that seems to question why her daughter would know what I like for breakfast. For some reason I feel the need to explain.

"Wow! Your daughter has a good memory! We only had breakfast together that morning in Gettysburg."

"She told me about that weekend. I know she had a great time."

"My friends thought I was crazy taking a girl to a battlefield. They didn't think it sounded like a very romantic destination."

Again, I get a look from Mrs. Hunter. Maybe I shouldn't have used the word *romantic*.

"She enjoyed it anyway."

"She and I were having a great time until she got that call."

"Call?"

"Yes. Her roommate called to tell her she had a letter from St. Agatha's."

"Oh, her acceptance letter I would guess."

"As it turned out, and Giselle . . ."

Mrs. Hunter smiles and says, "We call her G."

"G?"

"Yes. Her dad always called her Gigi and somewhere along the line it became G."

"I like it. Anyway, G got so excited when her roommate read it to her. And I could tell she was going to go for it. I was happy for her, but I knew it would change things for us, and so did she. Within a few weeks she had moved back here, and a couple of months later, I'm back in Missouri."

"She had to do it, you know, Dale?"

"I know. I took me awhile, but I know."

I put some cream cheese on my bagel while she sips her coffee. I see her looking out at her back yard.

"Your yard is nice, Mrs. Hunter. Someone's done a lot of work out there."

"I've done most of it."

"And your house, it looks like you've given it a lot of loving care."

She nods and takes another sip of her coffee. I chew on my bagel and try to think where we go from here. There's so much her daughter has told me about their lives here. She's told me how they had to move here after her dad had lost his bout with cancer. Her aunt and uncle live in the house just north of this one, and they owned this property and offered to sell it at a price Mrs. Hunter could afford.

The silence is starting to get uncomfortable, so she asks me about my week. I'd shared most of it with Giselle last night as she took me on a tour of the town, but I don't mind telling it again to Mrs. Hunter.

"It was good. I got to see my friends in Philly for a couple of days. I went to the shore with some friends for a few days, then I came up here. It's been great. I needed the break."

"I wish you didn't have to leave today."

"Me too, but I need to get to Ohio tonight. I promised a guy there that I'd stop by and then I'm flying out of Columbus tomorrow afternoon."

"So, have you and G made plans for this morning?"

"I think we plan to finish sightseeing, and then we

are supposed to go to some place that has unbelievable hamburgers."

"Oh yes, Goochie's."

"That's the place."

"You have to go there if you come to Pleasant Valley. Out of town guests are required to have a Rembrandt's Pizza and a Goochie burger."

"We had Rembrandt's last night, so it looks like I will check all the boxes."

I finish my coffee.

"You want a refill?"

"Sure, if there's plenty left. I don't want to take G's, though."

"Why don't I just make us a new pot."

As she gets up to do that, I look at her and think how much she and her daughter look alike; both of them pretty and petite with reddish-blond hair, although Mrs. Hunter's hair is a little darker now. By looking at her I can picture how Giselle might look in twenty-five years. There was a time that I dreamed I'd be part of that picture, too. Then nursing school called her to New York, I went home and became infatuated with Sarah, and the dream was shelved. Last night when I saw Giselle again, I got it down and started dusting it off.

Mrs. H has the coffee going and offers me another bagel while I wait. I tell her I've had plenty, and it sounds like I need to save room for the Goochie burger. We chat for a couple more minutes and the coffee maker finishes its job. She grabs our cups and walks to the counter, and as she does G walks in. She's wearing an oversized t-shirt, perhaps her older brother's, and I like the outfit, but I don't think her mom approves.

"You didn't need to get all dressed up on our account, dear."

"Sorry, Mom, I'll go get something else on, but I need some coffee first."

She comes over to the bench where I'm sitting and slides in next to me. I have a flashback to our time in Gettysburg, and that in turn makes me question why I'm leaving today.

Mrs. Hunter brings coffee for the three of us.

"Here you can take this upstairs while you change."

"In a minute, Mom."

I'm enjoying the little scene and she certainly doesn't need to rush on my account.

"So, you two have a morning of sightseeing and then a Goochie burger lined up."

"That's the plan. I showed him most of the town last night, but I saved Riverside Park for today."

"Good idea. It's much prettier in daylight."

G looks at me. "Okay, tell me what you think of what you've seen so far."

I have this temptation to tell her that I like what I'm seeing, but I believe she is asking about her hometown.

"As I told you last night, I like it. It's a beautiful town. I could see why it would be hard for anyone to leave it."

"Well, I graduate next spring, so I might have to."

I want to tell her that they are begging for nurses in Missouri, but it's not the time nor place.

"Honey, there will be plenty of jobs around here if you want to stay."

"I know, Mom, and I'm not too worried."

She gets up, goes to the counter, and fixes herself a plate. I catch myself watching her, and when I turn my attention back to my coffee, I see that Mrs. Hunter has been watching me. I grab my cup and start drinking. It isn't so much that I want more coffee, as it is that I am hoping the cup will cover my face. I'm sure it's turning red at this point. She grins at my discomfort then slowly picks up her own cup.

Giselle fills her plate and rejoins us. Then she insists that I tell her mother the Walker Farm saga.

"You sure we have time for that?"

"You need to tell her. She'll love it."

And so I do. It takes some time. She has lots of questions—good ones for the most part. It takes so long for me to tell my story that G leaves in the middle of it to go upstairs and get showered and dressed.

When I finish, I say, "And there you have it."

"That's quite a story."

"I think so, too. Probably nothing worthy of a novel or a movie, but a good story."

"And you'll be looking for a new job then."

"Most likely."

"Our bank vice president is retiring next year. You could apply for that. I'd bet they would hire you in a minute with your background."

"Banking, huh?"

"Yes."

"I've kind of been there and done that, Mrs. H. Is it okay if I call you that?"

"It is, and you should think about applying."

"I will."

We get up and I help her clear the table and put things away. By this time, Giselle is back downstairs and ready to resume our tour. I head up to brush my teeth so we can go.

As I stand in the little bathroom and look at myself in the mirror, I think of what it would be like to be the vice-president of a small-town bank. It wouldn't be the worst life, but I would much prefer that it be in Missouri. Pleasant Valley seems nice, but I don't think I'd want to live in an area whose winters are as difficult as they are here. And there's no guarantee that Giselle and I would pick up where we left off. *If we don't, where will that leave me?*

I walk into the kitchen and the two of them are talking. Giselle looks at me and says, "Mom tells me you're going to be the next VP at our bank."

"Yes. Apparently and the best part is I don't have to apply, do any interviews, or even be offered the job—none of that! I just take the position."

"You'd get it if you wanted it."

"I appreciate the confidence. Are you ready to go?"

"Let's go!"

44

W E'VE SEEN A COUPLE OF PLACES we didn't get to last night and still have one more place to go before lunch. Giselle wanted to save Riverside Park for last. She thinks it'll be the highlight of our little tour. When we reach the entrance, she has me pull into the long narrow parking lot that runs alongside the river, and points to where she wants me to park. Before we get out, I take a moment to enjoy the view, and it is amazing.

We get out of the car and walk to a bike trail that runs between the parking lot and the river. As we walk south along the trail, Giselle takes the lead, and we see a wide waterfall tumbling over a small dam. I have to admit the view of Giselle in front of that waterfall makes the scene unbeatable. We step off the trail to enjoy the scene and let a couple of bikers pass. Opposite us is a stately three-story red brick building that looks to be hundred years old or more, and it's reflected in the clear water above the dam.

"What is that building?"

"That's the old Holman Hotel. It closed in the 1970s and sat empty for several years, then a non-profit bought it. They've converted it to a theater and arts center."

"That's a pretty nice deal for a town this size. Is it used a lot?"

"It's used for concerts, plays, exhibits, adult education classes, wedding receptions—well, you get the idea."

"It's a beautiful building, and the view of it reflected in the river is like a postcard or a watercolor painting."

"It really is. I tend to forget how pretty it is until I get to show it off."

"Your whole town is nice, G. I can see why you'd want to stay here."

"You think I want to stay here?"

"It sounded like that would be your plan when you were talking with your mom earlier."

"I might. Right now, I just want to finish my degree. And what about you?"

"Me?"

"Yes. Last night, you were talking last about changing jobs. If you did, would you be willing to move?"

"Yeah, maybe. Maybe out west this time. I've lived in the east and Midwest. Maybe it's time for me to go west."

"I don't think you'll leave Missouri again."

"You don't?"

"No."

"You never know. Maybe I'll go for that bank job here in town."

"Bank job? Are you planning to apply for a position or stage a robbery?"

"Applying for a job would probably work out better, I think."

"And you'd never apply."

"You don't think so?"

"No."

"Well, I am wondering if it's time to go a different direction."

"Like I said, you'd never consider moving here."

"You never know."

———————

Half an hour later, we pull into Goochie's parking lot. It's in need of some updates, but places like this always have the best food. We walk in the door and the guy at the cash register welcomes us with a big booming voice. I have a déjà vu moment; then realize he could be the twin brother of a guy who runs a steak place I like in Philly.

"Welcome to Goochie's." He points at Giselle, "You, I know," then pointing at me, "but you I don't know! You're new here!"

"Yessir I am, and I've been told I can't come to Pleasant Valley and not come to Goochie's."

"You were told right. I like you now. Come in and sit down. Sit anywhere you like," again, he speaks as if we are hearing impaired.

There are a half dozen tables open, but we spy a booth on the far wall and make our way there.

"I think we can talk here," says Giselle as we take our seats.

"Yes, getting away from the noisy greeter guy is a good idea."

"Oh, that's Goochie. He's a good guy. He's just a little loud."

"A little! And what kind of name is Goochie?"

"I think it's short for Guccinelli, or something like that,

and people just started calling him Goochie."

"Okay."

"So, you've enjoyed our little tour of Pleasant Valley?"

"I have, and the bike path along the river looked like it would be a good ride. I'll have to . . ."

"Bring your bike next time?"

"I was going to say that, yes."

"Good, then you'll come back."

"I'd like to if there is an open invitation."

"There is."

"That would mean I'd have to drive; that is, if I wanted to bike."

"Yes, or if you'd rather fly, we could find you a bike here. My friend Brad has one you could use."

"Tell me about this Brad guy."

"He's a high school friend. I told you about him once. He's a nice guy. Reminds me of you, actually."

"Oh yeah, I remember you mentioned him one time. Maybe it was when we went to Gettysburg."

She pauses a second, turns something over in her mind, then looks at me and says, "Dale, I loved everything about that weekend."

"So, did I. Perfect day, perfect evening, perfect night, great breakfast—and then we're driving home, and all of sudden everything changes. Sometimes I wish you'd never gotten that acceptance letter. I hope you don't mind my saying that."

"No, I understand. But I *did* get it, and I knew it was what I had been waiting for."

"But that was it for us."

"It sort of had to be; don't you think?"

"I don't know. Anyway, back to Brad. Are you seeing this Brad guy?"

"A little. It's all very low-key, Dale."

"I'd have settled for low-key too, you know."

She laughs. "No you wouldn't have."

She's right. I wouldn't have.

Our server arrives with our glasses of water and menus.

Giselle says, "We know what we want. We want two cheeseburger specials with the works."

The server whose name is Desireé looks at me to see if I approve.

I hold up my hands in surrender. "Hey, I'm a first timer, Desireé. So, I'm going with what she recommends."

"You won't be disappointed."

And with that, Desireé heads to the kitchen. Then she turns back around.

"I forgot your drink orders."

This time, I speak up, "We'll both take diet Cokes."

Desiree looks at Giselle and when she sees her nod, she takes off again.

We sit here looking at each other and it feels like we're back where we left off—back to where we were before that morning in October, but there are miles between us now and no easy way to resolve the distance.

A few minutes later, we have our drinks but not our food.

"So, where were we?"

"You were telling me you had huge regrets at leaving me for nursing school and you're ready to drop out and move to Missouri."

"I don't think so, and isn't there someone there you're already interested in?"

I should have told her last night, but I didn't. I consider my answer. What do I really want her to know?

"There was, but she is more interested in my brother."

"Your brother, Dave?"

"Yes."

"I don't even know where to start asking about that."

"Don't then. There's nothing good that can come from talking about it. I took a week off to come out here and specifically *not* think about it for a while."

"Has it helped?"

"Very much."

She smiles and looks at me.

"Have I helped?"

"More than you know."

"So, things will be okay when you get home?"

"*Okay?* Probably. *Good?* Probably not for a while."

"I'm sorry to hear that."

"It's okay. Let's change the subject."

"Sounds like you had fun at the beach with your friends."

"I did. I would get up and watch the sunrise over the ocean each day."

"That sounds wonderful."

"It was. I'd sit there with my coffee and soak it all in. Most days I had the beach pretty much to myself."

"I have this picture of you sitting there, relaxed, watching the waves come in and the shorebirds skittering about."

"It was very much like that. I had time to myself to think about things. Including you."

"I wish you'd come here sooner than last night."

"I thought about it, but you're in school. What was I going to do while you went to class?"

"I could have missed a class or two for you."

"I know you, and you would *not* have done that. You're too conscientious."

She doesn't have a comeback for that. She knows I'm right.

"Well, I don't like it that I only get you for a night and a morning, while your friend, Mariah, and her fiancé, Carlo, got you for almost a week."

Before I answer her, Desireé checks on us and informs us our order will be coming out soon. She asks if we need refills on our drinks and we say we're good for now. When she leaves, I get lost in my thoughts for a moment.

"You're awfully quiet, Dale."

"You have me thinking about the drive today. I'm not really looking forward to it."

"Just stay here then! You can get up early and go to Columbus tomorrow. You can always see Jack another time. He won't mind, and I'd enjoy having you around for a few more hours."

I think about it, and I am tempted to change my plans, but then I say, "No, I promised him I'd show up today, and I would have to leave super early tomorrow to get to the airport on time. It'll be an easier drive from Jack's."

"I understand."

"To be honest, though, your invitation is tempting."

She smiles and says, "Well, I'm glad to hear that."

I smile back at her and reach out and take her hand.

"This is nice. I've missed you."

"Me, too. Thanks for coming up to see me."

"No need for thanks. I've enjoyed this a lot."

"Please come back."

"I will. I need to meet this Brad guy and see if I approve."

282

"You would, and he would like you."

And with that, Desireé arrives with our burgers and fries.
I take a bite, and the cheeseburger is exceptional. I try
one of the fries, and it is as good if not better than the burger.
The food tastes so good I focus on it. We both do.

Several minutes later she says, "You seem to be enjoying
your burger."

"Wow! It is so good."

"I know!"

"I may have to come back just for the burger."

"*Just* for the burger?" she asks, smiling.

"And the fries."

"Just for the food?"

"Well, that and the bike ride you promised me."

"So, for the food and the bike ride?"

"Yes, and to check out Brad."

She has a smile at this point and says, "I think you're
forgetting something."

"Let me see. I mentioned the food, and the bike ride, and
Brad. Yeah, I think that covers it."

She smiles more broadly now, and says, "You should come
back in September. It's beautiful here in the fall."

"It's a deal. But it might have to be next year."

"That's fourteen months away."

"Yes."

"A lot can happen between now and then, Dale."

"True, but I'll still put it on my calendar."

"Okay, but I wish it were sooner."

As we finish our food, I change the subject and ask her
about her classes. As she talks about them, I listen to every
word, and wonder how different things could have been if

she hadn't gotten that letter, and if I hadn't gone home and pivoted to Sarah for a time.

———————

Desireé has cleared our dishes and we are enjoying refills and not wanting to leave.

Finally, Giselle looks at me and says, "So, I guess I have to let you go."

I think she could almost talk me into staying at this point. I've had less than a day with her and I want more.

"Yes, and I guess I'd better settle up with our server and get back to your house and grab my stuff."

"I suppose."

I look at her and realize that maybe I should not have given up so easily last fall.

"You could come with me."

"Tonight?"

"Sure. You owe me a trip to St. Louis now that I've been to Pleasant Valley."

"Tonight's a bad idea, but sometime soon maybe."

"Well, you said you didn't want to wait fourteen months."

"I don't know when it would be though."

"I'll buy your plane ticket, if that makes a difference."

"That's nice of you, but it's more about figuring out when I could get away."

"Do you have a fall break?"

"We do."

"There you go."

"But you said you might come here in September."

"Probably not until next year though."

"Let me think about it."

I know if she thinks about it, it won't happen. This is like a sale. I need to close the deal.

"So, when is your fall break?"

"The second week of October."

"That's a great time of year in the Midwest. I'll start looking for a ticket when I get home."

"Ooookay."

And the way she says, "Okay," tells me I will have a challenge ahead if I'm to convince her to come.

An hour later I am on the road to Ohio, making good time and still on schedule to meet the guys for dinner. Saying goodbye to Giselle wasn't easy, and I was this close to calling Jack to say I wouldn't make it. If I told him that it was for Giselle, he would understand. I try to be a man of my word though, and I told him I'd be there tonight. He may have moved some things around on his social calendar for me. It's the right thing to do, but I hate it.

I think about the fact that maybe there might be something with Giselle after all, and I think about how this changes things with my brother. If, and it is a very big if, *if* I were to rekindle something with Giselle, then what is the point of my still being angry with him? But then, as I think about it, *this changes nothing*. It's always been about him and me—two brothers, one of whom has treated the other poorly and never offered to make it right.

45

Saturday, July 26

"**F**INISH YOUR PIZZA. We've got a big evening planned." No sooner had I arrived at Jack's place, than he and Sean took me to their favorite pizza joint somewhere west of Akron. I didn't have the heart to tell them I'd had pizza the night before and it was much better than theirs.

I finish my pizza and the rest of my second beer. "Okay, guys what are these big plans?"

"We're taking you to a driving range."

"A driving range. As in golf?"

"Yep. We're playing in a two-person scramble tomorrow and we need some practice."

"It's Saturday. You didn't have time to practice today?"

"We wanted to, but a bunch of work stuff came up."

"Guys, I'm not a golfer."

"We'll have you hitting the hell out of that little white thing in no time," says Sean.

"I don't think you have any idea how bad I am at golf."

"Come on. You'll love it."

I left Giselle for this?

Reluctantly, I agree to join them because it appears I have no choice. So, after Jack pays the bill, we are out the door.

Jack climbs in the passenger seat of Sean's Suburban, I get in the back, and we're off for an evening that I had no idea was coming. Sean takes us down a state highway for a few miles until we make a right turn on a gravel road. It doesn't exactly seem like a road one would take to get to a driving range. Good thing I trust these two.

We go a mile or so farther and I see some lights ahead. It's either our destination or Sean has changed his mind and we're going to watch a little league game. I'm assuming it's the range, and as we get closer, I see I'm right.

We pull into a large gravel parking lot that has eight to ten other cars in it. Ahead of me I can see several tee boxes, half of which are filled with men and a couple of women working on their games. I study them for a minute, and it becomes apparent that many of them need the work. I feel a little better. I will still be the worst golfer here, but not all that far behind a few of them.

While I've been watching the golfers, Sean and Jack have gotten out of the Suburban and are making the walk over to a small white building that serves as an office and snack bar. I follow them and as I study the building, I see that it may have been a double-wide trailer in another lifetime.

"How did you guys find this place?"

"Oh, the guy who owns it is a friend of ours. His dad owns a farm, and they carved the driving range out of the northeast corner of it. They were looking for a way to make a little more income without adding a lot of work, so they came up with this. I think it's doing pretty well."

"So, a farm to golf conversion, huh?"

"Yep. A partial one, at least."

"Interesting."

We go inside and a middle-aged woman is working the counter. She perks up at the sight of the Nolan brothers.

"You two! You're here on a Saturday night? What's going on?"

Sean says, "We heard you were working, so we told the other girls they were out of luck."

She smiles, flattered by the remark even though she knows that Sean is full of it.

"So, you boys want the medium or big buckets tonight?"

"Three big buckets, Selene."

I tell them I don't need to hit that many balls, but they ignore me.

"Who's your tall friend?"

"That's Dale from Missouri."

"Hello, Dale from Missouri. What are you doing here with these two?"

"Hi, Selene. Nice to meet you. Actually, I lived next door to this guy"—nodding at Jack—"in Philadelphia, and I decided to stop by and see how he's doing."

"He's always doing well, from what I hear." She looks at Jack and grins.

Sean says, "You hear right, Selene. Now what do we owe you."

"I'm just going to charge for two buckets, since your friend here is your guest."

Thanks, Selene."

"Just make sure you two come back."

Sean says, "We always do."

And with that we head out the door and back to Sean's Suburban. The guys get their clubs and change into golf shoes. I look at my Nikes and decide they will have to do, since socks are my only other choice.

I carry my bucket of balls and follow Jack and Sean to the tee boxes. Just south of the mid-point there are three open spots together, so we take them. Jack is in the middle and I'm on his right, closer to the office. Jack hands me a driver to use.

"You sure you don't want to use this club, Jack?"

"No. Sean hits the ball well off the tee. It's about the only good thing he does—well, that and hitting a few putts now and then. I have to carry us on the fairways, so I'm going to work on my short game."

Sean comes past Jack, and it appears he wants to coach me a little before he starts hitting. He models how to set up, and then advises me on how to stand, how to grip the club, where the ball should be, how to bring the club back, and how to move my hips as I swing. It's probably four more pieces of information than I can process. I practice without a ball for a few swings, and Sean decides I'm ready for the real thing. I get a few balls out of my bucket and put one on the rubber tube that's inserted into the fake turf. Sean steps back, and I try to replicate what he's told me. I take a swing, and the ball goes straight; not too far, but straight.

"Hit one more, Dale."

I do, and it lands in about the same spot.

"Okay, you're good to go. I'm going to go hit a few."

I turn around to watch Jack hitting a few balls first. He's smooth and the ball seems to jump off his club with no effort on his part. Sean sets up in the box behind Jack, and I watch the two of them taking swings. The few times I've tried it, I have found golf to be difficult. They make it look easy.

I turn back and put a ball on my tee, and as I do, an older gentleman in front of me turns around and begins a conversation.

"So, I take it you're just learning this game."

"Yes sir, I am. I'm here with these two guys. They're practicing for a tournament tomorrow and brought me along."

He says, "Golf's a deceptively difficult game, but it can be a lot of fun."

"Yeah. I don't think I'll be playing much golf."

"You don't?"

"No. I'm not a golf kind of guy."

He gives me a look and says, "May I ask what a golf kind of guy looks like?"

Behind me, Jack says, "Yeah, exactly what do you mean there, Dale?"

Now you've done it.

"I apologize if I came off the wrong way. I guess I mean that I don't have a lot of talent nor the patience for this game. I usually choose to jog or ride a bike or just work out if I have free time."

"Oh, I see."

He says he sees, but I think my choices for physical activity interest him just as much as golf does me.

I get ready for my first uncoached shot and try to do a mental run-through all the things Sean told me. The old guy is getting ready to hit one as well. I watch him hit while I get set up. He takes a nice, easy swing and the ball goes straight and farther than I would have guessed. It's my turn, so I take a deep breath, mentally visualize my steps, and proceed to almost miss the ball on my swing. In fact, it would have been better if I had. I catch the ball on the toe of the driver and send it to my right narrowly missing the old guy and coming to rest against the office. The golfer who is standing nearest the ball picks it up and looks my way. I turn around and look at Jack as if he is the one who hit it. He has his hands on his hips with a look of "don't even try," leaving no doubt that I'm the culprit.

"That one kind of got away from you," says my neighbor.

"Yes, and I'm very sorry."

"Just relax and try it again. You'll do fine."

I tee another ball, apologize to it as I do; take a huge breath; raise and lower my shoulders in a motion that should relax me; tighten and loosen my grip on the club to further relax; and then slowly take the club away from the ball. I get to the top of my swing and feel like I want to kill that little white thing sitting there on the tube, so I proceed to lunge at it rather than swing through it. Somehow, I make good contact this time, and I watch it sail about 50 yards, then make a perfect left turn and go another 50 or so. I would have to do a geometric calculation involving hypotenuses and squares to know exactly how far it went, but at least the golfers to my right are safe.

Jack says, "I'm not sure I've ever seen a ball hook exactly like that, Dale."

"I tried to tell you guys I'm no good at this."

"We didn't believe you."

"And now?"

291

"Starting to," says Sean.

I set yet another ball on the tee tube and wonder what its fate will be. I do all the relaxing things I've been trying to do, take the club back at a nice pace, then start my swing. I feel excited about this one, and I want to see where it goes, so I look up early to enjoy the majesty of my hit. In doing so, I lift both my head and my torso, which makes me miss the ball entirely. Again, the upside is that no one else was injured, and there is the possibility that I can pretend it was just a practice swing.

The old guy says, "I think you scared the hell out of that ball."

"Yep."

"Mind if I give you one bit of advice?"

"You mean like, put the club away, return the rest of the balls to the office and go sit in the car?"

"No. No. I was going to suggest you try a different club. No one can hit a driver. Even pros struggle with that club. Get out your 5-iron and start with that."

I turn around to Jack. "Mind if I switch clubs?"

"Not at all. I just finished with the 5-iron. You're welcome to it."

I trade clubs with him, put a ball down and step up trying to figure out what I should do. My new friend/volunteer golf instructor steps over to help me out. He talks me through what I should do, and he doesn't leave until I've hit a few and I'm doing what he wants me to.

I take my time with the remaining balls and do a little better. Probably one-third of my shots are acceptable, with another third being borderline, and the remainder being balls that I top, slice, or hook. Still, that's much better than what I would have done with the driver.

The old guy finishes up and gets ready to leave.

I tell him, "Thank you for helping me out."

"No problem. You have some ability, but you definitely weren't ready to hit the big boy."

"No, I was not!"

He walks off and I hit my last couple of balls. Jack and Sean have been taking more time between shots than I have, so I get to watch the two of them finish. Jack is consistent. To me, all his hits are good ones, but he seems less than satisfied with a couple—a couple I would have gladly claimed. Sean is more erratic. He's all power and not a lot of technique; much like my brother Dave with a bowling ball in his hand. The two brothers carry on a conversation between hits, with most of it being trash talk. It's obvious they've practiced golf and trash talk over the years, and they're good at both. It's fun watching them go back and forth. I miss that.

When they finish, they throw their clubs in Sean's car and take a seat on the rear deck to change shoes, all the while discussing their strategy for tomorrow's two-man scramble. They're still discussing it when we get in the car and start towards Jack's place.

"Okay, so, once again, here's how it's going to go, Sean. I'll hit first, and if I give us something we can play, then you can cut loose with your driver. If not, get out your 3-wood and play it safe. Got it?"

"So, I'll be hitting my 3-wood all day?"

Jack laughs and shakes his head.

"No, I am sure I'll have us in good shape most of the time, but when I don't—on those *rare* occasions I don't, you need to put one in play."

"Okay. Got it."

"I'll get us on, then I need you to hit some putts. If you do, we'll be going home with some hardware."

"So pretty much like every other time we play, then?"

"Yep."

We drive a little farther and Sean says, "You two old guys done for the night? It's still early."

I say, "I have an early afternoon flight tomorrow, so I'll need to get up and get going."

"It's not that far to the airport. Come on. It's like ten o'clock. The night is barely getting started."

Jack says, "I'm with Dale. I'm going to have one more beer then call it a night."

"Why don't you stay and have one with us, Sean?"

Sean says, "If you two aren't going out, I have a friend I need to stop by and see."

I start to ask about his friend, but Sean is Jack's brother, so I'm sure what kind of friendship this is. Still, I can't resist giving him a little bit of a hard time.

"Where does this guy live?"

"What guy?"

"Your friend."

Sean looks at his rear-view mirror at me and says, "Good one."

46

WE DRIVE THROUGH THE TOWN OF WILLMORE, the Nolan brothers' hometown. It's a nice community of about 20,000, located about halfway between Cleveland and Columbus. We pass through Willmore and get to Jack's place, which is just past the city limits on the west side of town. Sean pulls up to the old two-story farmhouse which has been Jack's home since he moved back in January. He drops us off, then leaves to see his friend. I get my suitcase out of my rental and follow Jack inside.

"I still can't believe you bought yourself a hundred-year-old farmhouse, Jack."

"Don't you like it?"

"Yes, I do. I like it a lot. It's just not what I would have guessed you'd buy."

"To be honest, it wasn't what I set out to buy. The place belonged to my aunt and uncle. They sold their farm to their neighbor, but he didn't want the house and was going to tear it

295

down. My aunt and uncle talked him into letting me have the house and lot for next to nothing. There were a few updates needed, but I've been knocking those out on weekends."

"Wow. I would never have imagined you redoing a house."

"I know."

I set my suitcase down and look around the place.

Jack gives me a couple of minutes, then says, "Take your stuff to the upstairs bedroom on the right, then meet me out on the porch for a beer."

The guest room looks nothing like a room I think Jack would have. It has an old four-poster bed with an oversized quilt that must have taken someone months, if not years to sew, a vintage walnut dresser with a mirror, and an old rocking chair with an afghan thrown over it. The bed looks so inviting I want to climb in and get some sleep, but Jack is waiting downstairs and there's a beer with my name on it.

I go downstairs and through the kitchen to where Jack is sitting on his screened-in porch. He hands me a beer and I take a seat. We tap our beer bottles together and toast to our days in Philly.

"I like this porch. Did you do this?"

"It was already screened in."

"Do you sit out here much?"

Jack looks at me for a second and says, "I do. Sometimes I'll bring dinner out here and enjoy it. That is if I'm having a sandwich or pizza or something similar. Some nights I sit out here just like this—sometimes with a friend and sometimes just by myself. It's nice to be outside and not worry about the bugs eating you alive."

"Tell me about the guest room upstairs."

"Oh, that's the room Sean and I would stay in when we'd

come visit our uncle and aunt. I kept some of their things when they moved and put most of them in that room. It just seemed right. It's nice having something of theirs still here, you know?"

"Yes, I do. It's almost like a shrine to your aunt and uncle."

"Yes, or like a museum of stuff from a better time."

I sip my beer, listen to the crickets, and watch the fireflies outside. It is so peaceful; it makes me want a place like this of my own.

Jack says, "You know, after you switched clubs, you weren't hitting them all that bad."

"My best shot wasn't as good as your worst, though."

"I don't know about that. I think you sell yourself short."

I take a deep pull on my beer and say, "So, Jack. Tell me about Philly. How was your victory lap around K&S?"

Jack finishes a sip before answering, then says,

"It was perfect. I walked in there and they escorted me to Truman Smith's office. There was another person there, someone I'd never met before, and she didn't say much. Smith started off by asking what I had been doing since I left in January. I told him how I had a great job and that the business I was working for had taken off since I joined them, I didn't mention it was my brother's business."

"That was probably wise on your part."

"He told me that was great to hear, and then he told me how much they appreciated my making the trip and that a lot of their clients had been asking about me. I told him it was nice to hear that. Then he said that they had been too quick to let me go, and they regretted the manner and the timing of it. I told him that I thought they had made a mistake, too, but life goes on."

"What did he do after that?"

"He explained what they had in mind for me if I came back, and to be honest, it was a nice offer. I let him finish and then told him I had no interest in working there."

"Oh boy, now it's getting good. What'd he do?"

"He was shocked and asked me why I had bothered to come in to talk. I looked him in the eye and said that I wanted to hear what he had to say, and I wanted to see some of the old crew. He gave me a blank look and I stood up and wished him a good day and walked out."

"Well, I guess that closes that chapter."

"It does, and it feels good."

"So tell me, are you okay with all that happened?"

"Yeah, I am. Walking into the place made me realize it's not the same place, and I'm happy where I am."

"So that was good, at least. Was that it, then? You didn't do anything else while you were in Philly?"

"Later that night I went out with some of the old gang for wings and beers."

"Who all was there?"

"Most of the people we hung out with."

"Kylie?"

"Yep."

"So is Kylie doing all right?"

He looks at me with a bit of a smile.

"She's great."

There's something there I should ask him about. I turn my bottle of beer around, stare at the label, take a swig and wait for Jack to say something else.

Jack looks at me and says, "So fill me on everything back in Missouri."

I tell him of my problem with Dave.

298

"Well, that's a nice little mess."

"Yes."

"How do you see that situation ending?" he asks.

"What do you mean?"

"It seems like someone is going to have to make the next move, and I feel like it might be you."

I sigh. "I don't know. This trip has me going back and forth on what I should do."

"Well your brother doesn't seem to see that he's caused a problem."

"Worse than that, Jack, it doesn't seem to bother him that *I* think he has, even if he doesn't. We're the Barnhart brothers, and it should mean something to him things aren't right."

"And you'll end up making it right again."

"I suppose, or maybe there's a middle ground."

"As in?"

"There'll be a time we'll be together, and without realizing it things will fall back into what they were before, and we'll just move on."

"Will you be satisfied with that?"

"I may have to be."

We finish our beers, and I'm ready to head up to my room when Jack asks how my work has been going.

"We might need another beer."

"Sounds like we do."

47

Sunday, July 27

"LADIES AND GENTLEMEN, if St. Louis is your final destination today, we want to thank you for flying Southwest."

"So, this is where we get off, I guess."

"I guess so."

I've been sitting next to a retired English professor and the two of us have talked the entire flight as if we are old friends. He's coming in to see his son, and I am coming home.

"It's always good to get home, isn't it?"

"It usually is."

He digests that for a moment, and says, "But not today?"

"No, not really."

"Well, it's hard to come back from a vacation, especially if it's been a good one."

"It was. I was all excited to go when I left last week, and now it's over."

He looks at me and says, "You are at some sort of crossroads, aren't you?"

I'd shared very little about my situation, and I'm impressed with his intuition. "I might be."

"Good luck. I think you'll figure it out."

"Thank you. I hope I do."

We leave the plane and head different directions: he to find his son, and I to find the shuttle that will take me to my car. While waiting, I text my parents to let them know I'm home. Mom texts back and asks how the trip was. I tell her I'll call when I get back to my place. I'm not quite ready for the "We're so glad you're home, how was it?" conversation.

The wait for the shuttle is short and it takes me right to my car. I spend the drive to Chesterfield reliving last week. As I do, I realize that I will be going back to New York next summer, if not sooner, which makes me feel both better and worse. Better, because it can and will happen. Worse, because it will be a whole year before it does. I make a vow to work on getting Giselle to come here, and to get it set up so that she can't say no.

As I pull in the driveway, I see Phyllis standing outside with a man that I've seen a few times before. I stop just short of his car and get out to say hello.

"Welcome back!"

"Thanks."

"Dale, I put all your mail on your kitchen counter."

"Sorry you had to do that. I should have had them hold it for me. But thanks."

"It was nothing, and everything looked okay on your side."

"Thanks again, Phyllis."

"Did you have a good time?"

301

"I had a great time."

"But it's always nice to get back home, isn't it?"

"That's what they say."

Realizing she hasn't introduced me yet, she says, "Dale, have you met Max?"

"I don't think we've been introduced."

"Max, this is my neighbor, Dale. Dale, this is my friend, Max."

We step forward and shake hands. Max is thin and fit for a guy his age. He has salt and pepper hair and a nice smile. He makes a good first impression.

"So, Phyllis what's been going on around here, besides the grass growing and needing to be cut?"

"Don't worry about that, Dale. It's your first night back. It can wait."

"I may mow it anyway. I've been sitting all day, and the activity might do me some good."

Max asks, "Wait, you mow the lawn for Phyllis?"

"I do."

Phyllis says, "I had a lawn service, but I fired them. They'd let it get way too long, and when they cut it, they left dead grass everywhere. It was a mess, and they didn't even trim. Dale told me he'd do it for me if I bought him a mower and a trimmer, so I did, and he's my lawn guy now."

I give him a sheepish look. "I actually enjoy mowing lawns, and it gives me a bit of exercise."

Max says, "Phyllis, I hope you gave him a break on his rent."

"I tried to offer him a deal, but he didn't take it."

He looks at me.

"What can I say? I like to mow."

"You may be the ideal tenant."

Phyllis says, "He is." Then she pauses for a minute and her expression changes. "Dale, I have something I need to tell you."

"Okay."

"Max has asked me to move in with him and I've said yes—*and* we plan to get married later this fall!"

"That's great, Phyllis. When is all this supposed to happen?"

"The move-in part of it will happen in August."

"August!"

"Yes, we know it's soon, but we're ready to do this and now is as good a time as any."

Max says, "I had a huge crush on this woman in high school, and I let her get away. It won't happen a second time."

"I know this is sudden, Dale. But I know it's right."

"So, what are you going to do with this place?"

"I'll take some time and get my side ready to rent. I hope to find a good tenant in the next few weeks."

"Whoever it is, they won't be as good as you, Phyllis."

"I'll do my best. It's never fun trying to find a new tenant though. You can check them out, but you don't really know much about them until they move in."

"I'm sure that's true. And after your experience with me I'm sure you will be extra cautious!"

"That's not at all true. You've been great."

I smile and try to think of what to say next, but before I do—

"Wait! I have an idea that would solve a lot of our problems. Why don't you buy my duplex?"

"You want me to buy this place?"

"Why not? Think about it. It could be home for you and an income property."

"I don't know what to say, Phyllis."

"Think about it, please. And check with your company. They handle mortgages, right?"

"Yes, they do, but I don't know if this is something I want to do right now."

"I'll give you some time. I think you should do it."

"Okay. Let me consider it."

"Please do. *Really* think about it, okay?"

"Okay. I better get inside. I need to start my laundry then get going on this lawn. You two have a nice evening, and congratulations."

"Thanks, Dale. I'm going to miss you. You've been my best tenant, and it's not even close."

"Thanks, and Max, it's nice to meet you. I hope you realize how lucky you are."

"I sure do."

I go over and give Phyllis a hug. I am happy for her, even if I will miss her.

I get in my car and pull into my garage. When I get inside my phone rings. It's Mom, of course.

"Are you home?"

"Yes, I just pulled in."

"Great. How was your trip? We want to hear all about it."

"Right now? I'd like to unpack and do some laundry."

"Well, I'm sure you have things you need to do! Anyway, that's okay because we want you to come up next weekend."

"Okay, I think I could do that, but what's the occasion?"

"Well, your brother and DJ will be moving to their new

house the week after next, so we thought it would be fun to have a dinner together to celebrate the big move, and while we are doing that you can tell us about your trip."

"Sure. That would be nice. Would Sunday be okay?"

"Sure, but you're not coming up Saturday?"

"No, Phil has talked me into entering a triathlon with him on Saturday."

"Have you ever done one of those?"

"No, but I'd like to give a try, and this one is for novices."

"That sounds like fun, I guess."

"I think it will be."

"We're looking forward to seeing you, Dale. It's been too long."

"It's just been a couple of weeks Mom."

"It's been *three* since we came down to see you, and longer than that since you've been home."

"Okay. So, church and Sunday dinner then?"

"Yes. And we want to hear all about your trip."

"I'll work on my story and try to leave you mesmerized."

Dad joins the conversation at this point, "That sounds about right."

"Hey, Dad! I didn't know Mom had me on speaker."

"Yeah, I've been listening in. Glad you're home safe and sound."

"It was a nice trip. And now, back to the real world I guess."

Dad asks, "Do you have a busy week coming up?"

"There's nothing big coming up as far as I know."

"Good. Good. Well, we will let you go. See you next Sunday."

"Sounds good. Love you two."

"And we love you."

I decide to work on laundry before mowing, so I strip off my clothes, add them to the other dirty clothes from the week, sort the pile as Mom taught me to do before I went off to college, and throw the dark stuff in the washer. I find some old shorts and a worn-out t-shirt to wear for mowing. It's gotten warmer since I got home, but I don't mind working up a sweat. Maybe it will help get me ready for next weekend's triathlon. For sure it will give me time to think about things. Without a doubt, a guy does his best thinking while operating power equipment.

While I mow, I think about Phyllis's offer and wonder why I'm not interested. There are several advantages to doing it, the main one being I'd have more control over who lives next door. If I buy the place though, it means I'm making a long-term commitment, and I am not sure that's something I want.

48

Sunday, August 4

I CHECK MY CLOCK AND IT'S ALREADY EIGHT. I never sleep this late, but yesterday's triathlon has taken a toll. I was proud that I completed all three events but know I need to train more before I do another one. Of course, the week out east didn't help. I took it easy on vacation.

I rouse myself and get out of bed, and as I do I pay the price for yesterday: Sore shoulders, abs, arms, legs—the works. I can barely get out of bed, let alone take a shower and make breakfast. But I need to power through because I've promised my parents I'll come for church and Sunday dinner, and the Barnharts keep their word.

I haven't been home since the day I tried to work things out with Dave. When they came down to see me over the Fourth, we took in some of the activities around the city. It was a nice weekend, full of things to do, and not unbearably hot. We avoided much talk of "the situation." Mom and Dad didn't bring it up, because, maybe for the first time as parents, they don't have an answer. One of our strengths as a family has always been our willingness to face tough situations head-on. Now, with two adult sons at odds, they aren't sure how to pull that off, especially since I'm not budging this time. No doubt, part of their inviting me today is the thought that church and Sunday dinner will help. Since they can't solve the situation, they hope family time together will do the trick.

I head to the shower and let the warm water wash over me; hoping it will help me feel better. As I step out of the shower, I realize I am still moving slowly, and it's getting late. I know I can't make it for church and wonder if I'm up to making the trip at all.

I wrap a towel around me and go to my bedroom to get my phone. I pick it up and call Dad. I explain to him that there is no way I'll make it for church, but I'll still try to make it for Sunday dinner. He is a little disappointed but says they will be glad to see me when I get there.

I know after talking with Dad, I can't disappoint him again, so I pop four ibuprofen tablets, hoping they'll knock back my soreness. I have a few regrets about doing what I did yesterday, but I am determined to do it again when I get the chance.

I pour a cup of coffee, fix a bowl of cereal, and sit down to breakfast. As I do my towel comes loose and drapes itself over the top of the barstool. So, here I sit, nothing on and too sore to care, hoping the breakfast and ibuprofen will help.

I slowly finish breakfast in silence, put the dishes in the sink, get dressed, and start for Spring Mill.

When I pull into my parents' driveway, the front door opens, and DJ comes out to greet me. He waits until I get stopped this time, a lesson learned from earlier this year. I scoop him up, every part of my body still smarting. He wraps his arms around my neck while I hug him and pat his back.

As I hold him, I realize how much he's grown since that day he got in trouble back in February. He's a half a year older now, so that's to be expected, but I don't like it—he shouldn't be changing this fast. Of all the parts of our problem, not seeing DJ might be the worst, and in the few seconds that hug lasts I decide it's time to square things with my brother.

Mom and Dad come out right after DJ, so I put him down and we all exchange hugs—hugging being one of the primary activities of the Barnharts.

"So, what's for dinner, Mom?"

"We're going to try something new. It's a casserole recipe I found on-line."

"Great."

"All you need to do is come in and fix the salad."

"I'm fixing the salad?"

"You always do a good job, and we can talk while you're fixing it."

"Then it looks like I'm fixing the salad!" I look down and my nephew is still standing by me. "DJ, you want to help?"

"I do!"

We go inside and make our way to the kitchen. As we pass the family room, I can hear Dave on the phone. I can't tell if it's business or personal, and I don't really need to know.

In the kitchen, Mom has everything ready for me. Since DJ wants to help, I pull a little stepstool up to the counter, and he climbs up beside me. Dad takes a seat so he can join the conversation while watching the salad being made.

DJ scans everything Mom has laid out and announces, "I don't like those."

"DJ, I tell you what, let's take some of the lettuce from this big bowl and put it in a little one for you, and then you can make your *own* salad."

"Okay!"

We find him a bowl and I put some lettuce in it. I ask him if that's enough, and he decides it is. Then I start slicing a green pepper into the grown-up's salad. I offer some to DJ, and he declines. I get the same response with a yellow pepper, mushrooms, a cucumber, and a tomato. I know before I ask, the feta cheese will be a no-go. Finally, when I offer him a carrot, he decides he would like a little bit of that on his salad, but he wants to slice it himself. I put a small piece of carrot on the cutting board and watch as he cuts it into smaller pieces. When that's done, he picks up the cutting board and dumps most of the pieces into his bowl—with the rest falling on the counter. I clean that up, then ask him what else he would like. He thinks maybe he'd be okay with some regular cheese, so I go to the fridge, find a block of mild cheddar. I cut off a slice and put it on the cutting board, and he gets to work on it. When he has enough, he dumps it all in his bowl. I pat him on the back and tell him, "Good job, buddy."

He pats my shoulder, mimicking me, and says, "Thanks, buddy."

As we finish, Dave comes in and, ignoring me, says, "What can I do to help, Mom?"

"It looks like Dale and DJ have the salad ready, and the casserole and rolls are on the table. I think we're set, except for what everyone wants to drink."

"I'll take care of that." He starts filling our glasses, and then looks at me and says, "Well, look who's here. It's good to see you, Dale."

"You, too."

It's a generic sort of greeting, but it's a start.

DJ takes his salad and sits down, while I take the adults' salad to the table. The rest of us take our seats and Dad says a brief prayer. He doesn't always do this, so it marks this meal as a special occasion. Maybe Dad's decided I need to do penance for missing church. Maybe it's his plea for family harmony. Maybe he's thankful we're all together. And just maybe it's all the above.

———

I barely get started on my salad when Mom and Dad pepper me with questions about my recent trip. I try to keep my answers short. Still, the recap takes most of our meal. Dave doesn't say much, and that might be a good thing. Normally he would pick something—some specific detail, and like brothers everywhere, give me grief about it, but not today. Maybe it's because we're off to a good start and he doesn't want to jeopardize it. Or perhaps he's just not that interested.

When I finish, I decide to toss him a bone.

"So enough about me. Tell me about your new place."

"Well, we just closed on it last week, so I'm just getting started on what I want to get done. I've only got a few days between closing and move-in, so I'm having to re-prioritize. I'll do what has to be done before we move in and finish the rest afterwards. It's not ideal, but I'll make it work."

I ask him what needs to be done before the move, and he spends what's left of our meal together telling me.

"That's quite a list. Are you doing it all by yourself?"

"No, I've had a little help from some guys I've helped in the past and Sarah helped me yesterday."

"That's nice."

Dad says, "Dave, you should take your brother to see it after we eat."

"Do you want to see it?"

"Sure."

"Okay then."

We get up and start clearing the table, and I remember I haven't told them about Phyllis and the duplex.

"I forgot! I might have some news."

Mom says, "Could you hold that for a minute? I baked some cookies, and we have ice cream. You could tell us during dessert."

"Sure, Mom. No problem."

We finish clearing the table while she gets our desserts ready. She knows us well; the Barnhart Boys love cookies and ice cream—all of us, since birth.

We sit down with our desserts and while we enjoy them, I fill them in on Phyllis's offer to sell the place to me.

Dad says, "So, what do you think?"

Before I can tell him I probably won't buy it, Dave says, "I don't know. Rental properties can be a pain, especially if you get a bad tenant."

"Well, I guess that would be my problem, Dave."

I get a frosty, "Yes, I guess it would be. I was just trying to say that in my line of work I've talked with a lot of landlords, and I hear about their problems all the time."

"I'm aware there can be problems, but I think maybe I can handle anything that I'd need to take care of."

"Okay, just wanted to share what I knew."

"Okay, you did, but I don't remember you asking me for advice while you were looking for your house."

"No, I didn't."

Any progress we made has just been lost, and it is my fault. The fact that he's buying his second house and seemed to feel I'm not even capable of buying my first place was too much for me. And on top of that, now I'm wondering if I should go ahead and buy the duplex.

We finish dessert and Dad says, "You boys clear the table. Your mom, DJ, and I are going to take the dog for a walk."

Walking Duff is usually my job, but Dad is doing this to give us a chance to regroup.

Dave says, "We can do that, and when we finish, I'll pull up pictures of the new house and show Dale."

Things have changed in the last couple of minutes, and I'm no longer getting a tour. Dad and Mom notice, but they don't comment.

Dad gets Duff ready for his walk, and within a couple of minutes, the four of them are out the door. Since It's already heating up outside, it will be a short one; lasting no longer than it takes for Duff to do his job.

Without a lot of conversation, Dave and I get the dishes to the sink, where he goes to work rinsing them and putting them in the dishwasher. I take charge of putting away the leftover food. Before long, we have everything done.

I take a seat at the island and check out things on my phone.

Dave sees me waiting, gets his laptop from the other room, and comes to the table to join me. He opens his realtor's site and locates his house. The first few images are exterior views of the house and yard. As I see them, I recognize the place, having been by there a few times over the years. I didn't pay a lot of attention to it before; after all it was just another old house, but as he shows me around, I can see why he likes it. It's a cute little bungalow on a neat old street and located just south of Grant Park. It's old, but the pictures show it to be well-loved.

"Dave, it looks like a great house and a great location. I have to say though, I thought you'd be buying something a little newer."

As I say that, I realize my comment could sound negative and make things worse. To his credit, Dave keeps us where we need to be, "I had a lot of help when I was house-hunting. My advisors all really liked this one, so I went with it."

"I assume you got it for a good price?"

"I think I did. I didn't steal it, but the price was fair, and I got a couple of things thrown in before we signed the contract."

I think about Dave and DJ moving out and realize it will be a big change for my parents when they do.

"This place is going to be quiet when you two leave. I bet Dad and Mom will miss you."

"I think you might be right, and to be honest we'll miss them. I don't know what I would have done without them these past few months. They helped when I was late getting home, or when I had to go on an emergency call, and sometimes when I just needed a little break."

"They love DJ, and I'm sure they haven't minded and will still do that when you need it."

"True, but he and I need to get on with the next phase of our lives, and this new house is going to be the right place for it. Of course, Grant Park is close, and DJ loves that."

I can tell Dave's happy to be making this move, and, although I am a bit jealous, I find I feel more happy than envious. We've had a bit of moment here—a comeback from what happened few minutes before—and I feel like now might be the time to settle things between us: a time to make things better. Before I can say anything, he has a question for me.

"So, you had a great time out east."

"I did."

"You saw all your old friends?"

"Yep."

"Including, and I'll try to get their names right, Martha and Giselle?"

"Actually, it's Mariah and Giselle."

"So, how'd it go with them?"

"It went fine, and why the sudden interest?"

"Can't I just be interested in my older brother's romantic life?"

"Yes, you can. It's not like you, but you can."

He has a little smile.

"Dave, I feel like there's a little more to your question than an interest in my love life."

He's quiet; thinking carefully about what he wants to say.

"Okay, there is more to it, and here's the deal. I was hoping that maybe you'd get something going with someone and you'd get over obsessing about Sarah and me.

It's time for you to move on, Dale. All you're doing is making Mom, Dad and Sarah unhappy at this point."

"But not you?"

"No. I'm not unhappy, I'm just irritated. You need to get over this."

"So, let me get this straight. You're saying that it's time for me get over you and Sarah?"

"Yes, you got it. That is exactly what I am saying."

"Well, first of all, it's not you and Sarah, it's just you. And the funny thing is I was just about to tell you that I'm ready to let it go, and now you've ruined the moment."

"Me! What the hell did I do?"

"Hmmmm. Where to start? Okay here goes—"

As I start to explain, Mom and Dad walk in.

"Wow! It's a scorcher out there. Was it this hot yesterday when you did that triathlon thing?"

I want to finish what I started to say to Dave, but I can't do that with our parents and DJ around.

"Yeah, Dad. It was. Luckily, the last event was swimming, so I got to cool down some."

Dave says, "I don't know why you'd want to do something like that."

"I don't know, Dave. Maybe just to compete . . . or to test myself. Either way, I enjoyed it."

"But you said you're sore today."

"I really am."

"Doing something that makes you sore that you don't have to do doesn't seem too smart, if you ask me."

"Well, I don't believe anyone did."

Luckily for me the others are here, because I know what Dave would say next if they weren't.

The room gets quiet—uncomfortably quiet.

Dad tries to break the tension. "Hey, let's play some Rack-O. It's been a while."

I'm not interested in playing games, but I love my parents and I know Dad is just trying to cut the tension.

"Sounds good, Dad."

Dave declines the offer saying he needs to go do some work on his house, and he wants to know if he can leave DJ here with us.

"Sure. He can help his uncle Dale."

"You want to help me, DJ?"

"I do!"

Dave closes his computer, gets up to leave and is quickly out the door. Any opportunity that existed earlier is gone, and this time it's on him.

Mom brings in the card game and we take a seat at the table, with DJ on my lap. I hear Dave's truck start as he gets ready to go to his new place. I wonder if he's going alone, then ask myself why it matters.

Dad deals first and DJ helps me put the cards in my rack. As we play, I tell him what card I want pulled. He discards it and inserts the new card in its place. We play several hands and he and I win a couple. He gives me a fist bump when we do. When we don't win, he tells me we'll win the next one.

After an hour, he gets tired of playing. My legs, which were sore earlier, have now grown numb from his sitting on my lap, so I'm happy to call it quits. I look at the clock, and, although it's not that late, I think I'm ready to make the drive back to my place.

I stand, try to get the blood going in my legs again, and say, "Well, guys, this has been fun, but I think I'll take off."

"So soon? It seems like you just got here."

"I know, Mom, but I might try to mow the lawn tonight. It's been a week and I want to get it done."

Dad says, "I still don't know why you agreed to do that; and for no money!"

"You're the last person who should give me a hard time about that! You're like the king of yard work!"

"He has you there, dear. Honey, why don't you at least stay and have some more casserole? There'll be plenty of daylight when you get back and it will be cooler."

I know she's right, and I know that if I leave now, it's because I'm frustrated with Dave. I haven't been home in weeks, and I need to stay a little longer.

"I tell you what, Mom. You put some of that casserole in a container for me to take, and I'll hold off going for a bit."

Mom takes the deal.

She gets up to work on my take-home, and says, "I'd like a soda. Anyone else thirsty?"

"Yeah, I'll take one if you have any."

I know she does from putting food away after lunch. She grabs a couple out of the fridge, one for me and one for her. Dad prefers water. DJ gets some apple juice and entertains himself with his toys while the adults sit at the kitchen table and talk. We talk about everything. We talk about *The Gazette*, about the latest local news, and about politics. We share some family memories; and it all helps to make up for how the rest of the day has gone.

When the conversation finally starts to lag, I look at my phone and check the time. I tell my parents it really is time to go now. Mom gets up to make sure I take the casserole and salad that she prepared. My evening meal is set. I'll enjoy it after mowing—that is, if I do mow. It's oppressively hot by now, and it's supposed to rain tomorrow and cool off, so I maybe I should wait.

I say good-bye to my parents and give DJ a big hug and get ready to leave. As I back out of the driveway, the three of them have come out to wave goodbye. I'm almost out of the drive when Dad signals me to stop.

I stop and roll down my window. He walks up to me and says, "Why don't you come up again next weekend?"

"Dad, I'm going to wait until Dave and DJ are completely moved. How about two weeks from now instead?"

"Two weeks?"

"Yes, but I have an idea. Why don't you and Mom come with DJ to my place and stay next weekend? It would help Dave if he doesn't have DJ to worry about while he's moving."

"DJ might be staying with his other grandparents, but if not, we'll take you up on it."

"Please do. I've got the second bedroom set up now, so there's a better sleeping situation for you. DJ can sleep on the sofa-bed."

"Knowing your nephew, he'll want to sleep with you instead."

"Yeah, I know, and that would be okay. My ribs have recovered enough for another night with him. Oh, and bring Duff too if you want."

"We'll come for sure, and we'll let you know about DJ."

"Great. See you soon either way."

As I make my drive home, it dawns on me that Dave didn't ask me to help him move. He helped me move back to Missouri at the end of January, and I should return the favor. I debate whether to call him. Instead, I text him.

E.N. Klinginsmith

Do you need me to
come and help you
move next weekend?

There's no answer for a few minutes, and then:

No, I'm good. Thanks for asking.

I owe you one for
helping me in
January.

It's okay. I was glad to get you
home.

It was a big deal and I
appreciated it.

Glad to do it.

49

Wednesday, August 14

I step in her door and yell, "Anyone here?"

Phyllis calls out, "Yes, "I'm back here."

When I get to her empty bedroom, I see her standing there with a box in her arms.

"Here, let me take that for you."

She hands me the box.

"Is this it?" I ask.

"Yes, it's the last one."

"It looked like your movers were loading the last of your big stuff when I walked by just now."

"Yes. We're almost done."

"You excited?"

"Yes, and just a little sentimental."

"I guess we always feel that way when we move."

"I suppose so." She looks around. "It's not like I'm leaving lots of memories behind. I only lived here a couple of years, but still."

"I think this place was important to you. You had a rough time before you came here, and when you bought the duplex and then took over the daycare business, I think you proved to yourself you were going to be okay."

"Your analysis is good."

"No charge. I owed you something after all of the times you listened to me these past few months."

"I'm sorry it hasn't gotten better for you."

"It's getting there. I'm sure we'll be fine in time. I mean, eventually I'll just get tired of feeling mistreated."

"Well, it wouldn't be the best outcome, but it would get things back to where they were."

"I don't know if we'll ever get *there*, but we might get close."

We start down the hallway of the now empty unit. I know that plans are for the painters to come in soon and get it ready for the young couple that will be moving in. Phyllis has a niece who was recently married and they're moving here.

"I met my new neighbors the other day."

"What did you think?"

"They were nice, and I'll be lucky to have them next door. Not as lucky as I have been these last six months, but lucky."

"Oh, it will be good. They're closer to your age. Maybe you can do some couple's things with them."

"That would require a little work on my end, Phyllis."

She smiles at me. "I'm sorry. I didn't mean that to come across the wrong way."

"Oh, it didn't at all. No apology needed."

"Have you heard anything from your friend in New York?"

"You are not going to believe this, but I've talked her into coming here for a few days in October!"

"Great!"

"Yeah. I was sure she wouldn't do it, but I bought her a round-trip ticket, and she couldn't say no."

"Ahh, good plan," Phyllis approves.

"As it turns out."

"I can tell you're excited about it."

"I am. I had a chance to see her hometown last month, so now it's my turn to show her where I live."

"And you hope she'll like it."

"I know she will."

We step outside and I hand the box to one of the guys. He walks up the ramp and finds a spot for it.

"So, Phyllis, I will see you around."

"You will. I'll be here on the second of each month if I don't already have your rent check!"

I smile at her little joke. "Maybe I won't pay you just so you'll have to come by."

"I will be here during the updates to make sure things are going well for the kids."

"Okay, please make sure at least a couple of those times are outside of working hours, so I can say hi."

"I'll do that. And you have to bring your friend by when she comes to see you."

"Definitely. I want you two to meet."

And with that, I give Phyllis a hug and get ready to go to my side. I'll see her again, but the next time I do she won't be my neighbor, and it won't be the same.

Before I get too far, she calls out, "Are you still thinking about buying this place?"

"It depends on the day, Phyllis. Give me a couple more weeks to think about it, okay?"

I don't want to tell her that I will be moving on from Morgan*Plus* someday, and I don't know if I want to take on a mortgage payment until I figure some things out.

50

Saturday, October 12

GISELLE AND I ARE ON THE ROAD to Spring Mill. She came in Wednesday night, and I've spent the last two days giving her a whirlwind tour of St. Louis. I saved the trip to meet my parents for today.

"For some reason, I thought you lived closer to your parents."

"It's not too far: only seventy-five minutes from my place to theirs on a good day."

"I look forward to meeting them."

"You'll like them, and I know they'll like you."

I look at her. Knowing my parents—two people have never met a person with whom they couldn't hold an extended conversation—I think our afternoon and evening together will be okay. If not, Giselle has an early flight tomorrow, and we can use that as an excuse to leave early.

"So, tell me, have you enjoyed these last three days?"

"Every minute of it! The farthest west I've ever been before was Gettysburg. It's nice here, and the weather's been great. The trees are beautiful. Ours are already starting to lose their fall color."

"Okay, we've established that the weather and the scenery have been good. Anything else you've liked?"

"Obviously getting to see the Arch. I've seen it in pictures a hundred times, but it's much more impressive in person."

"Annnnd?"

"Oh! The Italian food at that place on the Hill was great."

"And the toasted ravioli?"

"Not really a fan of that."

"So to recap: the weather, the Arch, Italian food on the Hill. Nothing else?"

"One more thing! I thought that old courthouse was interesting. You were a good guide. I remember hearing about Dred Scott in school, but that's about all I remembered. I learned a lot. You could teach history, I think."

"Lord help the kids if I did."

I get the laugh I was looking for, and it feels good.

"I hate to think you're going home tomorrow. It seems like you just got here."

"Well, at least I've spent three days. As you will recall, I just got a night and a morning with you."

"Okay. I concede this round."

"Then you owe me a couple more days."

"And I will make that good, I promise."

"It can't be next fall. It has to be sooner."

She spends the rest of our drive trying to think of reasons

I should come see her sooner than September. Finally, she settles on her graduation in May, and I have to say yes to that.

We pull into my parents' driveway around two. I'm a little surprised they aren't standing outside waiting for us. Knowing them, they are probably just inside the front door. When we make it to the door, they are right where I pictured them.

"Mom, Dad, this is my friend Giselle. Giselle, these are my parents, Dale and Pat Barnhart."

"Dale Barnhart? I think I might know another guy with that same name."

Dad smiles and says, "Yes, but I bet he's not nearly as good-looking as me."

"Oh, I don't know about that, but I can see where he gets his good looks."

And she's off to a good start.

"Come on in Giselle. We are so happy to finally meet you. Dale has told us so much about you."

I worry that maybe she doesn't like the idea that she has been the subject of our conversations. But Giselle says, "Well, that's nice to hear."

So, I guess I needn't have worried.

"Come in. Would you like something cold to drink?"

We decide that iced tea sounds good, and Mom goes to the kitchen to get some tea for everyone. Giselle follows her to help; her stock rising by the minute.

Dad and I take a seat in the family room.

"She's cute, Dale, and seems really nice. I can see why you like her."

I give him a smile in return.

When Mom and Giselle come in with our tea, we start talking and the conversation flows easily, as I knew it would. They want to know more about her than what I've told them. They ask her about her hometown, which leads to her life story. I had told them that she was born in Paris when her dad worked there for a short time, which is why she has such an unusual name. They know she lived in Upstate New York with her mother, sister, and brother. Giselle fills in the blanks for them, including the difficult years when her dad was battling terminal cancer.

Of course, Mom wants to hear Giselle's version of how we met, so she asks about that.

"I had a close friend from high school, and she and I continued to be close through community college. One day, we were talking and decided we should move to a city and try living there for a few years. We'd spent most of our lives in Pleasant Valley, and we needed to branch out a little. I made a list of cities I'd be willing to try, and she did the same. Philadelphia was the highest-ranking city on both our lists."

"So, you just picked up and moved there?"

"Sort of, yes. We went there over spring break of our last year at Valley Community College and applied for jobs we thought we'd like. We each got offered a job; mine was at the bank, and we went back down a couple weeks later and found an affordable apartment close to our jobs. We moved in right after we graduated Community College, and I spent the next two years being a teller at the bank where Dale and I met. I decided I didn't have any future in the bank and what I really wanted to do was be a nurse. So, when I got accepted at St. Agatha's I moved back home, enrolled in school, and I'll finish next May."

Mom says, "That's quite a story. Dale did something similar. He told us he wanted to try living somewhere besides Missouri, so he went there to go to graduate school. We thought he'd eventually come back here though, and happily for us, he did."

"Yeah, it is a bit similar."

"So, you two have that in common."

I say, "We do. And we both left at about the same time, so there's that, too."

Giselle nods her head, then finishes her tea, and I think it's time for a change of pace.

"Okay, you two have asked all the questions you're allowed for one day. Why don't we show her Spring Mill?"

Everyone likes the idea, so we pile in Dad's car and off we go. Dad has decided to drive and be our guide, which is a good thing. He knows and loves this town more than anyone. We make Giselle sit up front so that she'll get the best view of things. I take a seat in back with Mom. After a few minutes, I realize there isn't a lot of leg room for a guy over six-foot-two. Dad has found about a dozen more landmarks to show us than I realized we had, causing the trip to be longer than expected, and I am starting to cramp. Finally, we reach the Spring Mill parking lot, and I'm the first to get out for the walking tour.

The old mill is one of the few scenic spots in our area. In the last part of the nineteenth and early twentieth centuries, the mill was active. People brought grain there to be turned in flour and feed. The city took over the property and turned it into a park several years ago. They got it just in time to rescue the two-story building before it fell completely into ruin. The mill was shored up and painted a red that was its original color, based on the few bits of paint still found on its exterior.

The spring that powered the mill is not a big one by Missouri standards, but at one time it was one of the larger ones north of the Missouri River. Something of a geologic nature happened before I was born, maybe a shift in the limestone due to a small earthquake, and that has restricted the amount of water that comes out of the ground. Still, there's enough flow to turn the old wheel. If you allow your mind free rein, you can picture the wheel turning more quickly and hear the old millstone doing work inside.

"This is so pretty. I wondered how your town got its name. Thanks for bringing me here."

"So, tell me, G, which place do you think is prettier, our old mill or the Holman Hotel?"

"That's not fair! You're putting me on the spot."

"It's okay. Be honest."

"Well, I like them both. Of course, I'm going to be partial to the one in my hometown."

Mom says, "Tell me about it."

I say, "I'll do better than that, Mom. I took some pics of it when we were there."

I get out my phone and pull up pictures from my trip. She agrees the place is pretty and insists on seeing other pictures I took while there. Giselle has to see them, too. It's another ten minutes before I can get my phone back.

We stop by a couple more places and it's time to go home.

"That was fantastic. Thanks so much for the tour."

Dad asks, "So how do you like our little town?"

I have this moment where I flash back to Giselle and her mom asking me the same question.

"I like it. It's interesting how towns seem to take on a personality just like people."

Mom asks, "How would you describe the personality of Spring Mill?"

"Well, I think it feels warm and friendly, and a nice place to live."

I know my folks love hearing that.

———————

We make it back home, and Dad lets us out, then parks the car in the garage. I suggest that it's a good time to take Giselle on a tour of the yard. My parents have spent time and money, and it looks great. They could be landscapers if they ever wanted to start second careers, and Giselle is duly impressed.

As we finish our walkabout, I ask my folks if they'd like G and me to take Duff for a walk, and they think that's a great idea. In no time, we have the dog leashed and we're on our way.

"The spring and old mill were pretty."

"But, not as nice as Riverside Park."

"Maybe not quite, but they were close."

We make it to a corner and wait for a car to pass. The driver and passenger give us the once over. They probably live in the neighborhood and are trying to figure out who the strangers are. It's funny, because they slow down and could not be any more obvious as they check us out. Finally, I wave at them and give them an exaggerated hello. Startled by this, they give me a feeble wave and speed off.

I say, "Wonder if we passed approval."

"Well, they took their time checking us out."

"Speaking of approval, you definitely passed the test with my folks."

"I didn't know it was a test! I like them too, and I'm so glad I got to meet them."

"Good. Hopefully, you like everyone and everything enough that you will want to come back."

"I do, for sure."

We keep walking around the neighborhood when I see a pickup that I recognize as my brother's passing us. He's obviously heading to my parents, and he's not alone. He honks and waves as he goes by. I give him a courtesy wave.

"Who was that?" Giselle asks.

"My brother and Sarah."

"Your brother?"

"Yes. And Sarah, I believe, and maybe DJ in the back. I couldn't tell for sure."

"Do you think they're going to your parents?"

"Most likely."

"Did you know they were coming?"

"I did not."

"Are you okay with it?" She sounds worried.

"I'll have to be. You'll like Sarah, and if DJ's with them, you'll get to meet that little guy. Sarah and DJ will almost make up for meeting Dave."

51

WE WALK IN THE DOOR and find Dave, Sarah, and DJ standing in the front foyer talking with Dad and Mom.

I say, "Hi, guys. I didn't know you were coming."

Sarah has a look of apology, so Dave takes over. "We kind of invited ourselves. We wanted to meet your friend. I hope you don't mind."

Giselle says, "Of course he doesn't, and I was hoping I'd get a chance to meet the three of you."

She holds out her hand. "I'm Giselle."

"Nice to meet you. I'm Dave, the younger, better-looking Barnhart, and this is my friend, Sarah, and my son, DJ."

Giselle shakes hands with the adults, and DJ, seeing that's the thing to do, extends his hand.

Dad says, "Maybe we should take this to the family room."

When we get there, Giselle sits beside me, then DJ insists on sitting between us, so we make room for him. He sits as close to Giselle as he can. She doesn't mind at all.

Of course, Sarah and Dave want to know all about Giselle, and she has to repeat everything she shared with my parents earlier. To her credit, she does it willingly and well.

Next, they want to know what she's done since she got here, and she tells that story for the second time this afternoon. Finally, Sarah wants to hear how she and I met. I am beginning to wish I had recorded our earlier question and answer session with Mom and Dad.

By the time she's retold everything and, in turn, asked some questions of Dave and Sarah, it's time to eat. Mom and Dad's dining room is nice, if a little dated. We don't eat there often, and when we do it's a special occasion. There are seven chairs at the table, and one that won't be needed is pulled off to the side. The empty seat reminds me that Alex isn't here, so I ask about him. Sarah tells me he's playing with his cousins at the Marshalls.

Mom directs us to our seats. She has given this some thought, I can tell, and we go where we are assigned. I'm sitting next to her, and on her other side is Dave. DJ is between his father and Sarah. Giselle is to my right and the girls are on either side of Dad. I know Mom really wants to sit next to Sarah and Giselle, but she has made the sacrifice, knowing her sitting between us will keep Dave and me in line.

Sarah and Giselle hit it off. They have a lot in common, starting with their being in school and scheduled to graduate in May. Each is interested in the other's college experience, and they compare notes.

Their conversation gets most interesting, at least to me, when they talk about what they plan to do *after* graduation. Sarah plans to interview near her hometown, and with schools near Spring Mill. Many of those districts have good schools where jobs are hard to get, so she's going to schedule as many interviews as she can to help her chances.

"And what about you, Giselle? Where do you want to work when you finish school?"

I don't know if it's coincidental or intentional, but for whatever reason everyone grows quiet when Dad asks that question, and all attention is now on Giselle.

"Well, of course I hope I've already lined up a job by graduation."

Mom says, "I'm sure you will. They need nurses everywhere."

Sarah presses the issue, "And do you have a place in mind? Do you want to work near your hometown? Back in Philadelphia? Or somewhere different?"

"Well, I've spent most of my savings on school, so it will be tempting to stay with my mom for the first year. That way I can save enough money to get my own place."

Dad says, "That's practical."

"Of course, I would like to be able to move out and be on my own sooner than that. I'll be twenty-five, and no one wants to live with their parents at that age."

We all look at Dave, because he has just moved out of Mom and Dad's house. He has to say something in his own defense.

"Okay. I think my situation was a little different, and I'm out now. Cut me a little slack, here."

I feel the need to pile on a little. "Well, it could have been worse. You could have been living in Mom and Dad's basement."

"That's true, but like I said I've got my own place now. And while we're on the topic of living situations, what are you doing about that duplex?"

"I told Phyllis I wasn't interested, and it turns out she may sell it to her niece. She and her husband have moved in the other half."

Sarah says, "How long do you plan to stay there, Dale?"

"I need to figure out what I'm going to do workwise before I think about where I'll live."

Mom says, "Well, there will be plenty of opportunities for you around here."

Dad adds, "And you know I need someone to take over *The Gazette*."

He never misses an opportunity to bring that up, and to be honest, there are days I think about it. Then I realize I'm not a journalist, and newspapers are struggling. Why would I want to take that on?

Sarah says, "You'd be good at that."

Dave says, "Well, he should be good at something."

Context is everything when you think about it. Before June, he could have made that remark and it would just have been part of our being the Brothers Barnhart. On most nights since June, I would have taken exception to it, and come back with a shot of my own. Tonight, as I hear it, it feels more like the old Dave and Dale.

"Speaking of good, Mom, dinner was great."

Everyone joins in complimenting her, and there's a little extra enthusiasm as they do, probably to make sure Dave hasn't started something with his snark.

Dad says, "Okay, men, let's clear the table, and give these three beautiful women have some time to talk."

336

Mom likes the idea. "That sounds great. There's fresh coffee and I'll take a cup. Sarah and Giselle, are either of you interested?"

Both are, so I am assigned the task of getting it for them, while Dave, Dad, and DJ get to work cleaning up.

Dave says that he and DJ will work on the dishes if Dad takes care of everything else. While they get started, I get out some coffee mugs, fill them, check with the women on their cream and sugar choices, then quietly serve them. They are in the middle of talking about some medical drama they all like, and I'm not sure they even know I'm there.

When I get back to the kitchen, Dad's sitting at the island across from Dave, who's rinsing dishes then handing them to DJ. The little guy carefully takes each dish then stacks it in the dishwasher. Dave checks on his work periodically and helps him organize whenever it's needed. Dad sips his coffee while they work. He looks at me as I enter and gives me a wink and a contented smile.

"Well, Mom is happy. After all these years with us, she finally has some women to talk to, and they all like the same TV show. Dave, I'm not so sure, but I think she might trade you and me for the girls."

"Could you blame her?"

Dad says, "I couldn't."

Dave looks at me and says, "It's been nice to have the real you back with us."

"The real me?"

"You know what I mean."

"I guess."

"C'mon. You've been angry since June. It's good to see you back like you were."

"And what if I'm not totally *back?*"

"You should be! Giselle's nice. You have something good there."

Once again, I want to tell him how he's missing the mark, but if he hasn't cared to figure it out by now, why go down that path again? It has been a nice evening for everyone, and there's nothing to gain by revisiting the same argument.

"She's great, no doubt."

"Think you can talk her into moving here?"

His question catches me off guard, and I don't know that I have a good answer for him.

Dad says, "That might be getting a little ahead of things, Dave."

"Well, Dad, you know Dale. When he's ready to propose, he pops the question."

The room gets quiet, and Dad's expression tells me I'm not the only one who sees how inappropriate Dave has been. Dad knows he needs to step in.

"That was out of line."

"Why? I wasn't wrong. It's kind of what he does. I mean he went to Gettysburg one weekend with Giselle, and he was ready to marry her. He never even had a date with Sarah and went to her house to tell her he was going to propose."

"Out of line, Son."

"Okay, okay. I'm sorry, but I'm not wrong."

I say, "No, Dave, you never are."

For a moment, we were right there. Again. And now—this.

"Why is everybody quiet?" DJ pipes up.

His granddad answers, "We've run out of things to talk about."

"Oh."

At this point, I don't see any reason to hang around. "Well, as fun as this has been, I need to get Giselle back to my place. She has an early flight, so we should hit the road."

Dad says, "We hate to see you leave so soon, but I can't blame you."

I go in and the three women are still happily engaged in conversation. I listen to them for a moment, hating to interrupt, but when Giselle sees me, she can tell something's on my mind.

"Is it time to go?"

"Yeah, we probably need to get you back to my place. You have a long day ahead of you tomorrow."

She stands up and begins the ritual of saying goodbye to Mom and Sarah. Giselle tells them how nice it has been to meet them. Mom and Sarah feel the same. Mom gets more compliments for the dinner. Then the guys come in and the noise level picks up. I enjoy the scene and let it go on for a few minutes, then I know I need to bring it to an end. I go to Mom and hug her goodbye, then Dad. DJ wants a hug, too, and I'm not saying no to that. I smile at Sarah and Dave and say my good-byes to them.

We're not too far down the road when Giselle says, "Thank you for today. I had a great time meeting everyone."

"Good. I hoped you would."

"Could I ask you something?"

"Sure."

"Did something happen in the kitchen?"

"Why do you ask?" I glance at her.

"You didn't look all that happy when you came in to get me, and I didn't really think it was that late."

"It was nothing big. Dave's always going to be Dave. It's amazing, really. He's on his best behavior all evening, and then he . . ."

"He what?"

"You know what? It was a great day, let's not ruin it."

"That sounds like a good plan."

After a few moments of silence, during which I've gotten us to US 61 and headed south, she says, "You know, I've enjoyed being here with you, meeting your family and seeing parts of you I hadn't seen before."

"Well, I like everything about you being here, too."

We have a few more moments of silence where I'm sure both of us are thinking about the day, or maybe about having to say good-bye tomorrow, or maybe both.

She says, "Dale, do you think we have a future?"

I look at her and laugh a little.

"Why are you laughing?

"Dave just accused me of being the guy who rushes things, and you're the one who's asking me about our future!"

"You didn't answer me."

I pause, choosing my words carefully and say, "I can't imagine a future without you."

"That's nice to hear."

"But the problem is, I can't picture where it would be."

I think I've confused her. She turns from looking at me to staring at the road ahead. I look at her and she is doing this little thing with her bottom lip she does when she's deep in thought or worried.

"You okay over there?"

"I am. I was thinking about what you just said."

"Well, can you see yourself living in Missouri?"

She says, "Can you see *yourself* living in New York?"

It's a stalemate, and I need to break it.

"So, Philadelphia, then."

"Oh, good God no!"

"I feel the same, and I don't know where that leaves us."

"Well, let's not worry about that now. I've had a great time with you, and you're coming to see me in May. That's all we need to focus on tonight, right?"

"Right."

After a few more miles, she says, "Dale, you know your brother and Sarah are going to get married?"

"How do you know that? Did she say something?"

"No. Just watching them together tonight. I can tell."

For some ridiculous reason, it bothers me to hear that. I take stock, realize who I have in the car with me, think how lucky I am she's here, and let it go.

"Yeah, I'm sure you're right."

"Had you not thought about that?"

"Maybe some, but it wasn't something I'd spent a lot of time on. I feel like whatever happens—happens at this point."

"So, you'll be okay with it."

"Sure. Why wouldn't I be?"

"Good. I needed to hear that."

52

Sunday, October 13

I ROLL OVER AND SAY, "TIME TO GET UP."

I get a sleepy, "I know," in return.

"You want to stay in bed for a couple more minutes?"

"Yes. Do you mind?"

"No. I'll go turn the coffee on and grab a quick shower."

I slide out of bed, go to the kitchen, crank up the coffee maker, and set out two mugs. A guy could get used to this.

Half an hour later, we're across from each other at my little kitchen table.

"I've had a great time, Dale."

As I look at her, I try to think of an original response—something better than just saying, "me too."

So I say, "It went too fast."

That's not better, but it's how I feel.

"I'm already looking forward to your coming to New York in May."

"I am too, but seven months feels like a long way off."

Another sip of coffee, a bite of bagel, a moment of silence, each of us trying to think of something to say that will lift our gloom.

"You can drop me off outside at the airport. You don't need to park and come in with me this morning."

"Are you sure? That's going to make our time even shorter. I can park and come in with you."

"No, I like it this way. It's quick and clean and defined. If you come inside, we'll talk, and it will be awkward, because we'll have to figure out how and when to bring it all to an end. I'd rather just pull off the band aid. Anyway, I'll call you tonight."

"Promise?"

"Yes, I promise."

I drop her off as she requested and watch her go inside. She was right, as usual; it was a better way to do it. As I make my way home, I'm thinking about our time together, I'm thinking about next spring, and then my thoughts turn to something I have planned for this afternoon. I get a call and answer without checking, "Hi! Did you make it through security?"

"Hi, Dale."

"Oh. Hi, Mom. I thought it was Giselle."

"So, you've dropped her off at the airport?"

343

"Yes, and I'm on my way home."

"Your father is taking me to see your grandmother, and we wanted to know if you'd like to ride with us. She'd love to see you."

"I'd love to, but I have something planned."

"Something planned?"

"Yes. A work project."

"Work? On Sunday?"

"I think I found a golf property for Morgan*Plus*. I'm going by to check it out this afternoon. I don't want them to know about it yet. I want to see it before I pitch the idea to them."

"Tell us about it."

"Well, it's out west of Pacific on I-44. And it has enough land adjacent to it that they could get their housing development, too."

"It's already a golf course?"

"Yes, and that's the beauty of it. The company who built it got overextended on some other properties and they need to move this one. I found it the same day it got listed, called them immediately, and scheduled a visit. If this works, the company will be years and money ahead of where they would have been with the Walker Place."

"Well, that should polish your star a little."

"It should, but I'm more interested in, how shall I say this, in winning the whole argument about Walker Farm, you know? Proving to them that I was right all along."

"Will they ever admit it if this turns out this is a better deal?"

"Most likely not. And you know what? If they don't, then that seals the deal for me. It'll be time to move on for sure."

"Oh gosh, I don't like hearing that. Still, I hope this works out for you. Will you call us later and fill us in?"

"I will, and you can tell me about your day with Gramma Spencer."

"We'll do that. Good luck."

When I make it back to my place, I have some time to kill, so I strip the guest bed and throw the sheets in the laundry. It's a Barnhart thing. My mother would have our guests' sheets and towels in the washer before their car had cleared our driveway. Maybe it's a way to cope with a quiet house.

While my washer is doing its thing, I find some leftover food in the fridge and make myself a quick lunch. As I munch on my sandwich, I pull up the website of the golf course, and it looks nice, from what I can tell. I'm not a golfer, so I might not be the best judge, but the pictures make it look like a place folks would want to play, and a place that Larry Morgan might like.

I check out the websites of other courses in the immediate vicinity and find several. If the websites are any indication, I'd say the one I'm going to look at ranks somewhere in the middle.

I finish my sandwich, put my dishes in the sink, then move the sheets to the dryer. I have time for a quick bathroom stop before I make the forty-five-minute drive to Belle Prairie Golf Club.

53

Monday, October 21

I CAN'T BELIEVE IT'S BEEN A WEEK since Giselle flew home. Even though she was only here a few days, I became accustomed to having her around, and my place seems so quiet and dull without her. I'm already looking forward to May and wondering if I should wait that long. Most likely I will, but it wouldn't take much to convince me to go there before her graduation weekend.

At least I had the golf course project to occupy my attention at work last week. Today's the big day. Today I should find out if Larry is going to make his move.

I got to work early this morning, and neither Larry nor Cooper were in yet. It's unusual that Larry wouldn't be in by nine, but not so much for Cooper. I'm anxious to hear what they have to say. They went to Belle Prairie on Friday to take a second look at the place. I expected to hear from them over the weekend, and I think no response from them is an indication that things didn't go well. I don't want to think that, but it's hard not to.

I'm sitting in my dreary little office, which I have grown to dislike more each day, and sifting through emails and news, more to pass the time than from any need to attend to them. I lean back and think about the last few days, trying to see where I might have gone wrong or failed to do something that would have won the day.

On Sunday, after dropping G off at the airport and taking care of a few things at home, I made my way to Belle Prairie Golf where I met Brian, the course operations manager. Brian and I bonded immediately. He's slightly younger than I am, and, in his shorts and polo looked more like a guy ready for eighteen holes than the man in charge of the place.

I inquired about the course and asked why it was on the market. He told me that the North Carolina-based parent company was no longer interested in managing a property in Missouri. I had communicated with him that Morgan*Plus* might be interested in the property, and when I walked in, he presented me with a folder of information I'd requested, and then we hopped in a golf cart and took a thirty-minute, two-beer tour of the place.

It's ripe for some significant updating. The clubhouse is functional, but it needs to tell prospective golfers, "This is a great place to play," rather than, "come in and pay at the counter." The carts and equipment are well-used, but not in immediate need of attention. The course is nice. Brian has begun some improvements and has plans for future upgrades. I'm no golfer, but even I can tell they're good ideas. It was obvious to me on Sunday that Brian has a passion for the place. He seems somewhat like the Jim

Lynch of Belle Prairie to me, and I think if Morgan*Plus* buys the property he should stay on after the sale.

He and I made plans to get Larry and Cooper to Belle Prairie on Thursday, and when Thursday came, I went with them in the hopes of getting them to see all the merits of the property. I had shown them pictures of the place on Monday, and they acted more than a little interested. For one thing, the course is already operating and making money. Another selling point is that the property is much larger than the course itself, and some work has been done to put in streets and utilities in the adjoining spaces to prep it for development. Just what Larry and Cooper were wanting.

But of course, it rained when we were there, and not just a shower, a full-on thunderstorm came in after we had been there less than thirty minutes. Brian, my ally now in trying to get a deal done, came up with a brilliant idea. One of the owners was flying in that night and the two of them were scheduled to play a round on Friday. He invited Larry and Cooper to join them, and they, golf-lovers that they are, jumped on the chance.

I expected to hear from them Friday night or over the weekend—but no word. Worry has replaced optimism for me. I want to get this done. It would be something of a vindication for me if it were to happen.

At nine-thirty, I hear a noise and it's Cooper coming down the hall to our office area. I'm trying to decide if I'm more like the young guy waiting to hear a girl's answer to his proposal or the patient waiting for his lab results. I think I might be somewhere in between and a little of both.

"Morning, Dale."

"Morning, Cooper."

"Dad's on his way in and he'll want to meet with us when he gets here."

I wait for more information but get none. Somehow, I think this is good. I think Cooper would relish my failure if it didn't work out and waste no time in telling me.

Ten minutes later, we are seated in Larry's office.

I'm optimistic, but still unsure what I'm about to hear.

"Come on in boys. Take a seat."

I sit and still have no hint of what I'm about to hear.

"Dale, when things didn't work out last spring, you told us you'd find a place as good or better." There's a moment of silence in the room, and then, "And you did. You found a nice course that's already up and running, and the streets and properties are developed and ready to sell.

"So, you liked it."

"We did. We got a chance to try the course out and we had a great time with your guy, Brian, and his boss, Lew. At the end of the day, we made them an offer that was just a little under their asking price. We also asked that they keep Brian on *their* payroll for a year, to run the place and help us with the transition."

"That's a great idea."

"It was Cooper's suggestion."

"Good job, Coop!"

"Hey, I might not be selling cars anymore, but I still like to deal."

"And they are going to accept the offer?"

"They already have in principle. We signed some preliminary paperwork, and we'll finalize the agreement in a few days."

"Does Brian know?"

"He does."

"I can't believe that guy didn't send me a text."

"He was under orders not to. We wanted you to surprise you this morning."

"Well, you succeeded."

"I want you to know that I'm impressed with your initiative on this. You went out, did your research, found a place, then set things up for us to check it out. You could have ordered some better weather on Thursday, though."

"Yeah, that wasn't great."

"It worked out okay—maybe better. It caused us to go back on Friday, play some golf, talk to Fairmont and get things worked out."

"That's great!"

"You know, last spring, after the Walker deal fell through, I had my doubts we'd ever find something I'd like as much, but Belle Prairie is nice, *and* we'll be making money on it right away. And there's more good news. We've told you that Brian is staying on for a year. When we get the deal done, we're going to offer to extend that by a couple more years, and I'm also happy to announce that Cooper is going to take over this project. He'll start selling lots and working with Brian to get the course upgraded."

"Congratulations, Cooper."

"Thank you, buddy. Hey, I think maybe, I owe you a lunch. Where would you like to eat today?"

"Surprise me."

54

Christmas Day

CHRISTMAS NEEDS KIDS OR SNOW, or better yet, both. We will have neither until DJ arrives. He and his dad are at Sarah's house. They were supposed to be here at noon but haven't made it yet. We've walked the dog, watched a couple of Christmas movies, had a nice lunch, and played some games, but there's been nothing Christmas-y about it. To make matters worse, our moods were already gloomy.

After I got here yesterday morning, I went with my parents to visit Gramma Spencer. I hadn't seen her for a few weeks, and I was shocked at how much her condition had deteriorated in that short period of time. There was a discussion with the staff about putting her on hospice care. That conversation, while not unexpected, was incredibly difficult, especially for Mom.

The drive home was quiet. I thought about taking my parents to see Walker Farm on the way. They've heard so much about it from me, and I was looking for something, anything really, to lighten the mood. It was late by the time we got to the exit and at this time of year not much daylight left, so we kept on going. I'll take them there another time.

We got home, had a bite to eat, and Dad made us go to the Christmas Eve service at church. I wasn't too excited about going, but Dad insisted. He thought the Christmas music might pick up our spirits, and it did help some, but the weight of the day was a lot to overcome.

We've decided to give Duff another neighborhood tour. While waiting for him to take care of things, I check my phone and see that it's three-thirty, and still no news from Dave. I text him.

Are you coming?

> *Sorry, Dale. This is Sarah.*
> *We're on our way. He's*
> *taking me and Alex to the*
> *Marshall's first.*

Okay.

I let my parents know they're close, and after Duff does his job, we make the turn on Azalea. As we approach our house, we see Dave pulling into the driveway. He gets out of his truck and Sarah gets out on the other side. She reaches in back and gets out a large, brightly colored bag. I look for the kids, but they aren't with them.

Mom is the first to speak, "Hi, you two! Merry Christmas!"

"Merry Christmas, Mom!"

"Merry Christmas, Pat. Merry Christmas, Dale and Dale."

"Where are the boys?"

"We left them at the Marshalls for a few minutes. Sarah wanted to come by for a minute and wish you a Merry Christmas in person, and DJ and Alex wanted to play with his cousins."

"I bet Steve and Anne will enjoy that."

Dave says, "Can we go inside? We have something to tell you."

Dad says, "Sure."

We all know what's coming.

When we make it to the family room, and before they tell us their news, Sarah takes her gifts out of the bag and hands them to us. Mom has something for her and Alex under our tree. Sarah takes them and puts them in the bag to open later, and we decide to hold off opening the ones she brought. There's an awkward silence, then Dave, who is too excited to wait any longer, says, "Mom and Dad, Sarah and I are engaged and we're getting married in June."

My parents are ecstatic and jump up to hug the two of them. I wait my turn and do the same, adding my congratulations.

"So, June you say?"

"Yes, that gives Sarah time to finish school and plan the wedding."

Mom wants to see the ring.

Dave says, "We're waiting on that until we tell the Marshalls."

"That's thoughtful of you."

"It was Sarah's idea."

Of course, it was.

Sarah says, "It won't be a big wedding, just family and some friends. But I'm sure, just as I say that, we'll end up with two hundred people."

Dave adds, "Sarah's sister Nichole will be the matron, is that right—matron? Anyway, she'll be the matron of honor, and Dale you are going to be my best man."

I was prepared to be asked by Dave, but I wasn't prepared to be told by him that I would be best man. It doesn't exactly sit well with me, but now's not the time.

Sarah says, "Once again, I'm sorry we're late. My sister and her family were there. We took turns opening gifts so we could see what everyone got."

I shouldn't have any resentment, but as I picture their perfect morning while the three of us were sitting here waiting, I do.

And then she looks at our tree and sees the unopened presents.

"Dave, you need to get me back. It's after four o'clock and your family hasn't had Christmas yet."

Dave says, "You're right."

"I am so sorry. You've waited all day. It's been my fault. I shouldn't have kept him so long. Time just got away from us."

Dave says, "We just lost track. I'll be right back with DJ. He's going to be pumped to see more presents."

As they prepare to leave, there's another round of congratulations complete with the obligatory Barnhart hugs.

They get in Dave's truck and the house gets quiet, but we know it won't be for long. Christmas will soon arrive courtesy of a little boy.

———————

The rest of the evening is great, thanks to DJ. He takes pure delight in every gift—and there are too many of them. The adults ride the wave of his joy, and it's Christmas after all.

I give him my gift last. He rips off the paper and looks at it. "What is it, Uncle Dale?"

"It's a drone, DJ. It can be used indoors, but you and your dad can go to Grant Park and fly it. Won't that be fun?"

"I want to see how it works."

Dave looks at me as if to say, "You started this, you finish it."

"Okay, let's get our coats on and we'll take it out front for a test flight, but just a short one." He's putting on his coat before I finish my sentence.

We get the batteries installed and head outside. The sun has just set, so there's some light but not much. We play around with the drone, and he gets the hang of it in a few minutes.

"Okay, buddy, let's go back in. It's time to have dinner." Reluctantly, he agrees.

"Thank you, Uncle Dale. This is my favorite present.'

"The rest of the evening goes too quickly, and by eight o'clock the little guy is ready for bed, with his grandparents not far behind.

Dave and DJ are staying over tonight, and that helps keep the feel of Christmas in the house for a few more hours.

They've been upstairs for over an hour now, dad reading to his boy. I'm sitting in the family room waiting for Dave to come back down. I've been checking things out on my computer, and when I look at my emails, there's one with a Christmas greeting from Giselle. I had tried to reach her earlier, but she was busy with her family. I text her and tell her I'll call tomorrow.

I get a beer out of the fridge and come back to the family room to sit. Normally I'd sit at the kitchen table, but the tree is here, and because I know its days are numbered now I want to enjoy it. I'm about half-finished with my beer, when Dave walks in.

"Get him to sleep finally?"

"Yes, he was tired, but he fought it for as long as he could. I think I read his books three times tonight. Oh, and thanks for the drone. He couldn't stop talking about it."

"I'm hoping it gives you hours of fun."

"No doubt it will."

"It's been a big day for him, and for you."

He sees that I'm working on a beer, so he goes and gets one, twists off its cap and sits down across from me.

"Dave, I was best man when you married Brit."

"Yes."

"And I was Drew's best man when he and Sarah got married."

"Okay."

"Maybe you and Sarah need a new best man. I didn't seem to be good luck for either of you the first time around. Maybe you should try someone new."

He looks at me with a bit of a smile.

"It wasn't you, and we really want you to do this. She'll have her sister, Nichole, up there, and I'll have you. It just makes sense."

"Makes sense, huh? You really know how to sweet talk a guy."

"I don't have much practice with sweet talking guys."

"Thanks for asking me. I'll think about it. In the meantime, think about one of your buddies or some guy who works for you. Hell, maybe it could be Dad."

"I don't think Dad would do that, and it would be odd." He pauses, then shakes his head. "You need to do it."

"I'll *think* about it."

"It would mean a lot to Sarah. She still feels bad how all of this went down. Help her out."

"Just give me a couple of days, okay?"

"Okay."

I let that sit, then try a new subject. "So, which bed is DJ in?"

"Yours of course. I need my sleep tonight."

"And I assume he's already sleeping sideways."

"I'm sure he will be by the time you get up there."

"Perfect."

I lift my bottle and lean towards him. He does the same and we tap them lightly in a toast.

"To you and Sarah."

"Thanks."

"One last thing."

"Shoot."

"It would have been easier for me to say yes just now, if you'd ever apologized and meant it."

"I apologized."

"It felt like words when you said it."

"Well, you know, for most of us words are the best way to talk."

I shrug my shoulders and finish my beer. He gets out his phone and checks to see if anything's come up that he'll need to attend to in the morning. I decide I'm ready to do battle with DJ, so I tell Dave good night, congratulate him one more time, then make my way upstairs. In a couple of days, I'll most likely say yes to his request. There's a point at which it's no longer worth the time and effort to care about this problem.

55

Mid-January

IT'S A LITTLE AFTER MIDNIGHT and I hear my phone. I know who it is before I pick up.

"Hi, Mom."

"The hospice person just told us that your grandmother most likely won't make it to morning."

"Mom, is Dad with you?"

"Yes, he and your aunt are here."

"I'll get dressed and get on my way as soon as I can."

"You don't have to. She may not even be here when you make it. I just wanted to let you know."

I think she called tonight because she wants me there, so I'm going to make the drive. "I'm coming. Have you told Dave?"

"Not yet."

"I can call him."

"Would you?"

"Sure. See you in a couple of hours."

"Drive safe, it's late."

"I know. See you soon."

———————

"Hi, Dale. Is it bad?"

"Yes, Mom just said Gramma might be gone by morning. I'm driving over tonight."

"I want to go, too."

"What will you do with DJ? Mom and Dad are in Columbia. You can't take him with you."

"He can spend the rest of the night at Brittany's parents. I told them I might need them soon. They'll be fine with it."

"Okay. Want to meet in Wentzville and drive together?"

"Yes. Give me some time to take care of things."

"I'll probably be there first. Text me when you're close."

"Will do."

———————

We make it to the Care Center around two-thirty. I called Mom as we pulled in, so she could alert the staff to let us in. We get to the door, and a security person is waiting for us.

"Hi guys, your parents are in your grandmother's room. You can sign in later. Just head on down."

"Thanks."

We walk into Gramma's room and find Mom, Dad, and Aunt T by her bed. Her breathing is ragged and labored, and the breaths are far enough apart you think each one will be the last.

We kneel beside Gramma's bed, and Mom asks us to say our goodbyes. She thinks her mom is waiting for something, and maybe it's us.

We each tell her we love her, and then we all watch quietly as she continues to labor. Aunt T says something to us, and a conversation starts. We talk for a few minutes, then the room feels different, and I look at my grandmother, realize she's not breathing anymore, and say, "She's gone."

There should be tears, and there will be tears soon, but there aren't any right now. It has been so horrible for weeks; there's only relief.

Aunt T leaves the room to notify the night crew. All the plans have been made and the staff has been informed. At this point, it's just a matter of putting things in motion.

Dave and I hug our weary mother and then our father who has been so supportive through it all.

Dad says, "You boys might as well head back. There's not much more you can do here, and you have to go to work tomorrow."

"We'll stay as long as you need us, Dad. What are you going to do?"

"We'll stay with Aunt T until they come and get your grandmother."

"What about her things? What happens with all of this?"

"We've already decided what your aunt will take and what we'll take. It isn't much. Most of what's left we're donating to a local charity."

We hang around until four when the funeral folks arrive to take Gramma's body. We get ready to leave, say goodbye to our aunt, then walk to the door with Mom and Dad.

Mom says, "Thanks for coming. It means so much to me that you did. Now drive safe."

"We'll text you when we get there. When are you going home?"

"We'll wait until daylight, then make the trip. I think we're both beyond being sleepy right now."

Dave says, "I'll come by with DJ this evening."

"We can order something out."

"He'll love it."

I say, "I'll come up, too, if you'd like."

"You don't have to do that."

"I'll see how the day goes. If it's quiet, I'll take off early."

———————

"Thanks for driving, Dave."

"No problem. I like the way my truck sits. The car lights don't bother your eyes like they do in a regular car—like that little thing you drive."

"That's true, and it is a surprisingly nice ride for a truck."

"Yeah, thanks." It's quiet a moment, then Dave asks, "Hey, have you thought anymore about what I asked you a couple of weeks ago?"

"I have."

"And?"

"Sure. If you want me to be your best man, I'll do it."

"Sarah will be so happy to hear that."

"Good."

"And I'll like having you stand up there with me."

"That's good, too. One word of advice."

I'm sure he's prepared for one more lecture.

"Oooookay."

"When the minister prompts you, just don't say 'I take you, Brittany.'"

Dave snorts, "Yeah, that would *not* be good."

It's another half hour until we get to Wentzville. Neither of us talk much. I don't know what Dave's thinking, but I've been reminiscing about summer trips and spending time with our grandparents in the little town of Carnahan, Mo. It was always two of the best weeks every summer. Now one of set of those grandparents is gone, the other pair retired to a house at the Lake of the Ozarks, and our parents are grandparents.

I feel bad for my mom—she's lost so much—and I don't like it that my parents are getting older. There is one thing I feel good about right now. I've said yes to Dave and closed that chapter. It went on too long.

56

The second Saturday in June

I'M SITTING HERE IN A ROOM down the hall from the sanctuary. The only other time I've been here was last night at the rehearsal. Sarah chose a church in St. Peters because it's half-way between Kirkwood and Spring Mill and equally new to both families. I think, as with so many things she's done, it's a good choice.

As I look at my phone to check the time, Dad walks in and asks where Dave is. I tell him Dave's in the restroom across the hall. Dad says the church is full and it's about time to get things started.

"I know."

"Dale, you look handsome."

"Thanks, Dad."

"Well, anyway, we'll see you two in there in a few minutes. I'd better get back and take my seat. They'll be walking your mom down the aisle soon and I'm supposed to be right behind."

364

"See you in there."

He leaves. The wedding will start soon, and I will be best man again.

After Dad leaves, the minister comes in to tell us that it's time to go, but Dave still isn't back from the men's room. I met Reverend McNeal last night and I like him. He's short and a little overweight with graying, thinning hair. He has a good sense of humor, and he's sharper than you think he might be when you first meet him.

"Where's the groom?" he asks.

"Bathroom, I think."

"Nervous tummy?"

"Maybe."

"Or too much celebrating last night. That happens a lot, too."

"I'm not sure." I shrug. "I went back to my place after the rehearsal. Not sure what Dave did."

"So, you didn't go with the guys?"

"No. Like they say, I've been there and done that."

He smiles at that.

It's quiet; I hesitate with what I want to ask, but then say, "Okay, since we have some time, I've been thinking about this wedding. Do couples usually have a big church wedding the second time around?"

"Sometimes. Not always."

"Seems like kind of a waste to me. I mean they've done the big ceremony already. They've got all the wedding gifts they need. Why don't they just have a private ceremony, or maybe a destination wedding and be done with it—you know what I mean?"

"Was that a question or were you just making a point?"

"I guess I meant it as a question."

"Long version or short for your answer?"

"Short please."

"Okay. When couples get married in front of a congregation, they're signifying to each other, to the folks gathered, and I hope to God, that they are committing their lives to each other. And just as importantly, the congregation is there to give the couple its blessing and its best wishes."

"And I would guess you're going to say that's just as important the second time around as it was the first."

"Don't you think?" he asks, smiling.

"I do."

"So let me ask you a question while we're waiting for your brother, who I'm hoping hasn't died or run off by now."

"Shoot."

"You didn't go out with the guys, last night."

"No," I verify.

"And you asked me about the ceremony, which has me thinking there's some issue between you and your brother."

"There was. There isn't now."

Reverend McNeal looks at me for a moment, then says, "Sometimes a ceremony can heal old wounds that aren't completely healed."

"Yeah?"

"It would be good if today were one of those days, don't you think?"

"I thought it had healed already."

"Not quite, I think."

Dave walks back in, looking better than he did earlier.

Reverend McNeal says, "They are ready for us gentlemen."

Dave says, "Then let's do this."

"Let's go get you married, Bro."

"Let's."

We step out into the hall and can hear the music coming from the sanctuary. It's a quick walk to the side door that leads to the altar. We follow the minister through the door and up the three steps to the altar; take our places there and, as we do, the music changes. Mom walks down the aisle, escorted by an usher with Dad right behind her. She makes eye contact with Dave and smiles, and then she looks at me and smiles again. It's a different smile, but the love's there just the same.

As I stand by my brother waiting for the other participants to make their walk down the aisle, I have a moment to check out the crowd. I know most of them. There are family members and friends of ours. Across the aisle from them, are Sarah's people, a few of whom I remember from when she and Drew got married.

Then I see Steve and Anne Marshall along with their daughter's family. They're sitting in the back on Sarah's side of the church. I'm more than a little surprised to see them there. They certainly didn't have to come today. Everyone would have understood. For them to be here to watch Sarah marry again must be painful, yet here they are.

They see me looking at them, and I get a slight nod from Steve, while Anne is stoic and stares straight ahead. I think about the courage they are showing just by being here. I think about what a wonderful gesture it is to Sarah and Dave, and how much I admire them for it. Their strength makes me feel petty for the way I was.

My attention turns to Alex and DJ as they start their walk down the aisle. The boys are each carrying a pillow with a fake ring on it. I have Dave's ring for Sarah and her sister has the ring for Dave. The boys were sad last night when they learned they wouldn't have the real rings, but someone promised them some ice cream and they soon got over it. They have their arms around each other's shoulders as they make the trip.

As I watch the two come down the aisle, I'm struck how much they look like brothers, and I realize they soon will be. I have a moment—maybe the first such moment in a long time; a moment of clarity as to what I should say tonight at the reception. I've been fretting about it—composing, revising, rejecting, and starting over. Knowing exactly what I want to say is a burden lifted.

When we reach the point in the ceremony where it is time for Dave to give Sarah her ring, he turns to face me. I pull the ring out of my pocket then start to hand it to him. He reaches to take it and as he does, I grab his hand, then pull him in for a full-on Barnhart hug. He's surprised for a second, then hugs me back and thanks me. I hand the ring to him, and he turns around to give it to Sarah.

The rest of the ceremony goes by in a blur. Before I know it, Dave, Sarah and the boys are being introduced as a family, and we are ready to head outside.

When we get there, Dave and Sarah line up to meet people with the rest of their families lined up facing them. This allows people the opportunity to come talk with us after congratulating the newlyweds.

I know all of us are watching the door to see when the Marshalls are coming out; each of us anxious to tell them what a great thing they have done today. It won't be easy, but the Marshalls have done the hard part. The crowd starts to thin, and I still haven't seen them. If they left without going through the line, who could blame them? Still, it doesn't seem like something they would do. Then, I see them coming out in the middle of a small group of folks from Spring Mill. Maybe they knew that it would be tough for Sarah, and they wanted their moment of congratulations to be more private. Maybe they just needed to gather strength for another difficult moment in their lives.

Led by Steve, they come to the couple, shake their hands, and congratulate them. At first the conversation seems reserved; formality a shield to protect everyone from emotions. Then Steve reaches out to Sarah and gives her a prolonged hug while Anne does the same for Dave. Somehow, amazingly, they all keep their composure. I'm not sure many of the rest of us do.

Drew's sister, Diane, follows and she and her husband congratulate the couple. Then she leans down and says something to Alex. His eyes light up and he nods a vigorous yes. She stands up and talks to Sarah and Dave, and soon, there's agreement that Alex and DJ will spend the night camping out in the Marshall's back yard. I don't know if Diane or Sarah came up with the idea. Regardless, it's brilliant, and I realize Reverend McNeal knew what he was talking about.

———————————

When all the guests have left for the reception, the wedding party poses for a few pictures, and then we follow. The venue isn't far from the church—just a couple of exits away on I-70. I make the drive alone, which I don't mind since it allows me to finalize the thoughts I had on the altar.

When I get to our hotel, I make my way to the ballroom where I find some guests, most of whom have already helped themselves to the appetizers and open bar. A few of them have chosen to pay for mixed drinks, not liking the free beer and wine choices. Why they would do that, I have no idea; but to each his own. As I make my way to get my beer, I'm greeted by friends who decide that today's a good time to remind me that I'm still single. I try different responses and they get less humorous as I go. Finally, when I have reached my limit, the Overtons corner me. The Overtons are a couple from Spring Mill my parents felt compelled to invite while hoping they'd decline. I've never cared much for them.

"Hey, Dale. When are you getting married?"

"Soon, I hope. I've ordered a bride and she is supposed to arrive any day now. I'd tell you her name, but I am not sure how to pronounce it. I know it has a bunch of consonants, including a few I've never seen before. It's okay, though, she doesn't speak English so I'm betting she can't say my name either."

I let that soak in, then continue, "I can't wait for you to meet her. She's got some cosmetic surgery scheduled first, but as soon as all that's healed, I'll make sure to introduce you."

Their eyes grow wide with surprise or shock. Whichever it is, it's perfect. I walk away, and I'd give anything to hear their conversation after I've gone.

Another couple stop me and tell me how nice I look. The guy says, "You look good. You don't fill out that tux as well as your brother does, but you look good."

370

After finally getting my beer, I walk by the McCoy's who are talking with some other people from Spring Mill. They stop me to tell me how handsome I look in my tux and what a wonderful wedding it was. I thank them and tell them they're right on both counts.

Ed says, "Well, you made a great best man."

"I've had a lot of practice, Ed."

Ed, who has a little sense of humor himself says, "Well, I'd say practice makes perfect, but then"—looking straight at me as he says it—"sometimes it doesn't."

I concede this round to him, then head out the door and cross the hallway to a door that leads to a verandah. A few of the younger folks are out there, and this looks more like my crowd. They see me and wave me over. For the next half hour or so, we share a few laughs and memories, some of which would have been better unshared.

One of Dave's friends teases me that my brother has gotten married twice now and I haven't even found one woman willing to marry me.

I say, "Can you blame them?"

"No."

The guy's wife, embarrassed by her husband's lack of tact, tells me she's sure there's someone out there who's just right for me. I tell her that if a guy like her husband can find someone as nice as she is, there has to be hope for me. I'm proud that I've complimented her and insulted him at the same time. I'm on something of a roll. Maybe my toast will go well after all.

I take a seat at the front table next to Mom. Our food comes out and it's not bad. I went with the chicken, as did Dad. Mom went with the fish. As we enjoy the meal, several people stand up to offer toasts to the newlyweds. I wait for the right time for mine. Before desserts are served, Mom gives me the signal, so I stand up, tap on my glass, and wait until I have the room's attention.

"Hello, I'm Dale, Dave's brother and the best man, but most of you knew that already—the best man part, that is." I get a polite laugh from the crowd. "I had a toast ready to go tonight but during the ceremony today I decided to go a different way. I threw away my notes and I'm just going to wing it." I look at the crowd while waiting to deliver my next line, then say, "I apologize in advance." There's a little more polite laughter.

"When Alex and DJ walked down the aisle today, looking sharp in their little tuxes, I thought how much like brothers they looked. And you know what? Starting today, and for the rest of their lives, they *will* be brothers. And man, if Dave and I are any indication, they are in for some great times, and their parents are in for a roller coaster.

"There will be some difficult times, no doubt, but if Dave and I are typical, I know that for every not-so-good time there will be a hundred great ones. DJ and Alex will be playmates, brothers, and, with any luck, they'll be best friends. And maybe twenty years or so from tonight one of them will get to stand up and be best man for the other like I am tonight."

I stop looking at the crowd and turn to Dave. "Today, I saw *my* best friend marry Sarah, who is one of the most fantastic people I know." I look at Sarah. "How he talked you into it,

Sarah, will always be a mystery to everyone here." I gesture to the crowd as I say this, and most are laughing now.

"Sarah, welcome to the Barnhart family. I know Mom is thrilled to have you join us. She's been surrounded by—and I hope all of you have had enough to drink, so that I can say this—she's spent her life surrounded by a fog of testosterone. She has to be so thrilled to have you to help her deal with that. And Sarah, I want you to know that while we may not be the greatest *family* ever, I know for sure you'll never find better people than Dale and Pat Barnhart."

I look at them and lift my glass as everyone does the same. "And I want to ask that all of you not hold it against these two nice people that they raised my brother and me. You have to know they did the best they could. And now, Sarah, you'll have *three* boys to raise. Lord help you. You're going to need it. Ladies and gentlemen, let's toast Dave and Sarah and Alex and DJ as they start their journey together."

Everyone toasts, and then there's a round of applause. I take my seat by Mom, and she nods her approval. Dad leans in and gives me a "good job." It no longer matters that things went wrong there for a time. They are better now.

———————————

As we finish eating, the MC starts the music. A few couples take to the dance floor. I'm talking with my folks and watching. If twenty couples are dancing, three of them aren't bad, seven of them aren't nearly as good as they think they are, and half of them shouldn't even be out there. Still, it's entertaining.

After a few songs, the Marshalls come over to collect Alex and DJ. The original plan had been for the boys to sleep in Mom and Dad's room tonight, so Dad accompanies them to get what they'll need for their campout.

After Dad is gone, I look at Mom and know exactly what she wants. "Mom. You want to dance to the next slow song?"

"I'd love it."

As luck would have it, the next song is a slow one. I stand, take her hand, and accompany her to the middle of the floor. While we dance, Mom tells me how much she enjoyed the toast and how glad she is that I agreed to be best man.

I wasn't sure she and Dad knew that it took me awhile to agree to do it, but it seems they knew.

"Oh, I needed to do it. It was no big deal."

"Well, you were great. Someday—"

I know what she's thinking. She won't be happy until I've found someone to share my life with, and she won't be *completely* happy until I've added a couple more Barnharts to the collection.

"I know Mom."

We're quiet then, and let the music take us where we need to go.

"You are a good dancer, you know that?"

I chuckle. "When you say it, it's a compliment, when everyone else says it, it's like they are surprised."

"Your granddad was a good dancer."

"Yeah, Gramma told me that one time."

"I wish they could have been here tonight."

"I know, Mom." I give her hand a squeeze.

"But I'm glad your father's parents made it."

"Yes, but I think they've already left."

"I know. Some things never change. We told them we'd pay for their room if they would stay, but they wanted to get home. You would think they'd have waited until after brunch tomorrow."

"I know!"

We finish our dance and I tell her I'm going to grab a beer and go outside for some fresh air. I ask her if she wants to go outside for a few minutes, and she thinks she might like to do that. We tell Dave and Sarah what we're up to, so they can tell Dad when he gets back. When we make it outside, we have it all to ourselves.

"Nice to have a little break."

"It is," I agree.

"It's such a nice night."

We check out the evening sky. The sun has set and the sky is getting dark enough that you can see a few stars, although not many show through the glare of the urban sky.

When we were little, Dad took Dave and Drew and me to a camping area an hour northwest of Spring Mill. Before we went to sleep that night, we watched the sky get dark. There was no moon, and we were away from the city, so for the first time in our lives, we saw the night sky as few people get to see it. We saw the stars, uncounted numbers of them, and we saw the Milky Way like some magical path across the sky taking our little minds to somewhere wonderful. Drew especially loved it, and he asked Dad why we couldn't have that sky in Spring Mill. Thinking about it now makes me miss him again.

"What are you thinking about, Dale?" Mom asks.

"I'm thinking about Drew. I miss him still."

"I know you do."

"And now Dave is married to Sarah. It's crazy."

"He'll be good to her. You know that."

"I do."

Neither of us speaks again for a bit. I take a pull on my beer, and she turns and looks again at the sky. It's just starting to get darker now and a few more stars show, but it's not the same as that night sky all those years ago.

The noise level picks up and it lets us know that someone, most likely Dad, is coming out to join us. The door shuts behind him and it grows quiet. I turn around and see him making his way to where we are.

"Hi, Dad. We just needed a break."

"So, did you tell her your big news?"

Dad knows something that I haven't told Mom yet. I had decided not to do that tonight. Today has been about Sarah and Dave. My turn is coming.

"Tell me what?"

And now I will have to tell her.

"When I went out to see Giselle a couple of weeks ago, I had an interview."

Mom says, "An interview? As in a job interview?"

"Yes."

"In New York?"

"Yes."

"With whom?"

"A bank in Pleasant Valley."

Mom asks, "How did it go?"

"Good, I guess. They offered me the position."

"Did you accept?"

"I'm considering it. I asked for some time; and told them that my current boss might be making me an offer."

"Well, that was sort of true, right?"

"Yes."

"I don't think I could stand it if you moved back east. Those couple of years when you were in Philadelphia were miserable. Hopefully, the offer from Morgan*Plus* is more attractive."

"It isn't bad."

"What do you want to do?"

"Here's the thing, Mom. You know how you have those refrigerator magnets about paths and journeys and destinations?"

"Yes, but you're going to have to tell me what they have to do with this."

"Well, I feel like I'm on one path and G is on a different one, and at some point I want to know if those paths will converge and become one. For that to happen, one of us is going to have to move, and I believe right now that needs to be me."

"Oh no!"

I realize I'm ruining a good day for Mom.

"I shouldn't have said anything tonight. This is Dave and Sarah's day. I'm sorry."

Dad says, "It will be okay." He looks at Mom, "When I was Dale's age, if it meant moving halfway across the country to be with you, I would have done that."

Mom knows he's right, and she knows the battle is being lost.

"But we'll hardly ever see you."

"I'll get back as often as I can."

Dad says, "Well, I was going to save this bit of news, but since we're sharing. You know I added a new guy to help me at *The Gazette*, and he and my other guy, are doing a good job. For the first time I feel like I have someone who might have a puncher's chance of saving the business. So, I can think about cutting back now."

"That's great, Dad."

"And, I have been thinking about buying an RV while we're still young enough to travel. So, while we're traveling about, we can go to New York as often as you like, Pat."

Mom asks, "If you take this job, will you and Giselle..."

"Not yet, Mom, but at least there's a chance this way."

"Well, I like her, and if you are going to make this move, I hope it works out, and someday we'll get to come visit our grandkids in this new RV I'm just now hearing about."

"Mom, it may be a while. She's starting a new job. I'll be starting a new job. There's a lot to work out. And maybe it would be good if I asked her to marry me and she said yes before we started working on this family you think we're going to have."

"Well, don't wait too long. You don't want to be old like we were."

"If being old means we'll be as good as you two have been, I think that would be just fine."

Before anyone can say anything else, Dave comes out.

"All right you three. We're missing you in there."

"Mom and Dad, you mean."

"Actually, I mean you. Sarah says I'm to tell you to get inside; that there's a dance you owe her. Some dance you always do at weddings and parties apparently."

"Oh God. I was hoping she'd forget."

Dave puts his arm around Mom. I'm on her other side and do the same. Dad stands next to me and puts his arm around my shoulder. We share one last moment together.

Just as we get ready to leave, my phone signals a text. It's Giselle. "Let me answer this, then I'll be in."

How was the wedding?

It was great.

Did u do your toast?

I did.

How did it go?

It was okay. Maybe better than okay.

Bet it was good.

I'll call you tomorrow afternoon and tell you all about it.

Okay. Looking forward to it. Have you decided?

I think I have.

Will I be happy?

I want to keep you in suspense.

Can't wait.

I want to tell her I'm going to accept the job, but I'll wait. I want to hear her reaction when I tell her.

I put my phone away and head back inside. When I get there, Sarah sees me and walks over and takes my hand.

"You didn't think you'd get off without having our dance, did you?"

"I knew you wouldn't let me off the hook."

"Let's go then."

She leads me to the middle of the dance floor. At her signal, the MC pulls up a song from the '90s that she and I have danced to a few times before, probably starting with the night she and Drew got married. We start slowly—a little rusty, and a bit awkward. As the song goes on, we relax and get into it. It's a long song, which is something I've never liked about it, but we hang in there and before it's done, we're doing well enough that we have a crowd around us.

When the song finally finishes, the people applaud, and Sarah gives me a hug that says all that needs to be said. She leaves me and walks back to where Dave and the two sets of parents are standing. She takes her place beside Dave and turns to look back at me, smiling. Dave points his index finger at me letting me know I did all right. I throw my hands out at shoulder height in a half shrug, as if to say, "This is what I do."

I start to join them, but as I do the two little flower girls, still up at this late hour, tug at my sleeves, wanting their turn on the dance floor. There's no way to say no at this point. The MC pulls up another song and off we go; one tall, gangly guy with two tiny partners. The crowd watches us for a bit, then I invite them to join us. Soon everyone is on the dance floor, including the older folks. There may be another song to come, but this is the evening's finale in every other respect.

Epilogue

T HE SKY IS CLEAR AND BLUE. It's going to be another hot mid-July day in Missouri, as it most likely will be in Illinois, Indiana, and in Ohio, where I'll spend the night. Looking down the river I enjoy the view of the sun reflecting off the Arch. Today it's a Gateway leading east.

The movers came to my place yesterday and added my things to those of a family moving to Pittsburg. Theirs will be dropped off before mine makes it to the small house I've rented.

I left my family this morning, exchanging a hug and a 'see-you-soon' with each of them before I got in my car and started this journey. There was no RV in my parents' driveway today, nor will there be. It was all a ruse on my father's part, caring and clever and meant to help Mom get through a difficult moment that night in June. But I know Mom and Dad will be coming my way as soon as they can. They'll want to see my new home and meet Giselle's family. They will want to see the fall color and make sure I'm okay.

E.N. Klinginsmith

It was harder to leave today than it has ever been before. When I went off to college at age eighteen, I knew I'd be coming home for all the various breaks on a college calendar. When I went to graduate school, there was the thought I'd return a couple years later with my degree in hand. This time is different, of course. I have a job and the promise of a lasting relationship if things go my way. This time, the path may not lead back home.

My thoughts are all over the place as I cross the bridge, and the sign welcoming me to Illinois tells me that Missouri and family are behind me now. Still, I know that tomorrow evening, Giselle and I will go to Riverside Park and together we'll walk the path along that river.

Acknowlegments

I'd like to thank the English teachers in my life, those I had as a student and those I observed as a principal. I've learned from all of you.

I also want to thank my friends, especially Roy, Linda, Russ, Dan, and Sharon, who love to read and share the titles of good books and the names of great authors.

Last, I'd like to acknowledge Yolanda Ciolli for encouraging me to take the idea of a story and keep working on it until it was worth sharing.

About the Author

When he was in ninth grade, Nyle Klinginsmith told his English teacher he had an idea for a novel. He even had an outline for the story. His teacher didn't doubt that he could do it, but advised him to wait a few years, gain more life experiences, and hone his writing skills.

After earning his degree at the University of Missouri-Columbia, Mr. Klinginsmith began his career with Columbia Public Schools where he served as a teacher, counselor, and administrator for thirty-eight years.

Some sixty years after announcing his intent to his teacher as a youth, he returned to his writing project. This first novel is the result.

Klinginsmith lives in central Missouri enjoying retirement with his wife, Barb.